Women's Voices, Women's Lives . . .

"Working has been a great learning experience; it has let me keep who I 'was' plus add who I 'am.' I feel more confident, brighter, more eager to share and learn and plan, more fulfilled. Working has taught me to be a better mother—to stress quality rather than quantity. I enjoy the time my husband and I share—we no longer take each other for granted. We are a couple who really care about and value each other. We are partners, co-parents, friends, and, foremost, lovers."

"Both of us recognize we need a 'wife' at home and so we pitch in together, which means a lot of give and take."

"The demands on a woman today are just too much! We must be successful businesswomen, loving partners, available mothers, expert housekeepers, thin and gorgeous, always young and athletic, intellectual and well-read. It's still a man's world—we just try harder."

"My life is hectic and busy, but the quality is A+."

"I would never consider not having kids. Children have been the most significant thing I've ever done. They have to be my priority, but I also love my work. I find it stimulating and exciting. I wouldn't put in the hours I do if I didn't enjoy my job. But it has to come second. There are times when, if a choice had to be made, I feel I can make it in favor of my children."

"My advice to my kids is don't get married until you feel your life is heading somewhere. I hate the thought of them saddled with young wives and babies. Do what you want to do before you become responsible for others."

"My husband and I both find that our relationship suffers not because of lack of love or desire, but simply because after the demands of work and the children have been met, there is often little energy left for each other."

"I don't think I would have been better off if I didn't work. I'm not sure my kids would have been better off, either. I would have been very frustrated if I hadn't had a career and I might have been less encouraging of their own development than I was. A frustrated mother can't be a nurturing mother."

"Sometimes I ask myself: 'My God, what am I doing this for?' I'm working my tail off for $28,000 a year, my kid says, 'Why aren't you home?,' my husband is eating cornflakes for dinner. I don't have an answer; I just work it through. I just tell myself to get back to what it is I really want to do; I tell myself I'm committed; I believe in what I'm doing."

"My husband is a firm believer that a woman's place is in the home—barefoot and pregnant—but he is coming around as I become a better wife and mother, and a happier woman through working."

"Society is still not ready for a dual-career marriage. I am expected, if not outright ordered, to make *all* concessions—his is the FIRST PERSON career in all aspects."

"I have a guilt complex about working. I don't have time to talk to my kids, really communicate with them. As they get older, I worry about not being there at the precise moment they may need to communicate, and that moment may never come again."

MOTHERS WHO WORK:
Strategies for Coping

Jeanne Bodin
and
Bonnie Mitelman

Ballantine Books · New York

 Published in the United States by Ballantine Books, a division of Random House, Inc., New York, and simultaneously in Canada by Random House of Canada Limited, Toronto.

Library of Congress Catalog Card Number: 82-90834

ISBN 0-345-30140-4

Cover photograph: © Angel Franco/Vision Fotos

Manufactured in the United States of America

First Edition: May 1983

10 9 8 7 6 5 4 3 2 1

Contents

For Murray,
and for my daughters, Joanna and Gail,
who will have choices to make.
J.B.

With love for Alan, Joanne, Steve,
and Geoffrey.
B.C.M.

Acknowledgments

This book was written entirely in our spare time—evenings, weekends, and on vacation days. Because of that, we are indebted to scores of people, both professionally and personally, whose help and support allowed us to work effectively and efficiently.

First and foremost, we'd like to thank the women who filled out our questionnaires and who agreed to be interviewed. Without them, we would have had very little to say.

To Lincoln Boehm, who helped us reshape and enliven a rather pedagogical rough draft, we are deeply grateful. His ongoing interest and enthusiasm for this project have energized us. He's been a real friend.

Carol Panzer worked intensively with us to create and produce the questionnaire, and her incisive comments and astute questions contributed to the ideological development of the book.

Our editor, Joelle Delbourgo, must be the quintessential editor. She respects the free flow of ideas, and she is herself a clear thinker. She helped us define our objectives and to eliminate the extraneous. Liz Sacksteder, too, asked tough questions and honed our analytical skills.

Our transcriber, Laurie Sterlacci, worked from tapes that were, at times, unintelligible. Jean Rosenwald, who typed our manuscript, not only met every deadline, no matter how impossible, but she also noted inconsistencies in logic, errors in grammar, spelling, and verb tense. She cared enough about the book to work diligently so that, in her words, we "would get an A!"

We are appreciative of the efforts of the organizations that disseminated the questionnaires: National Organization for Women; National Association for the Advancement of Colored People; National Council of Jewish Women; Planned Parenthood Federation of America; National Council on Family Relations; W.O.M.A.N. (Women Owners, Management, Administrative Network); Working Women, National Association of Office Workers; Cincinnati Working Women; Wellesley College Center for Research; Political Action Caucus; American Business Women's Administration; Center for the American Woman & Politics at Rutgers University; Manhattanville College Alumni Association; Financial Women's Association; Georgia Executive Women's Network; Georgia State University Alumni Association; Florida Women's Network; and *Working Woman* magazine.

Moreover, we appreciate the cooperation of the spokespersons from the following corporations: Intermedics, Inc.; the Stride Rite Corporation; the Polaroid Corporation; American Can Company; the Ford Foundation; and from the following government agencies: the Women's Bureau of the Department of Labor; the Bureau of Labor Statistics; the New York State Division of Housing and Community Renewal; and the Westchester County Office for Women.

We are, of course, very grateful for the understanding and good humor that our families showed during the creation of this book. They not only did the obvious—made dinner, took care of each other, and understood that our discretionary time was devoted to the book—but they also sustained us when our own "Superwoman" ghosts haunted us and we felt guilty or selfish or overwrought. They had a real pioneering spirit, and their commitment to us, and to the importance of our work, helped us all learn and grow from this experience. *Mothers Who Work* has been, in every sense, a family project, and we thank our husbands and our children for their part in it.

Briarcliff Manor, New York
November 1982

Introduction

We're working mothers, and have been for many years. Between us, we have five children and four stepchildren, ranging in age from four to twenty-two years old. We've combined careers and families, both as married women and as single parents, and we've been mothers who stayed home and cared for our children full-time while our husbands worked.

Over the years, we've pursued a wide variety of careers—both part-time and full-time. We have taught high school and college; founded a small corporation; written books and articles; worked in a large urban corporation; tutored homebound students; formed a catering business; started a crafts shop; and participated in community and other volunteer work. Like so many other women in our generation, our education and training were often secondary to the needs of our families. We've gathered our credentials under various circumstances: working full-time and going to college at night; working full-time and attending graduate school at night; and working part-time, taking care of a family, and getting a graduate degree. Indeed, we've pursued our careers in virtually every manner except an uninterrupted, concentrated effort to reach professional goals.

We've worked flexible hours in small companies and we've punched time clocks; we've been our own bosses and have worked for hierarchies of traditional organizations. We have, in short, typified the breadth of experience of contemporary American women in the 1980s.

Sometimes through our own choice, and sometimes as a function of circumstance, we have been active participants in the changing roles of women during the 1950s, 1960s, 1970s and 1980s. We've experienced these changes alone, and with others—friends, partners, families, colleagues; in city apartments and suburban houses, in postwar developments and in rural settings; near extended family and hundreds of miles away. Through it all, we have struggled with the substantive issues of family values and professional objectives.

We've often felt like pioneers and have realized that there have been real trade-offs in our lives. There has been pain, and there have been long soul-searching dialogues with self. Am I the kind of person I want to be? The kind of wife or partner and mother that I want to be? Am I concerned with my family's well-being at the sacrifice of my own? Am I too involved with my own needs and not appropriately concerned with the ramifications for my family? Is it possible to be a bright, independent woman and a good wife and partner and mother? Why is the struggle so often lonely? And is it worth it?

As teachers of Women's Studies and other related courses in high school and in college, we realized that women in particular, and society in general, are contending with complex cultural realities. Women in Western civilization have been socialized since biblical times[1] to be wives and mothers whose primary job is caring for the home and the family. The emphasis has been on filling the needs of husband and children; there has been little concern for the well-being of the woman. The economic, sociological, and psychological perspectives of the 1960s and 1970s have brought forth new expectations, and propelled women, either consciously or unconsciously, into a new dimension of role possibility—that of career woman.

Whether women went to work for financial reasons or wanted to work because of personal imperatives, they seemed to be experiencing guilt, ambivalency, and conflict on the one hand, and exhilaration, anticipation, and determination on the other. These subtleties intrigued us.

Because the world is changing so rapidly, and because roles and expectations are in constant flux, we hoped to discover for ourselves, and for others, roads that are smoother to travel than the ones we've so often journeyed. With that goal in mind, we sought out women all over the country, in all kinds of circumstances, who had combined careers and families with relative success. We hoped to learn from them what they felt they were doing right and to discover the source of their strength. We wanted to share the strategies that they'd used in effectively structuring their lives.

---

1. An interesting exploration of historical attitudes toward women appears in Susan Groag Bell's *Women: From the Greeks to the French Revolution* (Belmont, California: Wadsworth Publishing Company, Inc., 1973).

This is their book, their story. We're not professional psychologists, sociologists, or statisticians. But we are wives and mothers with a great deal of professional experience, and we have researched our subject extensively. We believe that there is intrinsic worth in an individual's perception of his or her own life.

We use the terms "working mother" and "professional" to refer to women who are generating income, even though we know that *all* mothers work inside the home as homemakers and nurturers. We have chosen to focus on the impact of work on family life and have investigated the subtleties of the role of wife and partner and mother instead of dealing with the nuances of professional life, because we're concerned about the future of the family. We're also concerned about the changing definition of family, considering the contemporary reality that so few families now conform to the mythic American ideal—that is, father working outside the home, mother as full-time homemaker, and their own children.

Moreover, the components of the family roles for women are more universal than are the elements comprising professional roles; a psychiatrist and a secretary may have little in common professionally, but they can share on many levels their experiences as mothers, and as women.

We stress that we are not talking about women who work solely for their own fulfillment or to express feminist political views. We are talking about the economic necessity of adults to provide for their families. Our fundamental concern has been to investigate the nature of the stress that working mothers feel as they provide for and nurture their families, and how they cope with the conflicts their dual commitments elicit.

We knew that working mothers have little discretionary time, and that they tend to sacrifice their own personal needs in order to take care of their professional and family obligations. One of the reasons we decided to write this book, in fact, is that even though we are friends as well as colleagues, we could not justify spending time together solely for social reasons. It had to be for some other, task-oriented reason! We suspected that other working mothers would feel the same about nondirected activity. If it's not filling family needs or earning money, we thought, working mothers would not take the twenty to thirty minutes needed to fill in the questionnaire.

That wasn't true. We must have hit a nerve, because the outpouring from working mothers was tremendous. The requests for questionnaires far outnumbered our ability to fill them. Women have written us long letters describing the intricacies of their lives—their frustrations and their accomplishments—as well as their personal survival systems. On a cross-country trip to one of our interviews, the flight attendant heard about our project and asked for a questionnaire. She then sent us an involved treatise on life as a traveling mother. At cocktail parties and school functions, at business meetings and in our classrooms, men and women asked for questionnaires, volunteered to be interviewed, offered suggestions for the book's content, and quizzed us for the "answers" we found.

Busy women set aside as much time as we needed in order for us to interview them. They would ask that all calls be held so that they wouldn't be disturbed. Those with whom we talked at home requested that family members respect their privacy during the course of our talk, and they gave us as much time as we wanted. Interestingly, some of the women we interviewed have subsequently appeared on national television or in national publications. For instance, one, a legislator, was later filmed speaking at a rally on social and political issues. The film clip was shown on the network evening news.

Whether the women we sought were highly successful and quite visible, or low-key and not professionally ambitious, they all seemed to feel a need to share with us the experiences they've had and to talk to other women who understand the difficult, relentless, rewarding task of being a working mother.

Part I

What Makes Working Mothers Work?

One successful professional describes herself and other working mothers as courageous and resourceful. Another characterizes herself and other mothers who work as barely hanging on.

Why is there such a gap in perceptions? Is one woman more capable than the other, or more stable?

Are contemporary American women truly efficient and accomplished, able to integrate family and professional needs with competence and care? Or, are working mothers clinging to the edge of sanity?

We wanted to find out. In view of the growing number of mothers who are or will be working, we wanted to explore the disparity in perceptions among them, and the effect that their work has on their feelings about themselves, on their relationships with others, and on the quality of their lives.

Millions of women are combining careers and families today. In fact, so many are doing it that one would think it is easy. But numbers aren't people; statistics do not tell the subtle stories of individual lives, of individual families all over this country who are analyzing and experiencing the impact of mothers who work.

The impact is great; the lives are complex. The more we began to investigate the gap in perceptions, the clearer it became to us that central to a woman's evaluation of herself as a working mother is an element so fundamental that it affects all else: her sense of self.

Sense of self.

It seems so simple, obvious in fact. An elementary step in the growing-up process that one would assume had been taken long ago. And yet, it is evident that women in our society are struggling with a developmental stage of self-definition that affects their view of themselves and the world around them. It shapes, in a most basic way, a woman's capacity to eliminate the conflict in her life, and the degree of self-criticism she manifests as she evaluates her role as wife or partner, mother and career woman. Indeed, it shapes her perception of herself as a woman, a human being.

Women today are trying to resolve their definition of who they are and what they stand for as individuals in a society that continues to characterize women in stereotypical ways. That process is in itself complex, but for contemporary women, it is complicated by the fact that those stereotypical roles are, in large part, untenable today—if they ever were tenable. Women, and especially middle-class working mothers, are attempting to clarify a muddled mix of values, expectations, behaviors, and priorities that have been and continue to be both internally and externally imposed. Society expects certain behavior from women, and an individual woman may expect behavior from herself that is in conflict with society's edicts. It is not always clear what one ought to do or what one wants to do or what one needs to do.

As working mothers, should women today consider themselves to be primarily nurturers or providers? As executives, should they transfer managerial skills to the home and supervise families in the same manner that is so effective at work? Women who are loving and tender at home need to become assertive and emotionally detached at the office—is it possible? And who is the *real* person? Which nature is truly one's own?

Families, too, are often confused by such role-switching and undefined changes in behavior. It is sometimes difficult to ascertain whether one is an independent, autonomous career person or a supportive, giving woman. They seem, in our society, to be mutually exclusive so much of the time. Reconciling such seemingly contradictory personal qualities can be confusing for many women, and certainly restructuring society's expectations about normal female behavior is no easy task, even for the strong-hearted.

In this book we define the role of provider to reflect these traditionally masculine qualities: independent, assertive, competitive, clear-thinking, self-motivated, risk-taking, goal-oriented, determined, resilient, cognizant of consequences, and decisive. The role of nurturer/partner is defined in terms of these traditionally feminine characteristics: adaptable, sensitive, loving, dependent, emotional, domestic, attractive, devoted, giving, empathetic, and submissive. An individual with a well-integrated sense of self should evidence traits that are appropriate to the situation, without regard for gender-based behavioral constraints.[1]

Working mothers face a myriad of conflicting messages from themselves, their families, their professional worlds, and society in general. The ability to perceive one's personal direction amidst a barrage of other directions is not simple.

As we began our research we had several suppositions. Some were obvious and prosaic, others were more problematic and abstract. We supposed that working mothers feel good about themselves and their families, but they understand that being a working mother means making certain sacrifices. Furthermore, we thought we'd find that they feel good about what they're doing, in spite of the fact that there are few support services, and society does not reflect the realities of their lives. Working mothers, we posited, tend to feel defensive both with themselves and with others, in varying degrees and at varying times, about their dual roles. We supposed that working mothers often feel isolated, and that they feel that they're doing everything alone, with little help from family members, work places, and the social structure.

We did think, however, that the more help that working mothers received with family responsibilities—either from family members or from hired help—the less stress they would feel. Tangentially, we thought that in families where there was a second or later marriage, there would be a higher level of sharing and, therefore, a reduced level of stress. In addition to shared family responsibilities decreasing stress, we presumed that a supportive work environment would alleviate conflict as well.

We also believed that highly successful, career-committed professional women would react to the daily needs and conflicts of family life in much the same way that successful men in our society have traditionally reacted, that is, they would be able to delegate calmly the responsibility for taking care of a sick child, or cope when a needed housekeeper quit, or any

---

1. These gender-based characteristics are adapted from a study by Inge K. Broverman, Donald M. Broverman, Frank E. Clarkson, Paul S. Rosenkrantz and Susan Vogel, "Sex-role Stereotypes and Clinical Judgments of Mental Health," Judith M. Bardwick, ed. *Readings on the Psychology of Women* (New York: Harper & Row, 1972), p. 320–324.

other important, but not life-threatening, event of family life occurred.

Women who felt successful professionally, in our minds, would have more positive feelings about themselves and their families than women who have negative feelings about their jobs. Moreover, we theorized that working women would feel better about themselves as professionals than they did about themselves as wives and mothers because the parameters of cognitive professional responsibilities are more clearly defined and more objectively assessed than the variables of affective personal responsibilities of wife and partner and mother. It's usually clearer, and more immediate, to see if you're doing a good job professionally than personally.

A crucial factor in the lives of working mothers is time. We knew that limitations of time would affect all working mothers, and we believed further that women with part-time jobs would feel that they had more time than women with full-time jobs would feel. Whether the lack of time was actual or perceived did not, for our purposes, matter. Whether a woman literally did not have the thirty minutes to drive her child to music lessons or simply felt that she didn't have enough time didn't fundamentally concern us. We were interested in the *stress* she felt because of the demands upon her time. We felt that part-time workers would feel less stress than full-time working mothers.

Additionally, we assumed that most working mothers would feel ambivalent about the impact of their working on their children, and that working at home would be less stressful than working outside the home. We speculated that commuting would bring additional stress to the lives of working mothers. In view of the added stress of working, we wondered whether working mothers might manifest such health-related problems as headaches, digestive difficulties, higher levels of tobacco and alcohol consumption. Moreover, we speculated on whether or not working mothers would show increased sleep disorders.

The single most significant factor that would distinguish the conflict felt in combining careers and families, we believed, would be age. We presumed that younger women (those under thirty-five) would be freer to pursue their individual priorities than would women in their late thirties and beyond. We thought that the younger women would have better integrated lives, and would feel less guilt and defensiveness about not being at home all the time with their children. We felt that younger men would be more adaptable to and feel less threatened by the professional goals of the women in their lives. We surmised that the socialization process that the younger men and women had experienced would have made them both more able to accept the changing role of women.

Demographic factors would, we felt, affect the stress levels of working mothers. They included: whether a woman was single or married; whether she was living in an urban, suburban, or rural area; whether she had family nearby. We also felt that the family income would substantially alter a woman's capacity to alleviate the stress of combining career and family. Furthermore, we considered that there would be a difference in stress levels between those women who worked primarily for personal satisfaction and those who worked for economic reasons.

In total, we hypothesized that working mothers would feel good about themselves and that they and their partners would *not* prefer them to be full-time homemakers. Finally, we believed that work has a positive impact on family life, and that even though the family structure has changed, the substance of family life is solid.

To test our suppositions, we sent out a survey to working mothers. Its purpose was to gather data and suggestions for coping with specific issues. To accomplish this, we included both objective and subjective questions; sections of the questionnaire had multiple-choice responses, and other sections were open-ended to give women an opportunity to describe their experiences in their own words. Based on our survey results and our suppositions, we interviewed several women who seemed to be coping effectively.

It was our belief that the more clearly defined a woman's sense of self—her legitimate right to be an autonomous human being—the better able she is to function both personally and professionally, that is, to resolve conflicts and to accept trade-offs. Knowing what matters to her and what her personal values, objectives, and priorities are, she is more capable of shaping her life so that it reflects *her* sense of who she is, not someone else's.

Such consistency of self-definition ought, we felt, to reduce the conflict, tension, and stress that exist in the lives of women who combine careers and families, and we set out to find out if we were right.

A Working Woman Is Not a Man

Why explore women's lives so carefully? Certainly men's lives are also complex, and everybody has problems, insecurities, anxieties, joys, and accomplishments. Yet over and over again, in professional as well as lay circles, women's lives are being analyzed, discussed, pondered, and shared.

What prompts an eminent elected official who travels extensively to wonder whether her being gone so much of the time will affect her four-year-old son's ability to have an intimate relationship as an adult?

Why does a small-business owner deny to her children that her business is financially successful, as successful perhaps as their father's?

Why should a divorced free-lance writer with two preschoolers feel anxious and torn because she has to work full-time in order to support them?

The reasons, of course, are as varied as the individuals involved. The layers of needs, expectations, roles, and values combine and regroup in a complex and fascinating interplay that requires careful scrutiny.

Defining the Issues

There are psychological issues which pervade every aspect of working Mothers' lives, and these issues affect their sense of self. They're reflected in concrete and abstract ways, in their behavior and in their attitudes. The issues are fundamental. They are: legitimacy and autonomy. Legitimacy allows the working mother to feel that her behavior falls within the established standards of her society. Autonomy permits her to be self-governing and capable of making decisions that affect her life. Without them, she cannot function as an independent, self-confident adult. These two issues are manifested concretely in the conflicts women face as they confront their economic and emotional responsibilities, and they're also manifested in the trade-offs that result from resolving these conflicts.

The trade-offs, whether recognized or not, are part of every decision that working mothers make, whether those decisions relate to legitimacy and autonomy, or to economic and emotional responsibilities.

It seems absurd at this point in our history, but the primary need that we began to realize we were addressing was a need that working mothers have for legitimacy in our society. After many lengthy, revealing conversations with a myriad of working mothers, and after compiling hundreds of questionnaires, we determined that women who are struggling to combine careers and families sense an undercurrent of nonacceptance, be it direct or indirect, on the part of the established order in America today. They seem to feel, somehow, that their priorities, lifestyles, and values are not being taken seriously, are not being validated by society. They feel that our schools, our government, our institutions, our organizations, and our industries do not substantively, seriously, and consistently reflect the realities of millions of American families, that is, that the mother works. Again and again, working mothers give examples of a message they hear all too often: the "normal" American mother is at home all the time and is *always* available to her family. Despite the reality of government statistics on working mothers (see pages 210-11), American society still seems to function according to a simplistic concept of "mother's place." She's at home at lunchtime; she can take children to doctors' appointments, after-school activities, and any special program during the week. And this, in spite of the fact that many teachers are themselves working mothers! Is this a reflection of unrealistic school boards, principals and administrators, or is it a manifestation of a romanticized vision of reality?

School forms assume that there is someone at home in case of an emergency; school organizations are often dependent upon a pool of available volunteer mothers. Most activities and services that involve children and the household are rooted in the assumption that there is a woman at home during the day. (A variation on this is the suggestion that a neighbor cover for a working mother. But neighbors work, too!)

Provisions can be made, of course, for these mundane elements of life; but the energy that individual mothers in home after home all over this country utilize in order to make arrangements is an inefficient use of time and resources. And the rigid framework of the society mandates their response—there are few people and places that provide for working mothers. The message is clear: Mothers are supposed to be at home.

Superficially, society pays lip service to the special needs of families with a working mother. The Polaroid Corporation, for example, is commendably offering a child-care benefit for its employees, but the income cutoff for such eligibility is low. Consequently only a small percentage of people utilize it. It is such restrictive and limited offerings as these which make working mothers (and fathers) feel that their needs are not being realistically met. Although some accommodations are being made to changing family structures, the bottom line of the message still remains clear to anyone who has lived through it—the normal mother, the caring mother, the *good* mother, is at home. Ask any working parent who's tried to find a pediatrician at 7:00 A.M. or 9:00 P.M. Ask anyone who's tried to make special arrangements for appliance servicing or child care on school vacation days. Ask a parent who's tried to find adequate day care for an infant or preschooler. Many people believe that times have changed in the past few years and that women's (and men's) roles are different and more flexible. But as far as substantive, *real* changes in provisions for families with working mothers are concerned, there has been little more than rhetoric. Ask any working mother. Or father, for that matter.

And so, working mothers feel, somehow, outside of the realm of society's prescribed pattern. They feel this way *in spite of* the fact that they are responsible, caring parents *and* hard-working, contributing wage earners.

It should be axiomatic to state that women work because they're adults, and, as adults, they're choosing from among the options available to them in order to provide for their families. However, some people still believe that women are working today because they see careers as romantic and the work place as a panacea for their immature yearnings. In fact, most women are working today because of an economic imperative. To judge that imperative as selfish or nonessential for women is as arbitrary as to judge a man's desire to provide well economically for his family as a function of his ego, or his need for status. People work, and work at certain careers, for a wide range of reasons—economic, psychological, physical, historical, sociological—and women, as well as men, are limited by certain constraints. For each person these constraints are different: a sole provider with four children has more of an economic imperative in choosing a job than someone with one child and an independent income in addition to salary. Gender should not be a factor in determining the degree to which someone's need to work is judged; yet, we found examples of women who consistently discovered that *because* they were women, their *need* to work was called into question.

Theoretically, then, the professional determinants for women should be as varied now as they are for men. Although that is true in some cases, women are still discriminated against because of widely held beliefs in the work force. For example, the working world and our social institutions still tend to be structured in ways that reflect the belief that men work because they *have* to and women work because they *want* to, thereby diminishing the commitment which many women bring to their jobs.

Let us not forget that most women who work today do so for economic reasons. They're providing for their families just as men have traditionally provided for theirs. They are fulfilling one of America's most fundamental values—the work ethic. Yet, at the same time that they carry economic responsibilities, they bear a vague sense of society's disapproval *because* they are working. In a sense, they're caught in a Catch-22. Society says that responsible adults provide for their families by working hard. Yet society also says that women should be at home meeting the family's emotional needs. Some of these women have no one else in the household who will provide for them; some of these women have husbands who *cannot* carry the economic burden by themselves. So, while working mothers are trying to act in an economically responsible way, society is, it would seem, punishing them because they're not available to their families during the day. It's a no-win situation, and these women often feel a lingering sense of guilt because they don't fit the myth. Ironically, the guilt stems from the fact that they are conscientious, caring mothers and conscientious, responsible adults! Society has given them two mutually exclusive messages, and they're in a double bind.

This is not to imply in any way that working mothers are crippled by this lack of validation by society. To the contrary, they seem strong and perceptive enough to pursue their dual roles in spite of the obstacles. Throughout our research, we were struck by the creativity and resiliency with which they lived their lives, determined their direction, and helped shape their children's lives. With very few support systems, and with barriers often thrust before them along the way, women are raising children *and* working with commitment, energy, and humor.

Some of them have helpful partners, others do not. Some are single heads of households. Some have financial resources; others are clearly in tough economic straits. Some women are highly educated and had been encouraged to pursue career goals from childhood; others are struggling with limited skills and a recalcitrant family. Some have a clear vision of their professional aspirations; others are working wherever they can find a job right now. But over and over, they shared with us their accomplishments and satisfactions, their limitations and their fears, in short, their sense of self.

Working mothers have developed inner resources and ingenuity on an individual level to overcome society's barriers. Not surprisingly, they are quite introspective as a group, and most of the women have some understanding of their own weaknesses, insecurities, and psyches, as well as those of their families.

They shared with us substantive aspects of their lives, private conflicts that less embattled individuals would have evaded or been unaware of. Some of the things they told us must have, at times, been painful to reveal. One woman suspects that, in the end, it was her increasing ability and success that dealt a crushing blow to her husband's ego, thereby causing their separation. Yet the woman loved her husband and, at times, felt that perhaps the price of her working had been too dear.

A sense of common purpose united us and the working mothers we questioned—they looked to us as a conduit; they wanted others to learn from their successes and failures, and they wanted to learn from somebody else. The emphasis was on the exchange of ideas for a common cause—a dialogue—rather than on idle chatter.

These women were eminently concerned about the well-being of their families. These were not people who lightly went off to work in the morning without a thought about their children. These were women who reasoned through each day carefully and juggled all kinds of complicated schedules in order to provide well for their families. Of course, each family is different, and priorities are never uniform. But within the parameters of a healthy, pluralistic society, these women felt a responsibility to their families as much as they felt a responsibility to their work.

What seemed to make their job so difficult, however, was the feeling that they were the pivotal person in the family, that it was their role to be the one to make arrangements for the children and to manage the home. Even if they had partners, or were involved in a shared living arrangement, most of the women felt a deep sense of responsibility to their perceived role as primary caretaking parent. They might not always be the one who called home to see if the children were where they were supposed to be after school, but they *felt* as if it were their responsibility to do so. The younger women (in their late twenties and early thirties) seemed better able to share the role of caretaking parent than the women in their late thirties and beyond; but still they acknowledged that they, in the end, felt more responsible for making child care arrangements, or for marketing or home management than their partners. Working mothers never seem to feel as free as working fathers have traditionally felt—the socialization process seems to have defined role responsibilities in ways that are difficult to break, and sometimes the socialization process and new, changing roles become inextricably muddled. In one case, a man who was president of a company and whose own wife had stayed at home when their children were young, found himself admonishing his female vice president because she was staying at home to care for a sick child rather than attending an important meeting at the office!

For working mothers, then, there is a constant tension between responsibility to family and responsibility to job, and that creates conflict. Unlike the traditional family, where a working husband has someone at home with an equal investment and commitment to his children, the working-mother family depends on outside help for caretaking. Housekeepers, no matter how competent, do not have the same long-term commitment to families that parents have. Neighbors, no matter how supportive, cannot supplant parental hugs when a child needs affection. The reality of nonparental caretakers is vivid for these working mothers. As a group, they verbalize the psychological, emotional, and physical impact of their working upon their families. As a group, they're more educated and psychologically aware than were working mothers of years past. And yet, they must work. They want to work. They feel a great responsibility to their jobs, in spite of their concern for the impact on their families. Again and again, the conflict resulting from this dual primary-responsibility position evidenced itself in conversations with working mothers.

In addition to their concern for their children and their jobs, working mothers also exhibited great concern for their partners. However, they seemed to feel that adult partners, although they needed time and energy, did not require the same kind of constant attention that children and jobs required. Some remarked sadly that the constraints of time and energy required them to focus on the urgent and immediate needs of children and jobs, rather than on the important, albeit more covert, needs of an adult partner in their lives. This theme surfaced often, and it was a source of ongoing concern for many; in some cases, it created breaches in the relationship. In other cases, the couples constantly worked at finding ways to spend time alone together in order to renew their closeness. Again, the problems created by working seemed to be candidly recognized in most cases, and efforts were being made to deal with them directly. Rarely did we find instances where women denied the stress that their dual roles were clearly causing them and their families. Perhaps it can be said that the caretaking values that have been traditionally instilled in women make them take the pulse of their families often, and make them ever-vigilant in their sensitivity to their family's needs. Unlike the proverbial male head of household in the past, who was not to be burdened with the emotional demands of his family because he worked so hard in the outside world to support them, working mothers (and many fathers, too, now) are acutely aware of their families' emotional state. At times that very awareness, and their inability to make everything smooth, bring unnecessary stress to working mothers. In short, they sometimes feel guilty because their role as provider takes away from their time as nurturer.

One of the keys to coping is flexibility. With knowledge born from experience, working mothers are keenly aware of how change is integral to life itself. Arrangements cannot remain constant. Housekeepers leave. School schedules change. Companies move. Secretaries quit. More than anything else, mothers who work expect the unexpected; they adapt. The frustration, uncertainty, and insecurity of having to depend on people and things in order even to get to work are part of the daily constants in working mothers' lives. Again, this is different from the traditional life of the working father—someone else made arrangements for the sitter who did not show up. Working mothers have to cope with the fact that children invariably get sick on a pressured day at the office; pipes burst at home during weather that makes commuting difficult; school plays occur when there is an important meeting out of town. Careful planning and a high level of organization do not mitigate against the unpredictable upheaval that frequents working mothers' lives. Because working fathers don't often have the sense of being the *primary* caretaker the way working mothers do, they aren't as conflicted during these upheavals. Working mothers usually carry their load with skill and humor, even though they have very little help. But there's stress inside. They feel the tension.

What makes things harder for working mothers is a general lack of understanding and support. They don't feel that their plight is taken seriously. Often they are made to feel that their tension is self-imposed, resulting from inefficiency on their part, or lack of established priorities. Sometimes they infer from society's attitude that their working is a frivolous indulgence, an attempt to find selfish gratification when they should be at home caring for children. Other times the implication is that working mothers are pressed for time because they are vain and preoccupied with looks, clothes, and cosmetics. It often seems that society does not recognize that the complexities of women's lives are legitimate.

The confusing, often mutually exclusive messages that working mothers receive from society are being transmitted constantly. Many women are capable of sorting out what applies to them and what doesn't. Many have their priorities clearly established, and they ignore the potentially combustible combinations of signals they receive. But, the fact remains that a large number are trying to fulfill old expectations as well as new ones, and some of the most intelligent and talented among them are resolving their lives in surprising ways. One woman, for example, who is a doctor and works full-time, gets up at 4:30 A.M. every day in order to take care of personal needs. Another one, also a professional, has her hairdresser come to her home in the evening in order to spend precious time with her husband *and* to be well-groomed.

Working mothers, then, tend to be women who take all their responsibilities seriously, and they care about how their work affects their families. We wanted to discover how they assessed the impact of work on their lives, and so we set out to investigate how working mothers were dealing with both the philosophical and concrete issues we had raised.

The complexities of the lives of working mothers are best captured in their own words. As their stories unfold, one perceives nuances which make each woman unique; yet commonalities of experience also emerge. Certain feelings surface again and again; similar responses emerge in life after life. There are universalities in the lives of working mothers; themes and patterns that are prevalent and widespread, transcending individual differences and sounding a recurring note with clarity and drama. Common concerns affect women all over the country, whether they live in cities or rural areas, whether they're affluent or just making ends meet. They touch professional women as well as part-time office workers who see themselves as temporary wage earners. They are significant and consequential, and they warrant consideration.

Planning Our Research

We wanted to bring women face-to-face with their lives; we wanted to discover the quantitative and qualitative impact of working on their lives. We wanted to know how working mothers structure their days; we wanted to know how they set their priorities in order to have productive, healthy family lives and successful, fruitful work lives. We knew that there were conflicts and trade-offs, and we wanted to find a representative number of income-producing women who would give us data and insight. To help us define the issues of concern we held two informal focus groups. We talked with women in their late twenties and early thirties who were middle-management and professionals in city and suburban areas. We discussed with them their concerns about being mothers who work. Their input was useful to us in focusing our questionnaires.

Who We Reached

We tried to find the greatest cross section of contemporary American women we could. We contacted all kinds of working mothers, from unusual women with extraordinary careers to typical ones with average jobs. In our survey, we reached artists, editors, financial analysts, bankers, small business owners, teachers, office workers, government workers, and people who had created jobs that defy categorization. In our interviews we talked to a nurse, a state legislator, a corporate executive, a real estate agent, professional women, managerial women, small business owners, a data processor, and others.

We heard from women who worked long hours and traveled extensively. We talked with women who had built careers around the hours that their children were gone so that they could be readily available to them when they got home. We reached mothers who spent a great deal of time away from home because their careers demanded it, and we encountered women who had given up opportunities because it would cause separation. We communicated with many different kinds of people in many different kinds of circumstances so that we could provide an authentic overview of how working mothers combine careers and families.

We selected a group of twenty-five women from all over the country in a variety of professional capacities and family situations and interviewed them, either in person or, in a few instances, on the telephone. These women were chosen because they exemplified some of the critical issues working mothers face, and because they seemed to successfully manage the particular area of their lives that we'd focused on. We wanted others to be able to draw from their experiences and to implement those strategies and suggestions that they found workable.

How We Reached Them

We sent out 750 questionnaires to women all over the country; 442 responded.[2]

The participants in this study were solicited through three sources:

---

2. The questionnaire is included in the Appendix beginning on page 237. It should also be noted that many questionnaires were returned to us after the compilation deadline and were therefore not included in the computations. Comments from those people have been included. Of the respondents to the questionnaire, 189 were from *Working Woman* and 253 were from the other two sources. Unfortunately, hundreds of requests for questionnaires in response to the Letter to the Editor in *Working Woman* were not filled because of time and cost restraints.

1. Participants who requested a questionnaire in response to a Letter to the Editor which appeared in *Working Woman* magazine in September 1981
2. Participants who were sent questionnaires through approximately fifteen national organizations largely selected from *Guide to Women's Resources* from The Office of Sarah Weddington, The White House, Washington, D.C. These organizations included the National Organization for Women; National Association for the Advancement of Colored People; National Council of Jewish Women; Planned Parenthood Federation of America; National Council on Family Relations; W.O.M.A.N. (Women Owners, Management, Administrative Network); Working Women, National Association of Office Workers; Cincinnati Working Women; Wellesley College Center for Research; Political Action Caucus; American Business Women's Association; Center for the American Woman & Politics at Rutgers University; Manhattanville College Alumni Association; Financial Women's Association; Georgia Executive Women's Network; Georgia State University Alumni Association; Florida Women's Network
3. Participants solicited through a chain, starting with people known to us sending questionnaires to their acquaintances, then to the second level's set of acquaintances and so on.

Whenever we used other people to solicit responses among their acquaintances, that person was asked to distribute questionnaires to women who were between twenty-five and fifty, who worked either part-time or full-time and who were committed to both their careers and their families. The contact person was requested to make every effort to distribute the questionnaires in as representative a way as possible so that marital status, family income, race, age, and profession were as varied as possible within the group of questionnaires distributed by any one person.

Our Questionnaire

Participants received a self-administered twelve-page questionnaire in the mail, which they returned anonymously or identified by name and address at their discretion. The study's purpose was noted in a cover letter.

The questionnaire areas included:

—Professional Life
—Personal and Family Life
—Service Needs Not Currently Met
—Demographics

The questionnaire solicited multiple choice answers to specific questions as well as the participants' general comments in each section of the questionnaire.

Looking at the Findings

The women in the survey averaged about thirty-eight years of age; 70% were between thirty-five and fifty-four years of age. Those who responded through *Working Woman* tended to be slightly younger.

In general, the sample was highly educated, with half having schooling beyond college, and only 22% had less than a college education.[3] Ours was an upscale sample; 56% had a family income of $40,000 or more per year (median family income is, at this time, around $22,000 for a family of four). Only one woman in ten reported a family income of less than $20,000.[4] Our sample is not representative; it tends to be within the upper socioeconomic group.

Three in four of these working mothers were married, 59% for the first time. Most had one (40%) or two (43%) children under eighteen still at home.

The majority lived in suburban areas (63%), although a good portion lived in central cities (24%) and rural areas (13%). Ninety-three percent of the respondents were White, 5% Black, 1% Hispanic, and 1% Other (race or ethnic group). Eighty-six percent of the respondents lived in a one-family house and 13% lived in an apartment. Eighty-one percent owned their own place of residence. Virtually every state was represented.

According to the Bureau of Census, U.S. Department of Commerce, in 1979 80.6% of employed women completed

---

3. Respondents through *Working Woman* magazine were somewhat more likely not to have a college degree (35% did not hold college degrees).

4. The *Working Woman* sample had a slightly lower income pattern, though still upscale on average.

four years of high school or more, whereas 18% completed four years or college of more.[5] In our survey, 100% completed high school or more, and 58% pursued higher education after college. Our focus is on middle-class women, and our data supports general conclusions about the impact of working on mothers of the socioeconomic category surveyed.

The issues of legitimacy and autonomy and the resultant conflicts and trade-offs are reflected in the relationship of women to their work and their families. As we analyzed the lives of women, we looked at the roles they play, the limitations they experience, the possibilities they envision, and the consequences they face. These can be internally or externally imposed; that is, they can be a function of a woman's inner voice or the result of her family's, her career's, or society's demands upon her.

Her roles are many; she is a person, a provider, a partner, a nurturer, and the pivotal person in the family. The limitations she encounters center around the limited time she has and the many demands her roles make on her. The possibilities that she envisions have to do with the changing structure of the family and society, and the consequences involved include the prices and trade-offs of having a career and family.

The great majority of working mothers feel torn to some degree between job needs and family needs. Yet most seem to deal with their stresses in a generally positive way. In our survey, three-quarters of the women didn't smoke, 60% were at or near the weight they'd like to maintain, most didn't get headaches or take antacids with any regularity.

Time, or the lack thereof, seemed to be the critical pressure to deal with. Less than half of the respondents got the sleep they'd like on a daily basis.

Only 12% of the respondents reported that they would prefer to be a full-time wife and mother (19% of the younger women and 25% of the divorced women). Husbands and partners seemed to be supportive of their desire to work, with only 19% of the respondents indicating that they felt their partner would prefer them to be a full-time wife and mother.

A bank executive with two children, one of whom is a preschooler, noted that in doing the questionnaire, she realized that all her professional answers were positive and her per-

5. U.S. Department of Commerce, Bureau of Census, *Educational Attainment in the United States: March 1979 and 1978,* August 1980, p. 5.

sonal ones were slightly negative. It prompted her to reevaluate her life: Should she continue to commute to her fulfilling job in the city, or should she take a less satisfying, less prestigious but more convenient job in the suburbs to be near her family?

A woman who is a psychologist and the mother of two teenagers commented, "I still am the one who carries the needs of the household in my head. No matter how busy I get professionally, I am always aware of where the children should be and what is happening at home. My husband seems to be able to focus entirely on his business life when he is away from home. I wonder whether other professional women have the same feeling of 'carrying the home needs with them at all times.'"

Many women are still trapped between what they were raised to believe was expected of them as women and their own individual needs and priorities. Furthermore, many women discover that what is appropriate for them as individuals may, in fact, become impossible for them to do because of restrictions imposed on them by society. Lack of day care, for example, or rigid promotion tracks or nine-to-five jobs are some ways in which society has structured the working world for the lives of men with a full-time wife at home, and not for the lives of women, especially those with children. In this way, the options for working mothers have been subtly limited, and the pressures increased.

Women As People

Due to the socialization process, women seem to have difficulty at times perceiving that their needs and priorities as people are legitimate, and society often countermands their sometimes tentative steps toward validating the needs that they do perceive. Women have tended to see the needs of others as more essential than their own needs, and their roles as caretakers, nurturers, and subordinates often supplant their role as provider, even when that role is necessary to their economic survival. Carol Gilligan of the Laboratory of Human Development at the Harvard Graduate School of Education has done some significant research in the areas of women, entitlement, and moral responsibility. According to Gilligan, women tend to feel selfish or immoral if they are acting in response to their own needs, rather than to the needs of those to whom they are close or for whom they feel responsible. This is a fundamental difference in attitude between men and women, and it causes some women stress.[6] Gilligan's work provides enlightenment in this most complex aspect of human development, and she points out the subtle ways in which men and women have been socialized to view entitlement. This has far-reaching implications in terms of women and work.

If a woman is still questioning her fundamental right to work, and if she has internalized society's message that women should be at home with children, she can become mired in so much self-doubt and self-criticism that she cannot feel entitled to make the kinds of decisions that are basic to working for a living. If a woman does not even feel that her right to work is legitimate, she certainly won't feel entitled to some of the things that men have traditionally accepted without question—things as fundamental as feeling entitled to the opportunity to train and work in the field of one's talent and interest, or as mundane as feeling entitled to relax and read the newspaper without interruption after a day's work. Women often question their right to work. They accept a man's entitlement, but some have difficulty in accepting their own legitimacy and entitlement.

A middle-aged woman with two children still at home is battling the issue of legitimacy even though she is a college professor and a state legislator. She told us, "Our society continues to place prime home and family responsibilities on the shoulders of women—which adds guilt to obstacles. Women are directed to be 'Superwomen' instead of human beings, particularly when married to successful professional men who must devote a great deal of time to a career." To the extent that she feels guilty about not taking on home and family responsibilities as she thinks she should, this woman is still plagued by the voice inside her that is questioning whether she is *entitled* to her career.

A suburban New York woman with three children who recently began to work part-time has resolved her feelings of entitlement in the following way: "My husband is a firm believer that a woman's place is in the home—barefoot and preg-

6. Carol Gilligan's book, *In a Different Voice* (Cambridge: Harvard University Press, 1982), and two articles about her research, "Are Women More Moral Than Men? Interview with Psychologist Carol Gilligan," *MS*, 1981, Vol. X, No. 6, p. 63–66 and "Why Should a Woman Be More Like a Man?" *Psychology Today*, 1982, Vol. 16, No. 6, p. 68–71, are excellent.

nant—but he is coming around as I become a better wife and mother, and a happier woman through working." She has balanced her husband's need for a traditional wife with their economic needs by working *part*-time.

A woman from Virginia cautioned, "Be firm. You know what you want for yourself. Do not let others sway you from what you want to satisfy their needs. Try not to let one role dominate over another. Do not let work take away from family." A California nurse said that she would feel better about herself if she could allow "some time for myself without guilt so that I can refresh myself and give positive time to my family and job and thus prevent burnout." A technologist from Maine likewise expressed the need for time by herself. "I have to make sure that I have some 'alone time.' One half-day on Saturday or after dinner some week night for two hours or so. This time may be used totally for relaxation or even catching up on chores. It is refreshing and stimulating and relieves me of confusion and demands for a while."

Autonomy and independence are also vitally important to working mothers. Recent statistics indicate that one out of two marriages end in divorce and that two out of every five children born in the 1970s in this country will grow up spending some amount of time in a household headed by a single parent. In most of those instances, that single parent will be a woman. The expectation that a woman will go from the home of her parents to the home of her husband and be taken care of throughout her adult life as a cherished wife is a myth that Margaret Fuller, the nineteenth-century writer, feminist, and activist, fought against more than a hundred years ago.[7] Yet the myth prevails, and our society has attitudes toward, policies concerning, and legislation regarding women that reflect this myth. In this country since its inception, and in Western civilization at least since the industrial revolution, women, even mothers, have found themselves in situations where they *must* work in order to provide for their families; yet this fact is still not reflected in our culture.

Taking control of one's life emerged as a common theme among our working mothers. One Missouri woman who has been divorced for twelve years discussed coming to terms with

7. In the mid-1800s, Margaret Fuller became literary editor of the *New York Tribune,* thereby becoming the first woman editor of a large newspaper. Author of *Woman in the Nineteenth Century,* she died in 1850.

her situation. "I found myself 'dead-ended' a few years ago. I had always been under the impression that 'something would come along' and that someone would recognize my special talents (whatever they were) and the whole world would open up. NOT SO! Nothing is that easy. I went back to school to work on completing a degree. I have twenty-three hours left, and I find that I am becoming very much in demand. I am single, my child is in college and no longer requires my constant supervision. I am mobile, I am thirty-eight and still attractive. And I am independent."

For some women, the opportunity to go from being a full-time wife and mother to a full-time worker constitutes independence. Said a woman from Minnesota with two children, "Working has given me a sense of development that I didn't quite feel before I began to work. The transition was difficult at first—but it has worked into a great learning experience that has let me keep who I 'was' plus add who I 'am.' I feel more confident, brighter, more eager to share and learn and plan, more fulfilled. Working has taught me to be a better mother—to stress quality rather than quantity. I enjoy the time my husband and I share—we no longer take each other for granted. We are a couple who really care about and value each other. We are partners, coparents, friends, and, foremost, lovers."

A Delaware woman reflected the attitude of many women. "I was a full-time wife and mother for seven years, and I was not my own person. By going back to work, I became 'me,' more than someone's wife or mother. I could not stop working now."

Attitudes toward work and oneself are summarized by an engineer from Massachusetts who is the mother of one child. "I am grown-up and able to support myself and take care of myself. While I am working I am learning more about my profession, and if for some reason in the future I have to support myself alone, I have a paying profession."

Our respondents indicated the need for determination in the face of obstacles. A businesswoman from New York suggested, "Being determined to make my way as a working person required patience and retraining of my husband and kids. Coping with the guilt and society's demand that I be at home for the sake of the kids, encouraging other women not to give in to chauvinistic demands of husbands whose egos are threatened, and giving my time, support, and guidance" were constructive ways she proposed to others who are trying to balance multiple roles. She continued, "I occasionally feel bitter and angry at myself and society for 'forcing' me to ignore an inner drive to excel in the business world. I feel I lost dramatically in the ten years I stayed home to raise kids. As a manager of a recruiting firm and as a career consultant, I deal constantly with women reentering the job market, and things have not changed much from the twelve years ago when I returned to the business."

A forty-year-old woman with two children explained her dilemma. "My personal conflict [right now] is wanting and being willing to work and being qualified (M.B.A. in finance) and not finding a job. It is emotionally draining and damaging."

Said a recently divorced Chicago woman, "Strong direction and action are musts for my life. The attitudes are good for my children also. I do get tense more often than I'd like, but I know that the first hundred years are the hardest!"

A woman from Colorado who is a manager dealt with the issue of success and self-esteem this way: "One of the most important elements of coping with multiple roles is a good self-image. If one has a good self-image, one demands, and in most cases receives, respect. This respect then has a 'ripple effect' on the whole household. In my own case, my partner and my children recognize the demands of my other roles and responsibilities, and they respond by sharing the household responsibilities as their own contribution to the family unit."

Independence and autonomy are essential for healthy adults; it is important to understand the place that they have in developing one's priorities and lifestyle. A Michigan woman who went to law school after her three children were in school summarized the need to set priorities and to "try to remember that human beings are more important than things." She went on to mention a recurring theme: Have a "sense of humor—in all areas."

In resolving the areas of independence and autonomy, legitimacy and entitlement, women stressed the necessity of making objective, realistic evaluations—what needs to be done, what needs *you* to do it, what your priorities really are, not the ones others expect you to have—and then assessing their own strengths and limitations realistically. A Minnesota hospital administrator illustrated the point. "I could write ten pages of thoughts on the evolution from full-time mother to full-time worker. It was hard—the first Christmas I worked I still thought I could sew four robes, do all the baking and shopping, and survive. The robes were given as partially finished gifts. Working is a different way of life—it takes practice."

It is not an easy matter to resolve these issues, however, especially within the confines of a work place and a society that tend to deal with women in restrictive, stereotyped ways; but in spite of the difficulties, the women who seem most successful and at peace with themselves are the ones who have worked through the fundamental issues of legitimacy and entitlement, and independence and autonomy.

These are women who, more often than not, define themselves in terms of their professions, their usefulness to society, their status, their economic position, and their individual contribution to their families and work places, rather than as someone's wife or mother. They seem to have a real, abiding sense of self and have come to feel independent and in control of their lives. They do not feel beholden to somebody else to define them or care for them. But they do understand the importance of interdependency in relationships. They see themselves as partners in cooperative ventures, as adults contributing to society. What's more, their families tend to see them that way, too.

Children see them as independent people who work *with* other adults in a participatory way, not as supplementary, superfluous individuals who matter *only* when one feels lost or in need of maternal love.

Women as Providers

Women in our surveyed age group have been socialized to believe that a woman's primary job should be that of wife and mother. They were not raised to see themselves as providers first. Nor have they, generally speaking, been raised to take themselves and their priorities and needs seriously. A man's attitude toward his job may be characterized by him as an *economic* necessity because he has been raised to see himself as a provider, while a woman's attitude toward her job may be seen as *personal satisfaction* because she was not raised to see herself as a provider. Legitimacy, entitlement, expectations—all are involved in these attitudinal ratings. The socialization process is a powerful influence, and it is possible that it affects some contemporary women's ability to analyze ojectively their reasons for working.

A management information system specialist who is married to a man in the military expressed the frustrations she feels. "Society in general is still not ready for a dual-career marriage, especially in the military. I am expected—if not outright ordered—to make *all* concessions. His is the FIRST PERSON career in all aspects."

The economic impetus to provide for the family is as real for many women as it has been traditionally for men. The misconception that women see careers as idealized embodiments of their fantasies, or ways in which to buy expensive clothes or vacations, still exists in our culture and is, at times, used to deprecate the role of woman as provider.

One Texas woman pointed out one of the compromises that women, just as men, have to make in order to make a living. "I was in graduate school and working full-time, but I have postponed my goals to take a position in marketing and advertising where I can earn much more money."

An Ohio professional said, "For intellectual fulfillment, I could be satisfied with a part-time job, but for economic necessity, I can't afford it." Added another Ohio woman, a secretary, "I feel very privileged to be a mother, and the rewards are many. I only wish my earnings as a secretary were at least adequate for a middle-class way of life."

Work as a Given. According to *The New York Times,* both the husband and wife are working in "52% of all married couples."[8] Few American families are comprised of what used to be considered the typical American family—a father working outside the home, a mother at home, not employed, and two children under eighteen. In fact, the 1980 U.S. Census figures indicate that 63% of American women are employed when their youngest child is in school.

In our survey, 85% of the 442 respondents work full-time, and 15% work part-time. This is true even though the sample is more educated and has a higher income than the average American. Whether these women see themselves as having jobs or careers, whether they are heads of households or supplementing the family income, whether they describe themselves as working primarily for economic reasons or primarily for personal satisfaction, the reality is that in the 1980s large numbers of American women are providers.

---

8. "Working Women: Easing Burden," *The New York Times*, Feb. 6, 1982, p. 21.

We asked our respondents several questions about their working lives, referred to in the survey as *professional lives,* even though not all of the women had professional occupations. There were eight categories listed on the survey, with space provided to indicate "Other" if they did not find their jobs categorized adequately. The categories were as follows: (1) Professional (e.g., attorney, editor, stockbroker, teacher, psychologist, doctor, engineer); (2) Managerial or Administrative; (3) Sales; (4) Secretarial or Clerical (e.g., bank teller, bookkeeper, cashier); (5) Artistic (e.g., artist, designer, writer, performer); (6) Service (e.g., hair stylist, chef, dental assistant); (7) Small Business Owner; and (8) Government or Military.

The respondents were in the following categories:[9]

Professional	46%	Artistic	3%
Managerial	27%	Service	1%
Sales	3%	Small Business	4%
Secretarial	10%	Government/Military	5%
		Other	1%

Many women have forged careers out of individual talents and necessities. One woman turned her hobby of baking into a successful bakery; others who loved to cook became caterers. Typists became transcribers; those who headed social committees of volunteer organizations opened party planning services.

Others trained for traditional careers such as lawyers, accountants, social workers, doctors, technicians, and nurses. Some women who had been trained, but who had taken years off to raise children, took their degrees and used them as a springboard for a new venture—a trained teacher became a textbook editor, for example.

Often careers just "happened." They grew out of opportunity and creativity. One woman, a former advertising copywriter with no business experience, started an advertising agency in partnership so that she could have flexibility, as well as income.

Work has become a given. A C.P.A. from Delaware said it this way: "My husband died when my kids were six and one.

9. It should be noted that *Working Woman* respondents tended to be more heavily managerial or administrative (34%) than the solicited group, which was more likely to be professional (53%). About one-third of the women work from their homes at least some of the time.

We started a team system for survival. Everyone pitched in and did what they could, based on age and ability. This resulted in the kids becoming more mature and responsible than their peers and gave us time for family outings." She went on to describe the anger and frustration that many other women expressed by the lack of support networks in our culture. 'Many articles dealing with working mothers address only wife/mother. I would like to see some emphasis on and acknowledgment of the problems faced by those of us who are mother/wife/breadwinner. Magazine articles describing Superwomen who have husbands contributing to the family coffer as well as doing their share of household and child chores leave me cold and angry."

A secretary from Georgia with five children and an income of less than $10,000 a year underscores the reality faced by other surveyed women. "I would prefer being a full-time wife and mother, especially since I have five children. I have had and still am having all kinds of conflicts with trying to get some financial assistance from my ex-husband. Working and trying to raise your children in a respectable manner with only one income is very hard."

An Indiana clerk in the U.S. Postal Service claimed, "If I don't work, we don't eat, and my job comes first, by necessity."

A New Jersey woman who owns her own business put it this way, "I'd have been a bad full-time mother—too much energy." Since she works for psychological, rather than economic, reasons, she seems to have felt some ambivalence about her job. She went on to tell us, "Have it accepted by everybody that work is part of your life. It saves fruitless talk about giving it up when things get hectic."

A North Dakota bank teller with four children and two stepchildren encapsulated the interaction between family and career: "I am paid quite well, but will never make much more than I am making right now. The job is quite definitely one with a limited future and no room for creativity except for brief customer relations. However, my family responsibilities are such that I can't afford to go to school or take a more interesting job."

The way one feels about one's profession and professional life is of significance in combining careers and families. Twenty-five percent of our respondents felt that they worked completely for reasons of personal satisfaction, while 15%

stated that they work primarily for economic reasons. Of the women in our survey who work primarily for economic reasons, 89% work full-time and the same percentage considered themselves successful.

Most women expressed an interaction between the two, saying that they work for both economic and personal reasons. Within this duality of purpose, however, the great majority of women considered themselves committed to a career (77%) rather than just holding a job to supplement income (19%).

It's important to understand that this commitment to career is significant for our purposes because it signals the degree of integrity and seriousness with which our respondents view their professions. It is also significant because it highlights the dual-role position that working mothers find in their lives—commitment to family and commitment to career. These women take their jobs, and their families, seriously.

For the most part, our survey group felt that they've achieved according to, or even surpassing, their expectations. Only one-fifth of the respondents said that they've attained less than they thought they would. The vast majority of our working mothers tended to like the work they were doing, and to feel that they were adequately trained for it. They considered themselves confident with peers, and reasonably assertive with supervisors.

Despite these positive attitudes toward their professional lives, and despite the fact that most of these women considered themselves successful, many of them stated that others see them as more successful than they judge themselves.

Close to half of our surveyed women supervised men, traveled with and entertained men as part of their profession, and they did so with minimal discomfort or awkwardness. In fact, 81% of our respondents found their work environments to be supportive. Whether or not that is a function of the increasing numbers of women in supervisory positions, and the growing networking that now pervades the work force, is a question that could be explored more thoroughly by industrial psychologists or others concerned with changes in the work place. For our purposes, however, suffice it to say that most of our respondents found their work environment generally supportive.

One important issue which affects working women to a greater degree than men is that of adequate remuneration. Women continue to be paid less than men. *The New York Times* reported that "median annual earnings for women in

1980 were $11,197 compared with $18,612 for men."[10] A woman in academia who is the mother of four children expressed it this way: "I'm well-known in my field—published extensively—have lots of media exposure (feature article, TV). Because of my visibility, it is assumed that money goes with it." She then described her inability to afford professional meetings and other budgetary restraints, and summed it up by saying, "It is humiliating to be watching pennies, scrounging to make ends meet, when everyone thinks you must be doing well financially. I'm reluctant to leave this secure, but underpaid, work at this time. I feel like I am counting the days to freedom."

Of course, women are not alone in feeling the frustration of inadequate remuneration, especially in academia, but it is certainly a fact of life that working mothers often confront. In all, only 60% of our respondents felt that they were adequately paid for the work they do, even though many more (92%) than that said that they were well-trained for the work they were doing. If their assessment of their professional training is accurate, there seems to be an inequity between the level of women's pay and the level of their training for the field, which indicates that there is still *not* equal pay for equal work. Clearly, adequate remuneration is a concern for most of the working mothers we surveyed.

When Mothers Are Single. Divorce has caused many women to revise their role expectations and definitions. According to a Midwestern manager, "I'd have preferred to be a homemaker as opposed to a working mother, but I'm divorced and have an infant to take care of. Economics have forced me to work full-time outside the home."

A woman from Connecticut who holds two jobs, one as a secretary and one as a government employee, pointed to a crucial factor in the lives of divorced working mothers: "I had no choice, since we have a very poor system for collecting child support from husbands."

Added an Idaho administrative secretary, with four children and a family income of less than $20,000, "I had always considered myself a full-time housewife, until divorce forced me to work. Now, I wouldn't enjoy not working."

---

10. "Working Women: Easing Burden," *The New York Times,* February 6, 1982, p. 21.

A divorced bank purchasing agent with two children addressed the problem of having to work because of a change in circumstances. "When I was married, I was glad to stay at home with my children and was against the idea of mothers working. Then divorce tore through my life, and I was forced to go back to work. I am very pleasantly surprised at the changes my working has made in all of us. The children are more independent now, and my self-confidence, which had reached an all-time low, is now high. I have never felt so good about myself and my life as I do now."

As difficult as it is for women with husbands or partners to manage their homes, care for their children, and work, it is all the more difficult for divorced or single women to handle all the roles and responsibilities. Not only must these women face the problems and logistics of home management essentially alone, but they must also deal with daily stresses and demands of caring for children without having another adult to help share the burdens (or the joys!). However, our survey indicated that, for the most part, divorced women do not experience significantly more stress in the areas of home and child care than nondivorced women. They do, however, experience more stress when it comes to such chores as housecleaning and slightly more stress in getting the marketing done, the laundry finished, and providing for car pooling for their children. This could be a function of their using much of their time and energy meeting the most essential needs of their families, and finding that they have little left for the lesser chores. Several women commented that life got somewhat easier for them when their children could drive and help with family errands.

The Impact of Working. The majority of women who answered our survey stated that work has had a positive affect on their own emotional well-being and sense of control over their lives, on their general relationship with husbands or partners, and on their children's development.[11] The skill development that comes from experience in the working world is increasing creative assertiveness in other areas of their lives. Office politics, salary negotiations, corporate hierarchies, promotions, and other aspects of working life enable women to become

11. Seventy-two percent felt good about themselves; 66% felt good about their children, and 56% felt good about their partners.

increasingly perceptive about and experienced in the formerly all-male domains of power and decision making.

Work had the most positive impact on the women's emotional development. Eighty-three percent felt very positive about their sense of control over their lives, while 85% felt positive about themselves emotionally. Slightly fewer (77%) expressed positive feelings about their role as mother, and 72% about the kind of wife or partner they were. A divorced woman reported, "I was forced to become a working mother because of a divorce. I have become a continually developing, more interesting and competent person. My children have benefited, and we are proud of each other." A sales representative from Hawaii found that she is "learning to be responsible for my life. What I truly want or wish for, I get, and when there is more to do I figure out priorities and then tackle the problem. I've written my long- and short-term goals down and review them regularly. I try really hard to keep a positive mental attitude."

Women who work primarily for economic reasons rather than for personal satisfaction were, however, from 10% to 20% less positive about most of the surveyed areas. It seems that if a woman works because she wants to, she is more likely to feel positive about all areas of her life than if she works primarily because of economic reasons.

It's interesting to note the differences between women whose primary reason for working is economic and women whose primary reason for working is personal satisfaction. Fifty-six percent of those working for economic reasons felt positive about the impact of their working on their general relationship with their husbands or partners; yet 78% of those who work for personal satisfaction felt positive in that regard. Of those who work primarily for economic reasons, 73% felt that work had a positive impact on their children's general development, while 84% of those who work for personal satisfaction felt that way. Furthermore, 77% of those who work primarily for economic reasons felt that work had a positive impact on them emotionally, while 93% of those who work for personal satisfaction felt that way. Clearly, the option of working for personal satisfaction has a more positive effect upon oneself, one's partner, and one's family than the imperative of having to work for economic reasons. Yet, even among mothers who work for economic reasons primarily, the vast majority believed that work has had a positive effect on their families and on themselves.

Women as Nurturers and Partners

In addition to their role of provider, working mothers play the traditional roles of nurturer and partner. Most of our respondents felt some conflict between their home and work lives, and in our survey they gave us specific examples. A woman with two small children "came close within the last few weeks to giving up my career when my child-care arrangements fell apart." A divorced woman with older children pointed out that she felt it was easier to work when the children were older and explained that her "life is a breeze now." Only two of her four children are at home, and "they cook and clean and notice when I've had a bad day at the office. Nothing to it now."

Several women expressed resentment that they had to ask their husbands or partners to help; they would have preferred that the men view house and family responsibilities as shared rather than her primary responsibility. Those that have been able to take the initiative and not wait for what should be done or what ought to be done seem to be able to develop more responsiveness and self-motivation on the part of their husbands or partners and their children. Delegation of responsibilities is an organizational skill that is often born out of time constraints.

Family Relationships. Our survey revealed that 72% of the women stated that their work has had a positive effect on their children's emotional development. Over and over again, women described the involvement of their children in the functioning of the home. Obviously, the older the children, the more they helped. Most of the respondents said that their children were more independent and more responsible as a result of their working. A divorced woman with two children who works and has almost completed her college degree stated that "my children have assumed a great deal of responsibility for themselves and the household. I do not try to be Supermom. I encourage them to be responsible. I feel that they have learned many skills earlier and better because of the responsibility. I am pleased with my life."

A mother of four who owns a home for adults in New York

explained, "I always make myself available to the children as much as possible and support them in gaining as much independence as they can handle. I feel that due to my working, the children are better off—they are more independent and get a well-rounded idea of life in general. I juggle my schedule to keep them on an even keel. A great deal of help for working mothers could come from the fathers, but training them is sometimes impossible!"

Many of the women surveyed felt that at least one of the two partners should have a flexible schedule to accommodate the children's needs. Fifty-five percent of the women would like more help from their partners in attending to the needs of sick children, although 37% said that they did receive some help in this area. A government worker from Iowa was grateful that her husband is a university professor—"He can work flexible hours, do errands, come home if a child is ill. He is also only five minutes from home. This is why he now manages more household business." A woman from California with two teen-agers felt "fortunate in having a job where I can make my own hours. Since I work close to home, I'm able to go to soccer games and award luncheons."

A Massachusetts woman with three children runs a one-woman advertising agency in her home. She said, "I have a very unique working arrangement. My business is five years old and very successful. I am able to grow at my own pace. I plan to expand slowly as my children grow. I am very fortunate to have a job I enjoy, time to develop professionally, time for my husband, and time for my children." She summed it up: "My life is hectic and busy, but the quality is A-plus."

Clearly, there are some prerequisites to functioning well at work and at home. A teacher from Long Island said, "Life is easier with a supportive husband. If you are career-minded, this should be discussed in great detail before marriage. Each party should be aware of the other's needs and goals, yet establish mutual priorities." An assistant director of a mental health agency in Missouri spoke about the closeness she now feels to her husband as a result of her career "There are a number of professional things that my husband and I share that enrich both my professional life and our relationship."

Although many women have difficulty finding enough time for their partners and children, they feel that the emotional state of the family is good. A bookkeeper and office manager from New Mexico who is married for the second time explained the relationship between work and family life this way: "My husband understands my need for personal satisfaction, and he is one of the basic reasons I have such high job satisfaction and can handle the stress of a job and a family."

In terms of their sexual relationships, our respondents gave inconclusive information. It may be that they were not as candid in this area as in other areas of their lives, or it may be that this issue is beyond the scope of our focus. In any event, it is significant that approximately thc same number of women (25%) felt that work had a *very* positive effect on their sex lives as felt that it had no impact.

Twenty-three percent felt that work had no impact on their husband's or partner's satisfaction with their sexual activity; 12% did not answer this question. A total of 48% of those surveyed felt that work had a positive effect on their sexual satisfaction. According to our respondents, 41% said that their partners were satisfied with their sexual activity, while 24% of the working mothers who responded to our survey said that their partners or husbands had negative feelings about the impact of work on their satisfaction with the women's sexual activity.[12]

In order to make a more definitive analysis of the impact of work on sexual activity, more research needs to be done. We believe that many people are not aware of the ways in which work demands and time pressures affect their sexual relationships, nor are they cognizant of the theory that highly successful people may be diverting their sexual energy into their work lives. But it is our belief that people who feel good about themselves and feel in control of their lives make better bedpartners.

A New York professional with two small children spelled out the problem. "My husband and I both find that our relationship suffers not because of lack of love or desire, but simply because after the demands of work and the children have been met, there is often little energy left for each other."

On the other hand, many people indicated that they set aside time for their partners by going away weekends or taking vacations alone together. Others created personal sanctuaries in their bedrooms, declaring the room off-limits to the children during evening or weekend hours. For many couples, con-

12. It should also be noted that married and divorced women responded similarly to these questions, except, of course, for questions relating to husbands.

sciously taking time for each other and their relationship solidified their partnership and created an environment that helped nurture closeness.

A professional with two children summed up the balance that couples are attempting to achieve. "A good marriage gets better if work inside and outside the home is shared. Home and family are as important, and need as much intelligence and care, as 'work.' 'Love and work' (Freud's phrase) are both crucial to a good life."

In every category—self, partner, children—70% or more of our respondents stated that work has had a positive impact. Working mothers feel good about themselves and their families and the sense of control that they have over their lives. Like men, they want some degree of power and decision-making ability in determining the course of their lives. It is to their credit that these women have positive feelings about themselves professionally and personally. They're experiencing some conflict in terms of family and career responsibilities, but it is not surprising in view of the fact that they're providers, nurturers, and managers.

Family Logistics. Women expressed that they felt conflict and stress because of their dual role of provider and nurturer and because of the fact that family responsibilities are not shared to the same degree that economic responsibilities are shared. Forty-three percent felt that housecleaning presented conflicts for their families, 23% mentioned conflict about the marketing, and 22% in getting the laundry done. Although 53% of these women's partners contribute to financial management and planning (and this includes the single women as well), 34% of our respondents felt stress in this area. Although 56% of our respondents had a family income of $40,000 or more, 81% of them managed the family finances, whereas only 53% of the husbands contributed to this mythically male domain of household responsibilities. Working mothers are not only responsible for purchasing detergent, but they also manage the financing of houses, cars, insurance, household goods and services, and other major family needs. To the extent that society begins to respond to the economic power of working mothers, there ought to be a growth of goods and services directed toward their needs, and their potential buying power.

According to our survey, 95% of our respondents take care of household management, 90% take care of meal preparation, 70% take care of housecleaning, 81% take care of financial management, 93% handle marketing and shopping, 78% take care of the laundry, 70% are responsible for child care, 97% are in charge of resolving family problems, and 84% take care of arranging for lessons and special activities. Many have some help from partners, children, and people outside the family. It should be noted again that 85% of the women work full-time.

Most women indicated that they would like more help from their husbands or partners, especially in the areas of food marketing (55%) and meal preparation (50%). Additionally, 57% would like more help with general home management, and 55% need more assistance when their children are ill. Many of the women noted that their husbands are accepting more responsibility than they used to, and they're learning to be more supportive.[13] Approximately one-third of our respondents listed the areas of meal preparation, child care (and care of sick children), arrangements for lessons and special activities, and household management as sources of conflict in their families.

Interestingly, over one-third of the women surveyed *did have* support from their husbands or partners in running their homes, in marketing, and in meal preparation. Twenty-seven percent of the husbands or partners helped with the cleaning, almost one-fourth assisted with laundry chores, and almost one-half helped with the child care. Shared goals, respect for each other, and commitment to the family seemed to underscore the relationships in which both the male and female were able to work together to provide for the home and family needs that were essential to the well-being of all the members. Although many women characterized their partners as helpful, 10% more of the respondents in second or later marriages said that their husbands helped with home and family responsibilities. No doubt women who had married at a later age the second time, or women who concertedly sought a more equitable relationship in the second or later marriage, found partners who tended to share more than the partners of respondents in their first marriages.

---

13. *Working Woman* respondents were twice as unlikely to have outside help as our solicited sample. Again, this difference may be a function of income—68% of the solicited sample had incomes over $40,000; 39% of the *Working Woman* sample were in that category. Thirty-five percent of the *Working Woman* sample recorded incomes of $29,999 or less; whereas only 20% of the solicited sample was below $29,999.

However, in first marriages, husbands did help at a somewhat higher rate with day-to-day child care and resolving family problems than in second marriages. It could not be determined from our data, but this may be a result of the fact that the children are more likely to be the woman's from her first marriage rather than the man's, and as the parent, she is more involved in child care and resolving family problems than her husband, who is a stepparent.

Perspective on sharing came from many women. A mother of three children from a rural area in Iowa explained, "I had the good fortune to marry a college graduate in 1960 who felt that his masculinity was not threatened by ironing, dishes, cooking, and child care. Two of our children are boys who have watched their father help out at home and now themselves do the dishes and laundry, just because it needs to be done, without being asked."

A woman who had remarried said, "We recognize each other's talents. Whoever is the most competent in an area is responsible for that area (if neither is better, you get the job if you object the least). This didn't work at first until we got our egos under control. The most important factor in our lives is being flexible and looking out for each other. It is very important to state what you are feeling when some area of your life seems burdensome."

A North Carolina professional with one child suggested that women must work for evolution rather than revolution. She has a supportive spouse and has learned to accept help graciously. "Both of us recognize we need a 'wife' at home and so we pitch in together, which means a lot of give and take."

An Ohio mother of two lives with a man who is not the father of her children, yet he "likes my children and admires me as well as loves me. He is supportive and does not make me feel inferior to him. My ex-husband did. My advice is to find a man who doesn't make you feel any guiltier than you already feel."

While only 10% of our respondents had outside help for general household management, 42% had some housecleaning help. Women in a first marriage, according to our survey, were more likely to have help than those in a second marriage or single women. The former were 10% more likely to have a combined income of over $40,000, which may account for the increased proportion of outside help. Also, women under 35, who presumably had younger children, were more likely to need outside child-care help. In view of that, 57% of the younger women had help outside the family for child care, whereas only 40% of women over 35 had help outside the family for child care. The kind of help changes as family needs change—young children require child care, older children may require car-pooling and special activities—but all of them require someone who manages and delegate the jobs.

Most of the women who don't have help outside the family said that they do not desire it, except in connection with child care. Forty percent of the women indicated that they have some outside assistance to meet the needs of their children, but only 35% felt that children should ideally be cared for by help outside the family. Obviously, working mothers have not altogether resolved the guilt they feel when they can't be home to care for children. Those who have reconciled themselves to hiring help and can afford it said that it reduced stress and allowed them to go to work with more peace of mind.

A suburban New Yorker recently hired a live-in housekeeper. "It has changed our lives dramatically for the better," she said. "It has given us back some of the flexibility we lost when we had to arrange for a baby-sitter in advance. And having the housework, laundry, and cleaning done makes everything workable." A director of an undergraduate program in the Washington, D.C., area has some assistance from "a dependable mother substitute who is on salary with benefits. If it weren't for her, I would be up a creek." She added that one of the benefits of her arrangement was that "my son and his father have developed a close relationship, since my work involves travel and they are alone frequently. My son is growing up within an equal marriage, and I hope it will make him see women as truly equal."

A young woman with a new baby was able to return to her job as a self-employed lawyer by taking the baby to work with her or trading off with her husband. "For the first three months, my husband and I traded taking him to work with us, although I had him most of the time because I was nursing. Later we had a baby-sitter care for him beginning with a half-day a week and increasing to three days a week. My husband and I each work four day weeks and we each stay home one weekday with our child."

The issue of who is responsible for the home has been uniquely resolved by a government worker in Iowa who has an eleven-year-old daughter. "I don't delegate responsibilities at home because it's not my responsibility. The three of us work out the family needs a day at a time, without rigid plans, each contributing as much as they can. We volunteer to do the things that fit our schedules and preferences. I think it would be just awful to 'run a household.' I'm not burdened by any sense of duty to put dinner on the table or clean sheets on the bed, unless the others are sick. You may think our home must be a mess. Sometimes it is, but generally it's neat and clean, the laundry gets done, good meals get cooked, and our various hobbies indulged. Best of all, we love one another very much."

About 25% of the children of these working mothers help with the meal preparation, housecleaning, and laundry, while about one-sixth help with the marketing. A large majority of the respondents did not feel compelled to indicate that their children should help. But those women whose children help felt that sharing family chores fostered a sense of fairness, independence, equality, and, the satisfaction of having contributed something essential to the family. Both married women and single mothers claimed that their children should and, in fact, do help.

An entry-level government worker with five children felt strongly that her primary goal as a parent was to have her children become self-sufficient, responsible, self-confident members of the community. "All of us cook one dinner a week. We all have two rooms to clean (or an equal chore) on Saturday. I ask the children to participate in painting, yard work, and so forth. I told them at the beginning that if one person had to be the servant, that person would shrivel up, and if some people did no survival chores, they, too, would be incomplete human beings." A New York librarian put it this way, "No longer is shopping and laundry Mom's job. It is for whoever has the time. This situation promotes a much more cooperative atmosphere."

A New York professional "assigns specific jobs to children on a monthly rotation system; for example, setting the table, taking out the garbage, clearing the table." A woman who lives on an island in Maine has "the children help with the meals, which makes them feel important and gives me a little extra time to read a bedtime story or listen to a report for school."

A divorced woman with two children who lives in an urban area of Texas said, "I make my kids take a large responsibility for chores, housecleaning, and meals—it's good for them."

A somewhat higher percentage of divorced mothers than married mothers felt that their children should help with the housecleaning, marketing, and laundry. The only areas where the children of these mothers actually help significantly more is in meal preparation, over 20%, and in arranging for their own lessons and special activities, where twice as many children help.

A librarian from Iowa felt that "while outside help would considerably ease the burdens of housework, I feel somewhat of an obligation to give my two sons the opportunity to share in all the responsibilities of household management so that they won't grow up believing that all they need to do is pay someone—usually a woman—to do all the menial, necessary tasks."

A Minneapolis adult education coordinator described her approach: "The prevailing technique we utilize in our family to cope with the multiple roles we all encounter is open communication. When any problem arises we are committed to working it through by talking. We come to a decision and each person contributes to making it work." A California woman in a second marriage told us that she copes with multiple roles by having a "supportive husband who contributes more than 50%."

A taxpayer service representative from Arizona said, "Delegate! Ask for specific help. My husband would have helped me more if only I had asked. Make each family member responsible for seeing specific duties get done." She explained, "I had little education, since we were married when I was sixteen. My husband is supportive (and kind of proud) that I'm doing well in my job, which is very technical. He was very much against my going to work at first. We still had four of our six children at home and finances were tight. But since I started working, I have much more self-esteem, and he has admitted that since I could support myself if necessary, it has taken a load off his mind."

Many of the comments attested to the fact that the most successful women were able to set priorities and eliminate the nonessential. A professional from Massachusetts suggested the following: "Reduce the number of stress-causing events. For example, give up having a tidy home, fixing gourmet meals, keeping up with high fashion. Concentrate your energies on what you feel to be priorities to you. Never assume the household is solely the mother's responsibility, and make clear how you expect others to contribute to the common good of the household."

Woman as Pivotal Person in the Family

In our survey, 59% of those women who work primarily for economic reasons indicated that they feel conflict about family needs versus career needs. In spite of the fact that most are working full-time, fully 94% of those working for economic reasons have *primary* responsibility for home management, giving them *two* full-time jobs. Ninety-six percent of those who work primarily for economic reasons feel, too, that they're primarily responsible for resolving family problems, meaning that they have the emotional, as well as the physical, responsibility for the family. No wonder more than half feel some conflict between family needs and career needs; they have no one at home taking care of the needs and problems there. They are the pivotal person. It's important to note that of those working primarily for economic reasons, *only 4%* indicate that they have paid help for household management. These women are carrying the primary responsibility for home, family and career, with very little support.

This lack of support and the pivotal position that they play in the family as primary caretaker combine to create anxiety and disquiet at times. In addition, most working mothers carry a remnant of society's traditional expectations of them as mothers who should be home in the first place. Consequently, they often feel more pressure than working fathers have traditionally felt. In addition, they are coping with the everyday realities of working—commuting; expenses, such as lunch and travel; minor problems and frustrations at work; child care arrangements; physical health.

Still another issue was raised by a New Jersey woman. "The allegiance question is hard to answer. I enjoy both parts of my life. To enter into each one fully in its time and not to resent the time taken from the other is a conscious decision."

Flexibility in one's professional life eases some of the tension of career and family. One woman offered this description of resolving excessive demands at work: "It took me six months to accomplish this, but I have 'organized' my bosses in such a fashion so that they are completely honest with me about what is a rush job and what is truly not. This has helped me a great deal in getting priority items finished instead of spinning my wheels on items that could have waited until something of more importance was completed. If there have been many priority items on my schedule, I try to reserve one half-day every week or so to catch up on other items that are cluttering my desk.

"I place a great deal of importance on honesty and being informed. I feel that as a working woman with commitments at home, I cannot be put in the position of having to stay late at the drop of a hat on a frequent basis. I simply informed my bosses that this is my situation and that, whenever possible, I would prefer to come in early to get extra work finished rather than to stay late to do the same. They generally respect my wishes and, I feel, have made every effort to do so because I took the initiative and pointed out the problems that I faced in being imposed upon late in the day."

Illustrative of this organizational skill born out of necessity was this suggestion from an administrator in Virginia. "At work I do my more difficult and time-consuming tasks in the morning when I'm at my best, leaving the afternoon for anything unexpected that comes up."

Another example of shaping work schedules to conform somewhat to family responsibilities came from a professional woman in California. "After returning to my job when the baby was six months old, I arranged with my employer to work seventy-two rather than eighty hours each pay period. I am off every other Friday, which gives me a three-day weekend. This gives me a head start on chores, personal maintenance, and so forth, so that Saturday and Sunday are free for activities with my family. It's not enough, but it's a beginning."

Essential to these women's schedules is the fact that they took the initiative to devise creative work arrangements. It is important for working mothers to assess resources and options realistically and then work within the constraints to develop professional situations that are as acceptable to them as possible. Although corporations, ordinary work schedules, and our society tend to reinforce a nine-to-five, five-day-a-week system, some women have been able to develop creative options by being realistic, assertive, and self-motivated.

Because of their ability to distinguish between what is truly necessary and what is falsely perceived to be important at work, it's possible that working mothers will influence the psychology of work that has often existed in America. Men who were free to expand their work hours to meet real or perceived needs to get something done, or who were able to work at inefficient rates because their time was not limited, may now be influenced by women who must be more productive and efficient simply because of restraints on their available hours for work.

Juggling all the responsibilities of the working mother's life is difficult and, as a mother of a five- and seven-year-old from Maine told us, "Each week is a new adventure. At least I'm never bored! I love my work, but I wish I were paid more and had more flexibility with my hours. I am very aware of how dependent I am on other people (particularly baby-sitters) to make my life 'work.' The logistics involved in making sure my children's needs are met, as well as those of my husband and myself, are sometimes incredible."

"No one ever said that life was meant to be easy. I suppose in some ways our lives have not changed that much from those of pioneer women, only the setting is different," an executive secretary from Michigan with three children told us.

"In general, I've found that logistics is by far the hardest part of working motherhood. There's nothing you can't accomplish for a price—my price has been money, because I'm unwilling to spend all my waking hours keeping things together. If money were tighter, I know I would not be so calm about it all. In the last several years I've become very militant about the plight of working women and displaced homemakers, and nothing I've seen since I've been back in the business world has made me feel very optimistic."

From a manager in New York came this appraisal about her professional life. "My sanguine answers about time result from a lowering of expectations. Tiredness plays a very large role in my life since I became a mother!"

Another woman added, "Know your limitations—say no when you just can't do another thing." A professional woman from Florida suggested a realistic perspective: "Give up things and commitments that are not essential. Don't bring work home or home to work. Develop friendships with women and families that have similar lifestyles."

Although the majority of women who answered our questionnaire felt that work has been good for them, their relationships with their partners, and their children, they candidly revealed that work creates tremendous time pressures. Most felt conflicted because they couldn't do everything they would like to do.

Too Little Time

The most critical issue in working mothers' lives is *time.* Time, as a limited commodity, places constraints on everyone, no matter how energetic, talented, intelligent, or ingenious. There are only twenty-four hours in a day.

According to the survey, the time demands of professional life on one's time were considered excessive, at least sometimes, by 60% of the respondents. Fourteen percent found professional time-demands usually *excessive.* Those who work at home, presumably because it's hard to separate work time from family time, and divorced women, were even more likely to feel the impact of professional demands on their time.

In a given day, time has to be allocated to job, children, partner, home, self, community, friends, activities, and any other interests and concerns that people have. Almost universally, women put themselves and their personal needs and interests way behind their professional and familial obligations. But in so doing, they felt a certain unease because, as working women, they are supposed to be healthy, energetic, well-groomed, and properly attired.

Despite the time constraints created by their dual roles, most of the surveyed women were clearly concerned with the quality of their family lives. Survey comments suggested that the women had established priorities, were well-organized, and were making every effort to provide for the needs of their children, their partners, and themselves. Many stressed that perhaps their homes weren't as spotless as they once were, but the people in the family were doing well and many families had become more cooperative in assuming household and familial responsibilities.

In order to understand the nature of time and its application to the lives of working mothers, it is important to understand that one's assessment of time can be related to the value one attaches to a particular activity. Time can be judged quantitatively, qualitatively, or in both ways; that is, helping a child with homework requires an investment of both hours and energy which far exceed the hours and energy needed for such things as roasting a chicken. As a result, women may feel they have enough time for domestic tasks and not enough time for children—domestic tasks are qualitatively and quantitatively less time-consuming than child care. Family needs can be viewed as expansive; they can fill as much time as one has. Such demands as domestic tasks are usually much more limited and probably require less time in actual hours and emotional investment, thereby resulting in an assessment of having enough time for domestic tasks and not enough time for children or husbands.

More women felt that they had time for personal care (62%), probably because of its limited scope, than had time for social activities (40%). Fifty percent of those who responded felt that they didn't have enough time for their children. Women with younger children felt more keenly the lack of time to care for their children. A woman from North Carolina who works and is also finishing graduate school explained it this way: "I don't feel like such a great mother right now because I am away so much. However, it's quality not quantity of time that counts. I am a much better mother than I was when I stayed home. I believe that my going to school and working will in the long run have a positive effect on the attitude that our children (a boy and a girl) have about women, their capabilities, roles, and intellectual abilities." Another woman, from Texas, who works in a family business, provided special time for her two older children by taking them out to lunch, shopping, or to some special outing one at a time while her husband babysat with the other.

The issue of time and children is one that individuals need to assess for themselves; each family is different, and each child is different. Realistic expectations and objective evaluations of children's needs are essential here, for women can fall victim to their guilt and can be overcome by demands for their attention. In the words of Thomas Jefferson, they may then "find nothing so dreadful as voluntary slavery";[14] it is important for working mothers to be attuned to the needs of their children, but not enslaved by them.

Thirty-nine percent of our correspondents didn't have enough time for their husbands and partners, and virtually all of them were concerned about it. More than 50% did not have enough time for friends and personal development. They were also concerned about making time for community involve-

14. "Declaration of Causes and Necessity of Taking Up Arms; July 6, 1775" cited in Henry Steele Commager, ed., *Documents in American History* (New York: Appleton-Century-Crofts, Inc., 1958), p. 95.

ment, hobbies, extended families, travel, entertaining, social or cultural activities, and their wardrobes, but these needs were considered less essential. There was not one area listed where some of the women did not feel that they would like to have more time; women who are working for personal satisfaction rather than primarily for economic reasons, however, were slightly more likely (about 10%) to have more time for everything, most notably their husbands or partners.

Single and divorced mothers have somewhat less time than married mothers to devote to family life. The lack of the resource of an adult partner with whom to share home and family responsibilities places additional constraints on their lives. It seems clear that divorced women try very hard to maintain a balanced family life for themselves and their children, and they want to maintain homes, care for children, take care of themselves and participate in community life. A divorced woman from Oklahoma who has two children explained the dilemma this way: "No matter how artful we are at juggling everything, it really is too much for one person to handle. My children and I are very fortunate in having a healthy, lively communication. We talk about everything (almost); we fight things out and resolve them, and we always muster support for each other." Another woman, the mother of two children, said, "I make the most of every hour of my workday to do my work, then do the same with my leisure hours with my family."

The Trade-offs

Our respondents seemed candid about the difficulties of their lives. They did not describe idyllic households with cherubic youngsters willingly aiding and solicitous partners eagerly assisting. They told us about the frustrations and the pressures they faced. But we were also assured by their comments and by statistical computations, that it is possible to combine careers and families in ways that are healthy and fulfilling. It's not easy, though, and there is a price.

Most of the women surveyed emphasized that one must compromise and reduce expectations in order to manage a career and family successfully. Individuals compromised in different ways, but the reality of compromise itself was pervasive. Women worked through the notion of "Superwomen"; consciously and deliberately they made professional choices that coincided with family responsibilities. An editor expressed it this way: "I like to do everything well. I'm used to working hard and reaching my goals; I suppose I'm a bit of a perfectionist. I had to give up the notion that my family, my job, my home, could be perfect."

Others voiced the same view. "Most of all get rid of your 'Superwoman' complex!" This California therapist went on to assert, "I have fallen for the temptation to expect of myself that I do everything, as much and as well as women who have careers without families or families without careers. It cannot be done! Compromises have to be made." A Virginia woman wasn't quite so sanguine. "I'm tired and I wish I made more money so I could hire help or I wish I could stay home and do it myself."

The trade-offs are different for each woman, but some recurrent compromises are: slower professional growth; not being there for their children; estrangement and anger with husbands or partners; the inability to pursue personal needs and missed opportunities. A woman from Texas put the conflict succinctly: "Working might not be the burden it is if my working were not a necessity and if my working made the difference in our lifestyle. My pay still does not allow for any extras or luxuries that would help my home life."

A large number of our respondents felt that work demands were excessive. A New York woman with two children stated, "I thoroughly enjoy my work and am certain that were it not for the demands of my family (and by demands I include the enormous pleasure I get from my children and husband and my desire to be with them), I would be more successful in terms of recognition within my profession. For example, I have little time for professional activities outside my office."

Many women make compromises in their professional lives which result in low pay and limited advancement. A Michigan woman lost her part-time job (thirty hours a week) because she couldn't satisfy her boss's time demands. Her pay would not support a sitter in order for her to work after school hours. "So here I am," she told us, "out in the middle of a recession, feeling mad and sad and guilty as hell, and strangely relieved. I really need a job for economic reasons—our costs have skyrocketed. If there weren't the children to consider, I would be working full-time by now. But I need a job during school hours only, they are few and far between, and it's either don't work or work the forty hours and hire a sitter, which I may bring myself to do yet. I feel very torn because the job has been good, but the kids have needs, too. I want to be there and be a good mother. So I guess the choice for this working mother is turning out to be the kids."

A lawyer told us, "I have had to slow my career growth somewhat to accommodate my family." A nurse from Northern California has had to live apart from her husband in Southern California because "I didn't want to give up my job." Another Californian, a C.P.A. who is divorced, told us, "I had to give up a job as an auditor to be a better mother. I miss the traveling and entertaining, but I expect to resume that type of work when my son is grown."

The California psychotherapist mentioned earlier also alluded to a career trade-off that most men in our society cannot even envision. "Having a family drastically changed my career plans. If I did not have children, I probably would have ended up in academics rather than in private practice. I immediately discovered how demanding it is to raise small children by trying to write a Ph.D. dissertation right after my first baby was born. I ended up taking six years off from my career. I value the tremendous importance of mothering in the early years of childhood and did not want to leave that job to someone else. I do not regret that decision, but I have experienced a painful period of readjustment at both ends of this time-out. It is difficult to give up your identity of professional woman to be 'just a housewife and mother.' To do that for a long time had a subtly undermining effect on my confidence and professional self-esteem, and it was not easy to return to my profession, even though I was fully committed to do so. I am glad I did it the way I did."

A librarian from Michigan defined the stress of having a corporate husband who is transferred frequently. "It is difficult to have a career when a corporation moves your husband around. Obviously he makes more money, so I take second place—and they [the corporation] don't care if I work. They view me as freeing him to be at work fifteen hours a day." A nurse from South Carolina who is married to a man in the military expressed a similar feeling that the impact of being transferred is frustrating for working wives: "Frequent moves made it impossible for me to use my GI Bill to pursue a doctorate."

A woman whose husband recently left her with two small children said that she was lucky to find a part-time job in her field, "but come any financial crisis in the company, I will be the first to be let go." Paradoxically, single mothers are often regarded as working to supplement income and therefore not in need of the same pay as the men in comparable jobs "who are supporting a family."

Although many women have compromised their professional goals, at least for the time that their children are young, some feel that they have compromised their family goals. This feeling was poignantly expressed by a Wisconsin woman who said that she would have preferred to be a full-time wife and mother. "I often feel angry with myself. My children are five and two and a half, and I see them growing up so fast. Perhaps there's always time to work, but they won't be little for long. But, on the other hand, the academic field is hard to find jobs in nowadays, and I wonder if I could get back in after being out for a while. And we've grown accustomed to my salary. Is it fair to my husband to be the sole breadwinner?"

A woman who told us that she feels good about herself and her relationship with her family still has lingering doubts about her choices. "I am happy, competent, and totally satisfied professionally. My insecurities are about child-rearing and motherhood, not work. Children are demanding, stressful, unpredictable, and omnipresent. But what greater responsibility do we have than to raise our children well?"

A medical transcriber from Maine compared herself to an elastic band being pulled in two directions. A New Yorker said that many times she "feels like the taffy in a taffy pull. I try to give each of the children, as well as my husband, a special time of the day when I focus only on that person for a certain period of time."

When the trade-offs seem to put the children on the negative side, the mother often experiences a great deal of guilt. "The worst problem is the guilt factor of not being flexible enough to do the things I feel I need to do to have time with the children. I wish I had the time so that my children could be a little less responsible and allowed to be kids," a woman from Michigan who owns her own business sadly declared. "I feel I've cheated my kids out of some of the joys of childhood experiences."

A New York mother of three who is a caterer put it this way. "My most difficult area of guilt, stress, pressure, is the children. Trying to car pool and juggle their after-school activities and in-school performances with my business schedule makes me very tense. I want to be supportive, but my mind is a million miles away on rentals and pricing menus and directing help."

A professional woman from Illinois expressed the feelings of isolation that other working mothers alluded to, especially those who work at home. "Although I have the ideal situation of working at home and setting my own hours, I miss the people and the social atmosphere of an office. I feel more like a full-time housewife because my only contact during the day is with other 'at-home' mothers."

Divorced women feel the trade-offs painfully. A professional from Maine who manages a department store wrote, "In reviewing this questionnaire, it is very clear to me that I find great satisfaction, pride, and a sense of achievement in my career, but I am experiencing great stress in reconciling its demands with those of my small child. I feel it is a tremendous task which leaves all three parts shortchanged—career, child, yourself. I'm sure I'm not alone in my particular situation, but it feels as if I am a lot of the time."

Other women noted that the price they paid for working and having children has been *self,* and many hoped that their husbands or partners would begin to share more. An air force officer from Nebraska felt that the problem is "always having the home duties fall on the woman as 'her' responsibility, regardless of her position outside the home. I have yet to see a couple where both adults work and the husband has the majority of the home responsibilities. I get so tired of seeing Superwoman trying to make ends meet."

A woman from California who has only recently gone back to work commented about the support her husband gives her. "He has only been partially helpful. Rather than offering to take one-half the load, he 'assists' me when asked. I guess I'm becoming more and more resentful of this situation. I have told him how I feel, but he prefers not to take me seriously. He likes the added income, but he wishes I were more available. At this point I am doing as little as I can get away with, and that's lots more than he does."

Although most of the women felt reasonably satisfied with their choices, a few obviously resented the demands being made of them. A retired nurse who has become the owner of a real estate agency in New Jersey posited, "The demands on a woman today are just too much! We must be successful businesswomen, loving partners, available mothers, expert housekeepers, thin and gorgeous, always young and athletic, intellectual and well-read. It's still a man's world—we just try harder."

A part-time clerical worker from Ohio added, "I have always believed the person liberated in women's lib is the man. As a woman takes on more financial responsibilities, she eliminates a lot of stress on the man." A professional from New York City who rated her relationships with her husband and children as somewhat negative "cynically believes the situation to be nearly impossible and expects it not to improve in our lifetime. I work almost as hard at managing and organizing my two lives as I do living either of them. One has to be super at *that,* most of all."

The solutions may not be as comfortable as one would like; the compromises may be painful. "We intend to have only one child," concluded a Rhode Island librarian regretfully. Some were sad and some felt selfish because they had come to this decision. But the realities of their lives made it clear that they couldn't have everything, and perhaps one of the things that difficult economic conditions brought was smaller families.

Clearly, many women are doing more than they can do either successfully or efficiently, and many feel overwhelmed, pressured, distressed, and guilty. Although some of these feelings are an outgrowth of ways in which these women were raised, and the values that they were taught, much of this anxiety does come from the very real pressure of their dual responsibilities. Unlike men, whose traditional focus has been career, most of these women have two equally demanding foci, and a tradition of serving others and responding to society's messages to them instead of asserting their own independence and shaping their *own* messages to themselves.

Central to working mothers' sense of well-being is the understanding that life is a series of trade-offs, of compromises. Many women have gained, through the vicissitudes of their lives, a certain equanimity. They know and accept the fact that they can't have everything. At least that's what they verbalize. Some are more astute than others about what they've traded off, and some are perceptive about the consequences of their actions, but consistently we found that women are in touch with what they want and, within the areas of their control, with what they have to give up in order to achieve that. Often having to give up something is unfair, significant, painful, or difficult. The prices they pay are indeed high.

Our concern is with *how* working mothers structure their lives, and not at this time with how society ought to change in order to be more responsive to human needs. That is not to say that we believe that no changes need be made in the work place, but the thrust of our fact-finding was the ways women combine careers and families *now,* not in the future. Just as our country resisted the unionization of exploited factory workers until the early part of this century, so it has not validated the needs and rights of working parents. Just as struggling unionizers continued to work at their jobs while they fought to change the system, so struggling working parents will no doubt have to survive within the present unjust limitations while they fight to change the system. Throughout its brief history, this country has withstood fundamental social change—we have become industrialized, urbanized, integrated, and we have extended the vote to females, none of which was intrinsically part of our society from the beginning. Change is possible, but it is a long time in coming. In the meantime, oppressed people struggling for individual rights need to have support systems; there is comfort and courage in sharing with others.

The Support Systems

Support systems can come from within or outside, and women seem to have a need for both emotional and practical support. Perhaps the need for emotional support stems from the lack of entitlement women feel to demand their rights without validation from those around them. Often they seem to be adamant about getting the emotional and indirect support they need, and passive about negotiating for practical, direct support.

Women are sustained by different support systems, from religious beliefs to understanding partners to outside assistance in caring for children and homes. Support systems for one's personal life can aid in eliminating stress that can carry over into one's work environment. Conversely, a supportive work environment can result in less stress in one's personal life. In fact, of the women who felt no conflict between family and career, 90% said that they had a supportive work environment. Similarly, of those who said that they had enough time for their husbands and children, at least 85% said that their work environment was supportive.

* * *

Having Emotional Support. Supportive husbands or partners were cited again and again in the questionnaires. A public relations director for a 36,000-student school district in Florida, with two children of her own, noted, "The most constructive help I have is a husband who is a full-time partner in our family. There is no such thing as his role or my role—the smooth running of our family is both our roles."

Added an administrative assistant for a consulting engineering firm in Louisiana, "My husband is very proud of my position and all that I have achieved for my personal goals." The mother of six children, she added that "I, in turn, am very supportive of him and his goals and personal wishes. To be a full-time wife and mother is not my aim in life. I love both my children and my job as well as my husband."

An administrator said that her husband, too, is supportive, and she has "thought many times how difficult my life could be without his help and support. I believe the men in this situation (married, with wife working, and children) are the key to 75% of the pressure."

A social scientist from Connecticut brought another dimension to the ways in which husbands or partners can be supportive. "My husband and I have similar occupations and thus are able to share our professional and family concerns. We are also fortunate to have excellent child-care facilities at the university with which my husband is employed, and thus he and our child are able to have better interaction than many fathers and children."

A Missouri systems analyst attested to the value of professional associations. "I belong to a women's organization of data processors, which is basically a networking organization. I make friends with women whom I perceive to have the same problems, and yet are successful."

A Massachusetts mother of three who is a commercial construction estimator and metal buildings coordinator suggested another kind of support network. "Women's magazines such as *Savvy* and *Working Woman* are reassuring and helpful."

An administrator who has an infant said that "talking to other new mothers and working women" provides sources for helpful ideas and gets rid of some of the frustration she feels. In addition, she compares herself "to a nonworking young mother I know, and I imagine her day with no one to talk to and no new ideas around."

Other people found that their support system came from involvement in religion or a spiritual life. Said a secretary from Michigan, "Our home has a deep spiritual foundation. My husband and I seek guidance from God and work out solutions together on even the slightest problems. Our relationship is not perfect, but it works for us. I feel that support from my husband gives me the confidence to perform as a working mother and wife successfully."

Many women's organizations and women's networks now help those who are forming career goals. They're responsive to and supportive of the special concerns of women, whether they're established in their careers or are entering the work place or making a career change.

Women helping women is widespread. And men do help women, too. But still, working mothers are largely on their own. Although formal, organized support systems would help alleviate the stress that working mothers feel, they don't exist on any wide scale. That is not to say that individual support services don't exist in isolated situations; they do. To a larger extent, though, we found that women have created systems to support their emotional and psychological needs, which are equally essential to their well-being.

Having Practical Support. Our survey asked about seventeen potential support systems or services that working mothers might like to have more accessible. The areas ranged from marketing and home delivery to communal kitchens. Although the survey results indicated that there was some interest evidenced in nearly all the categories, the areas where more than half the women expressed a need for support were:

—Adequate arrangements for a sick child at school
—Safe mass transportation
—Dependable help
—Flexible work schedule
—Housecleaning services
—Personal time off

In addition, younger women (with younger children) felt strongly about:

—Day care
—Sitter services
—After-school programs

In spite of the needs expressed in the objective data of the survey, the open-ended comments of the surveyed women did not describe support systems that they now have in their lives. Conceivably, this is related to the fact that such systems are not widely available. It is even possible that having support services to aid them as working mothers is something that many women don't consciously consider, so they don't even try to find them or discuss them. This could be a function, again, of feelings of lack of legitimacy or entitlement on the part of the women.

Fifty-one percent of our respondents wished that flexible work schedules were more available. Some women, in fact, had been able to shape their own work schedules, at least to some degree. Said a Connecticut administrator, "I have a flexible work schedule, and within limits, that allows me to juggle my schedule to fit my 2½-year-old son's schedule. I'm able to do all the activities that nonworking mothers do."

A professional woman from Minnesota who has one child and is expecting another added, "A flexible time schedule has helped us the most so far. I work from 6:30 A.M. to 3:00 P.M., and my husband prepares our daughter in the mornings to take her to a day-care home. I pick her up in the afternoons, and we have some time to spend together before dinner."

A much needed support system is the availability of child-care facilities for the middle class. A single parent from Virginia told us, "I feel there should be more day-care facilities offered by the businesses with whom working mothers are employed. This would eliminate travel time to and from sitters, mothers or fathers could spend lunch with children, and it could be less expensive than individual baby-sitters."

On-site day care would help a New Jersey professional in her early thirties, "More companies should provide on-site day care, which would lower employee absenteeism." This woman had several concrete suggestions. "I would like to see parental leaves of at least six months, then part-time work (in your current position) for around five years, with no loss of seniority." Moreover, she maintains that "day-care costs us twenty dollars a day; yet the maximum tax credit we receive is four hundred dollars [a year]. The total cost should be deductible." She suggested evening medical hours as well, a suggestion offered by many women.

As logical and desirable as these suggestions may seem to working mothers, it must be understood that businesses, and our society, are not apt at this point to implement widespread change because it benefits the family. Regrettable as it is that society does not seem to act upon its expressed belief in the importance of family life, the fact is that change does not occur because it is inherently just or humane or sensible.

A woman in Idaho found inexpensive child care by developing a babysitting co-op with other single parents in her university community. It wasn't ideal, but it was acceptable. Another woman told us that "near me is a condominium for people fifty-five and older—an excellent source for child-care help, household help, any help. Just hang up signs—there are a lot of older people ready, willing, and capable."

The women in our survey often cited physical fitness as a kind of support system. A marriage counselor from California summed up the view of many. "I use physical fitness to maintain my overall energy level—aerobic exercise daily, vegetarian foods, whole foods. I'd like to see women, especially working mothers, be more selfish in terms of health—carve out and demand time for physical care and exercise, meditation and friendship with other women. What's it all for if we aren't enjoying life?"

Is Life Simpler for Younger Mothers?

We had expected that younger women would feel more control over their lives and would experience less guilt than older women in combining careers and families. We had assumed that the younger women had different expectations about being wife and mother than the women over 35. Yet, in our survey, in which 30% of the respondents were under 35, only 77% of the younger women felt that they had control over their lives as opposed to 88% of the older women. Conceivably, feelings of control are a function of age; it could also be a result of younger women's expectations of more control not having materialized. But it is noteworthy that women under 35, presumably with more career opportunities and less rigid attitudes, had less of a feeling of autonomy than older women. However, the number of those who said that they had control over their lives was still high (77%).

Working mothers showed common response patterns regardless of age; that is, women under thirty-five tended to respond the same way that women over thirty-five did. It is interesting to note that although women under thirty-five were generally positive about themselves and their work, they were somewhat less so than older women in evaluating the effect of their jobs on themselves and their children.

Women under thirty-five felt a lack of time even more strongly than the women over thirty-five, especially in the areas of children's activities and their children in general. The women under thirty-five have a much stronger need for outside child-care help than the women over thirty-five. This most certainly stems from the fact that their children are younger and require greater physical attention.

In our survey, more younger women (under 35) had one child (54%) than had two children (39%). This could be a function of our demographics, or of the fact that women often start their families later now, or that there is a trend among younger Americans, especially those who are working, well-educated, and well-to-do, to have small families (in fact, only one child). But presumably, support systems, such as availability of child care, have become a factor in some couples' decision to limit their families. America's young people are opting to have fewer, or no, children. This trend is certain to have ramifications for our society.

It's conceivable that the generation of females that is now in its teenage years, and which is largely a product of parents who were aware of, and no doubt influenced by, the women's movement of the 1960s, will have attitudes that are different from those women now in our thirty-five-and-under group.

In general, then, it didn't make much difference in our survey whether women were under or over thirty-five, whether they were married or single, working part-time or full-time, were urban or suburban; they experience largely the same stresses and satisfactions. That is not to say, however, that there were no differences. But what was so striking in our findings was the universality of the experience of being a working mother.

They're Working!

What our society expects of women, what their husbands or partners expect of them, what their colleagues expect of them, what their children expect of them, and what they expect of themselves may seem irreconcilable to many women. But based on our research, there are those who have reconciled these expectations, and to the extent that they have resolved them, they experience less conflict and are better able to integrate their personal and professional lives.

It is our belief that the structure of today's family is tremendously varied. It ranges from the traditional family system of the 1950s, wherein only men work outside the home, women are homemakers, and roles are clearly defined by gender, to the egalitarian family where roles are less defined and where responsibilities are not gender-based. Family structure and the mother's role in the family depend upon education, training, individual motivation, economic conditions, marital status, and a wide range of psychological and sociological factors. Furthermore, the structure and roles may change from year to year or from one set of circumstances to another.

Every family is different. In some families, choices are based on individual determinations, not on society's expectations. Other families are attempting to respond to individual needs within a tight, traditional gender-based relationship. For the most part, contemporary working mothers and their families are attempting to find where they feel most comfortable, given their expectations and their individual needs. Finding one's place can be seen as a process, ever in a state of change, and yet characterized by certain identifiable qualities at any given time.

In the more equitable situations, roles are shared—mothers and fathers both work, mothers and fathers both nurture, and children are an integral part of the family, both emotionally and functionally. Each person performs tasks and takes on responsibilities for the common good of the family, not for the ego satisfaction of any one person. Some families are able to achieve this level with little strife; others experience a great deal of upheaval, anger, and resentment and still do not have a truly egalitarian household.

Most of the women we surveyed seemed to be moving toward more egalitarian family structures. Some of the movement is slow, some painful, but there is clearly movement. Most women felt that the change is positive.

An admissions officer from Missouri who has two children is just beginning to resolve the problems of the shared roles of provider and caretaker with her husband. "I feel that although most men enjoy the benefits of two incomes, they fail to realize the amount of time it takes to be a housewife and mother. Women have been, and are, taken for granted. Many men spend Sunday afternoon in front of the television while the working mother mends, cooks, and so forth. Women buy books like *The Total Woman* to 'guide' them through. But it's men who need to be educated on the needs of women—all women."

A Minnesota educator elaborated on the initiative and assertiveness necessary to actively shape one's life so that careers and families are combined successfully. "I have chosen to work in a field which allows me to work around my family. If you can get to a high enough position so that you can usually develop people's trust and involve others in understanding such needs as arrangements for a sick child, it works out. I usually don't *ask* if a need comes up, I *state,* 'I have to pick up a child and I'll be back in twenty minutes.'"

Optimally, families can evolve into the kind of smooth-functioning group described by a Massachusetts professional who's been married for over twenty years: "We began our married life in the traditional way, I with the kids, laundry, cooking, cleaning, and my husband with the job, lawn, maintenance. Many discussions later a more equitable way of doing things evolved. He loves to cook—I hate it; so he does it. He hates to keep track of the kids' schedules and pay bills. I enjoy it, so I do it. No one likes housework, so we all do it. The boys are very much involved in doing their part at home. There is an expectation that we all 'work outside the home' (kids at school, parents for pay), and no one has the liberty of sitting back and being waited on. We all vacuum and dust and empty trash and do dishes. There are no more slaves in our house. I have always felt my husband is top priority, my kids second, my job third, and my house fourth. My husband, fortunately, concurs with this priority list. Our jobs are careers, but not all-consuming. We give them our best but not twenty-four hours per day. Both of us could be making more money, perhaps, if we had made the job 'number one,' but where would we be *really?* The boys are happy, well-adjusted, outgoing, fun-loving, hard-working boys. I'm proud of them and they, in turn, are proud of me. We just moved to Massachusetts after thirteen years in Maryland for *my* job—not his. He had to hunt for one, but he's an engineer and he was able to get a good one. It has worked out for us—it wasn't always easy, but most of the time it's been fun!"

For this woman, her priorities coincided with her husband's. In other cases, it takes a great deal of trial and error, negotiation and compromise, to determine who and what comes first. But the issue is not so much what comes first as *how* families interact with mutual respect and caring to determine their common goals and how they can be pursued together.

There are always choices. Usually they're not easy, or clear. They require a sense of legitimacy and entitlement so that they can be honestly assessed. Decisions should be made by independent, autonomous adults who analyze situations in terms of *mutually* defined family goals. It can be done; many families are doing it. The ways in which specific women have made the choices to balance their lives, and to help combine careers and families, can best be described by the women themselves. We interviewed several women to find out how they, and their families, work.

Part II

Letting Women Speak for Themselves

As soon as it became known in our personal and professional circles that we were planning to interview working mothers, we were besieged with suggestions. "Interview my wife; she's one of a kind." "I know someone interesting you should talk to." "Talk to my boss, she's amazing." "An unusual woman works for me; she's a good candidate for you." "My mother is incredible, she's been combining a career and family for years."

The pride and enthusiasm which consistently accompanied the proposal suggested to us that there are, in fact, many women who have effectively managed a career and family; yet each seemed to those around her an anomaly. It seemed to us that people believed that each accomplished woman had achieved success as an individual, and that her success was achieved in a vacuum. There was little awareness that many women, all over the country, have been juggling career and family for years. What struck us was that these women had little recognition, either individually or as a group, personally or professionally. It underscored again the isolation and estrangement that working mothers continue to feel, even in a society that seemingly has changed so much in the last few years. Again and again, we sensed that these working mothers feel atypical, unique, different from other people. Yet we found that they exist all over.

We selected twenty-five women from within our surveyed group to talk to. We wanted to find a representative group of people who lead productive lives and who have solved some of the common problems that women face today. Based on our survey results, we knew that most working mothers are concerned about establishing priorities, about relationships, about finding help and support, about time, and about trade-offs. More specifically, we knew that many contemporary women have one or more pervasive aspects of their lives which dramatically affect everything else: being a single mother; having young children; working from home; living on a limited income; having children first, then a career; establishing a career first, then having children; being professionally ambitious; being primarily home-oriented; having a second or later marriage. Additionally, we believed that there were some women living alternate or innovative life-styles who could provide insight and perspective that might not otherwise be readily available to others.

We looked for women in different kinds of careers and different family constellations. Demographically, we tried to achieve a cross-section in terms of race, marital status, profession, income, age, number and ages of children, geographic area, work situation, living arrangements. We chose people who seemed to address their lives with creativity, energy, and seriousness.

Without exception, the women we contacted agreed to be interviewed.[1] In most situations, our interview would begin quite formally, in an environment that could be characterized as professional. The women were their "public" selves, and they answered most of our questions circumspectly at first. As the interview progressed, however, they relaxed and became more candid and revealing. There was a feeling of our being friends discussing shared experiences. One professional, for example, told us that when she came home at night and there were problems with her children, she would be tense. She then laughed and said, "That's shorthand; you're a working mother, you know what I mean. I scream."

We did know. No matter how different people's lives seemed on the surface, we discovered that working mothers experience common joys and frustrations, doubts and triumphs. The women seemed to feel that we would understand what they were talking about; they trusted us to tell others what they had learned.

It occurred to us that perhaps working mothers have lost something that generations before have had—someone close to talk to. In extended families, women had other family members nearby, and although those ears weren't always perfect ones, they were ears! As full-time homemakers, women have

---

1. All names have been changed to protect confidentiality, and all the interviews have been shortened.

had neighbors or other friends with whom they could commiserate. But working mothers have so little time that they cannot afford the luxury of long lunch hours socializing or intimate telephone conversations. For the most part, they rarely take the hour and a half we spent together to talk to a friend.

We became that friend. Or so it seemed. Women often told us that "I've never said this before, but—" or "Right now, as I'm talking to you, I'm realizing that—" or "You've made me ask myself some questions I haven't asked in years." They appreciated our recognition of their efforts and our interest in them as a source for other women. They felt good about sharing their achievements and uncertainties with us, and we, in turn, feel quite honored that they have entrusted their hopes and fears, in short, their private selves, to us.

Ann Cunningham

Getting Started

Ann is the wife of a college professor and the mother of five boys. She lives in New England in a rural area about ten minutes from a large city. After years of caring for her family, she took a first, tentative step toward working outside the home by getting a job as a real estate salesperson.

I'm a real estate person at the local Century 21 office. I work eight hours per week in the office and put in as much as thirty to forty hours per week in the field, depending on family needs. My husband, Frank, a professor at the University, takes a lot of responsibility for the boys in the summer. If he were not available, in the summer I couldn't work full-time. My children's ages range from eight to nineteen; four go to school here and my oldest is away at school.

When I find work is beginning to be too much of a strain on the family I can back off. I can work at home, but it is difficult with the children around; when I'm available at home it's harder for them to think I'm really working. At the office, if I'm not on duty, I'm flexible enough to leave and pick them up at school and drop them somewhere. They'll say, "Mom, can you pick us up?" and I'll say, "I'm really busy," and they'll say "All the other moms are working." They really haven't grasped the fact that I'm working, because I still do most of the family things I did before.

It's not like Mom is gone from nine to five, because I can be home for days. I can do a lot of my work in the evenings. But there have been times when I have had an appointment I had to keep and I missed one of their games. They have to understand that it is part of my job; I can't always be there. They understand it intellectually, but they would prefer if I didn't work.

My husband would also prefer to have me at home. But he knows it's good for me and that whatever I bring in we can use. He would very much like a domestic person, which I am not; I never was. I love animals, but I am not the kind of person who can make preserves. I like to sew, but I didn't have any satisfaction cleaning house.

Although my working isn't essential economically, it is important. When I make a commission, it goes to pay off something or get something we've all been waiting for. Everyone appreciates it, but it's not a regular thing. The kids say, "When Mom gets paid we can go get new clothes"; but when Mom doesn't get paid they say, "How come you're working for nothing?" They don't take my work very seriously because I don't have a visible paycheck. It's difficult and sometimes I've thought I'd be better off in a job with a regular paycheck, but I'm not ready for that yet.

I'm going back to school full-time in the fall. I don't have a definite goal in mind, but I want to get a degree. I think I'm going to major in public relations. I'm forty years old and I need something more stable than the real estate business. I'll work while I go to school as long as I am able. The older kids are good about taking care of the younger ones. I have to learn to delegate more responsibilities; they're capable now.

The chores are a real hassle sometimes. I get very distressed with the kids if they are not done. They have to be reminded constantly. Take the animals, for instance. The kids are supposed to help and sometimes it's inconvenient, but I want them to learn to care about something besides themselves, even though it is more of a burden on me to make them feed the animals. They do it, but I have to remind them.

I have found that the working has changed me. If dinner is

not ready or I haven't washed the clothes, I don't feel guilty and Frank doesn't pressure me about things.

I think if I had gone to work when the kids were younger, they would have been more responsible. As it is now, my husband and I often do it for them rather than hassle them about it. They are better about doing things if I write it down and leave a note, but I still don't have it solved.

I also find it's frustrating to work hard and not make money at it. I like real estate and I'm putting in a lot of hours, but right now you can't make a living at it. I feel maybe it's not fair to take time from the family and have nothing to show for it. With five kids needing so many things, maybe it isn't fair to pursue something that isn't paying off.

I haven't found the perfect way yet. I'm really not organized enough. I keep trying to set so many hours a week for chores, but I have constant interruptions, so that whatever I plan to do doesn't happen. If I plan to get groceries on Tuesday, I end up getting a call to show a house. Or one of the kids says, "I have to go for sneakers." The only thing I can organize is my work. I make a list of the most important things that have to get done, the calls, and the appointments. As far as the house goes, it gets cleaned when someone is coming for dinner.

My advice to my kids is don't get married until you feel your life is heading somewhere. I hate the thought of them saddled with young wives and babies. We went through that, and it's much better to achieve educational goals and do what you want to do before you become responsible for others. They are growing up better informed. I think they realize that if they are going to live with someone, they had better share roles or it isn't going to work out.

If I had to do it again, I'd go to work sooner. Not that I'd want to leave the babies or kids, but I'd want to go to work part-time so that they would realize I'm a person and I need my own space and my own time. It's not difficult for them to realize mothers are people, and I wish I had started sooner because then they'd move over a bit. Working I feel alive and needed because I've added a new dimension to my life.

Elaine Dwyer

With Small Children

Elaine is a Midwesterner who moved to the Pacific Northwest a couple of years ago. She and her husband, John, are expecting a second child. They plan to have that baby at home, with the help of a midwife. Their son, Tommy, is a preschooler. A nurse, Elaine is adding to her professional credentials by going for her Bachelor of Science degree, even though the nursing certificate she has is adequate.

I am a float nurse; that is, I am not attached to any particular unit or group of people. I chose this position because I'm a student and I'm working part-time. When you belong to a unit, you are expected to work extra shifts when somebody else is sick. I thought it would make more sense not to have those strings pulling at me for whatever reason. Ultimately you're talking about patients who will not have the care they need if a nurse can't get to work. I didn't want to deal with the confrontations it would take to say, "No, I can't do it. My life is more important."

It has been a real transition. I graduated from nursing school in 1969 and have worked full-time ever since. I've always been totally involved in my profession until now. For the past two years I have been going to college also. When I went to nursing school the first time, I was in a diploma program, which is like a trade school, no college credit. The trend now in nursing, as in other professions, is to get a college degree, so the emphasis of my career now is more on school and not on work. It has been a struggle because I prefer working to going to school. But school will only last a bit longer, and I'll work as a nurse for the rest of my life.

There are frustrations with working and having a family. Before I had kids I used to think day care would be a real easy thing to do—drop them off, no big deal. Since I'm the oldest of thirteen children, I know what it's like to be around kids, so I wasn't in a real panic about child-rearing. It was when I hit nursing school and started learning all this developmental stuff that I really learned what I didn't know when I was helping to raise my brothers and sisters.

John's real family-oriented. That's one thing we've had to work out the past couple of years. He thought I was not spending enough time with him and Tommy. I listened and I started to really look at my hours and days. One of the ways I decided to handle that was to give up my weekend shifts so that on Saturday and Sunday the three of us can do things together. However, it also means more work for John, because I have more shifts during the week. I don't share as much responsibility for errands, and on Thursday and Friday he has all that responsibility. It is a compromise for him because the boys go for a drink on Friday night after work, and he has to miss it.

Day-care is difficult for me to deal with because my mom stayed home with us. She was always there. There are times when a kid really needs to have a parent there. Coming home from school is an important time for kids to talk, just to know that you're around. Now we drop Tommy off and pick him up, but when he's older and goes to school and comes home by himself, it's going to be hard to work out. There are after-school programs, but I am torn because I know both John and I need to spend time with our kids and I don't want day care to be a dumping ground.

I was really day care conscious even before I had a child. I interviewed day-cares when I was pregnant and found a place for the baby. The center I chose was in the north end of town, and even after we moved to the south end, I kept Tommy in the same day-care for stability because I really liked the people. It was in a home and the teacher had a license for twelve kids. She was like an aunt to me, yet we still had a business relationship. I decided to drive the extra miles and spend the extra money in gas to have security. I knew he was in a place where he was happy. He started going ten hours a week when he was four months old.

Day care is difficult because you miss so much of what they're doing, but I know if I stayed at home with him, I'd go nuts. Even though I respect the fact that my mom was there, I always knew I could never do it, I didn't want to do it, I didn't think I was the kind of person.

I try to spend quality time with Tommy. I think he wraps me around his finger because he knows when we're together he has my attention. Around the time he turned three, he and I started having serious problems. The twos weren't so bad, but the threes are. He's learning to be more independent and finding out what he wants to do. He will listen, but he's always testing limits. It drives me nuts. I know in school he has to be more controlled and it's normal for kids to act up more with parents. I think I'm soft and let him get away with more; I set limits because I know he needs limits, but he just breaks them.

Now I find myself doing more of what John has been doing from the beginning; that is, being more vehement with him when he's made me angry. It's difficult to keep things balanced.

John and I have tried to allow each other time to do things alone, but it doesn't always work out. Right now John is backpacking in the mountains for a week. The first year after Tommy was born I really wanted times when John and I could go out alone. We bought season tickets to a local theater two years in a row. This year it has not been as important because the three of us have such a short amount of time together that I've been willing to decrease the amount of time John and I have alone. When the second baby comes along we might get season tickets again.

I'm feeling the need to go away by myself now that John's been away. Maybe I just need to see some of my old friends in the Midwest. We moved from Michigan here three years ago, and it took me more than a year to feel comfortable. I'm still a little homesick. You make new friends, but you don't replace old friends. I used to see my mother at least once a month; I'm close to my mother. I don't have that anymore. Telephone and letters aren't the same.

John and I both decided to come here. We had traveled and seen the mountains and ocean; I really love the ocean. But I had an identity in my home town. Coming here was probably the most difficult thing I've ever done. After Tommy was born I had real trouble incorporating the role of mother and wife into my life without having the other roles that I was known in and knew myself in to fall back on. I had a couple of failures. I took a math admissions test to get back into school, and when I talked to the university, they told me my grade point was too low. Then I flunked the driver's test—all within a couple of months of moving here while I was pregnant. That was why I wanted to get back to work right away; I knew that was something to grasp onto. Since then I got my driver's license and was accepted into school.

John likes the fact that I work, that I carry my own weight. He looks at it in terms of economics; if something happened to him, I could support myself. However, when my activities infringe on what he thinks is the minimum we ought to spend together, that is when we will have a serious conversation.

He helps a lot at home. We split the laundry—probably not fifty-fifty—probably sixty-forty. He'd ruin my clothes. I'll wash the clothes, and he washes the sheets and towels. Cooking is probably the main problem we have. He doesn't like to cook and he won't use recipes, so there are only a few meals he makes. He doesn't like to participate in cleaning, but he does some of the grocery shopping. We usually do housework together. We don't have specific areas; I don't mind doing the kitchen if he does the bathroom. We both dust and vacuum. However, I don't think the house is as clean as it could be. Sometimes we argue about how clean it is, but we don't take time to do it. I think cooking is more of a daily conflict. We can't afford to go out.

Planning is the key to our home's running smoothly. I'm real good on plans but not on follow-up. I'd like both of us to do the planning. I'm not sure if John would agree. I know meal planning he would not agree to; he likes to be more spontaneous. He doesn't want to be told what to cook.

Our family is working well. When we're trying to work out the problems, whether they're solved or not I feel like addressing problems means that you're not ignoring them, and that's important.

I don't ever feel like work interferes, I guess because we haven't been in a situation where I have to work full-time. We don't own a lot of things. We don't go into hock so that we can have material possessions or take great vacations. If I had worked more hours, we could have afforded to go home for a visit, but I was really exhausted and I couldn't.

One thing I have no interest in is upward mobility. There may be some pressure on me to move upward once I have the Bachelor of Science in nursing. As a diploma nurse I didn't have such high credentials and I wasn't pushed, whereas ever since I walked into the School of Nursing, I've been pushed to get a master's and I'm not used to getting that push. I have no interest in a master's, but having a bachelor's degree does provide more options.

I do have an interest in doing some community outreach, maybe working with the elderly, which would mean I might have to be in charge of a group of people. That's going to be a conflict for me. If I choose to do something like that, I'll have to come to grips with all the politics of being a manager. I don't want that. My work commitment is as important to me as my family. It's not how much money I can make, but how much I can help people that matters. I'm also active in the American Nurses Association; they're calling it a union now. On average I probably have at least two meetings a week.

What's happening in my profession is that people are trying to figure out how to keep more nurses in nursing, so they are willing to consider providing services that will keep us at work, like flex-time and day care. I heard a nursing director talk about in-hospital day care and I was shocked. It is a contract demand made by the union that their hospital provide day care in the institution. I was on a TV program with a panel of nurses, and one of the people was a director in a hospital that is in the middle of bargaining. I don't know where that demand was on the list of priorities, but I know they have not settled that contract.

I think on-site day care would be terrific. If I could have lunch and go see my kid, I think I might have fewer guilt feelings.

You really have to want to do it all. I've always wanted a family, so I knew that this period of time was going to be hard. I've given up a lot—vacations and privacy, time John and I had alone—but it's not troubling me right now. I know that men and women don't have to fill traditional roles; it's not necessary. And I know that once I'm out of school, I'll probably be able to allow myself to have a little more time to do things that used to be enjoyable to me.

Maria Gomez

Venturing Forth at Forty

Maria lives in the Southwest. Maria and her husband Juan have two teenage sons.

I'm forty years old and my children are fourteen and fifteen. My husband works at an air force base in security. My oldest boy is in the ninth grade, and the other one is in the eighth grade. I work at a preschool and I've been there for six years.

I work nine to twelve, and two days a week I work until two. Six years ago I took this job after doing a lot of volunteer work at one of the private schools. My school is right in back of the school where my boys went in the third and fourth grade, and I decided to get paid for the work I had done as a volunteer. It had been ten years since I'd held a real job, although I had worked in an office for seven years before I had kids. I wanted to be close enough to my boys if they needed me. Since I wanted more children and my husband didn't want any more, my job also fulfilled that need.

My working part-time means I can still do what I was brought up to do—the role of wife and mother. I'm doing my own thing too, but I feel that the family comes first.

My husband is supportive of me. He switched jobs when I started working, so we started depending more on my money. It might not have been enough money if his new job hadn't worked out, but I didn't want to work full-time.

A year ago I started demonstrating different kinds of foods at the stores, foods like sauces or cakes. I started doing it for extra money because I still didn't want to go to an office. There are a lot of things we need, but I still want to be home with the family. By working on weekends I felt I would make my husband take over the house and take care of the boys while I was gone. I wanted the boys to communicate better with their father instead of me being the middleman all the time. Instead of mother doing everything for them, they now clean the house and have supper ready by the time I get home. They figured if mother was working, they should help out. It's worked out okay.

We both have our parents here in town. Our parents have helped us out financially and in other ways too. We never really had sitters; we didn't go out that much. But we could call the grandparents if we needed to. If I thought they were really sick, I'd stay home. If it wasn't too bad, then the grandparents would take them.

Having family nearby was good for the boys and good for us. They lend support and keep on telling us that things will get better. Both are very loving. I didn't have grandparents at all. I think the boys have been fortunate to have two sets of grandparents.

One of the things we did because our parents could sit for us was Marriage Encounter [weekend sensitivity sessions for couples]. We were one of the head couples. We had to spend a lot of time preparing, and our children were in the way. We did this for about a year and decided it was not what we wanted. We wanted to be a family, so we started doing a retreat for teenagers and we took our boys with us. We stopped when the boys got a little older because they were more interested in things like baseball. Also my husband decided that in order for us to get ahead he needs a degree, so he went back to college and he's now a senior. He's doing it very slowly because it's difficult for him.

He's very understanding of me; my house is not as clean as it used to be when all I did was dust and clean at home. I can be organized now, but it is not the same as being at home. Working takes a lot out of me. My husband's very supportive; he tells me, "Don't worry about it," when things go badly at work. He and I don't have problems communicating. I say to him, "What's wrong?" and he tells me and that's it. I used to knit a lot to get rid of frustrations. I haven't knitted for a long time; I think I'm relaxing more.

At work there's been a lot of friction. In the six years I've been there I've had six directors. With each new director there are drastic changes. That puts me under terrible pressure; it's always because of someone in authority, a director, never the children or a parent. I don't communicate very well with people in authority.

When this happens it causes problems at home, and the first thing my family tells me is to quit, but my love is for the children in the school, and I feel very responsible toward them. I feel like I'm not ready to leave them. I take a lot because I don't verbalize very well.

I took a course for women last year which taught me to be more assertive. It was called Turning Point. It did a lot for my ego. They tested my college aptitude, and I came out pretty high; I had thought I was just an ordinary student and could never go to college. The results showed that I could go to a four-year college, which I didn't think I could do. Not until I took the course did I realize I'm worth more than I thought I was.

I don't know yet if I will go. I like working with children, so it would have to be something that would lead me in that direction. I would like to teach poor children, and I know you need a degree for that. I can't afford to go to school because we still need money at home until my husband gets a little further on. I figure four more years and I'll have given the boys enough of me and then I can do something better. I think it's good that I started getting out into the world while I was still young. I'm forty now, but I was thirty-four when I started to work again. I was nervous then because I didn't think I could do anything. Now, I won't be so afraid.

When I was in high school the other girls all went to college. My girlfriends were going to be teachers, and I was going to be a mother, so I went to work and my girlfriends got their degrees. When we all got married they stayed home. I wanted to be the teacher, but I didn't have the degree. They had the degree and didn't want to teach. If I had known that I loved kids so much, I would have gone to college, because I would have gotten a better-paying teaching job.

As soon as the boys are out of school and my husband gets his degree, then it's my turn. Certain things scare me, but I think I'd like to go to college.

Beth Kerrigan

Building a Career Around a Family

Beth Kerrigan and her husband Jay, live with their two children in New England. Beth's priority is her family, even though she works full time in the business that she and her husband share. She's in her late thirties.

I'm one of those people who has lots of energy. I get up in the morning and get all the wash done and hung out before I go to work. At least that's what I do most of the time. I have to be at work by eight. I think I feel good because I don't eat any artificial sugar; I eat fruit, and I make my own bread. I buy pork from the butcher where it is smoked the old-fashioned way rather than injected. I eat bran and wheat germ every day so I know I'm getting certain things in my diet. I used to exercise, and when I wasn't working I walked three miles five days a week. When I went to work I did it three days a week.

I feel different since I changed my diet. Diets have improved for the family as well because I won't buy soda, ice cream, candy, or gum. I'm very faithful about getting enough sleep. I require a lot of sleep, and if I don't get it, I don't feel good the next day; I go to bed around nine-thirty or ten most every night. I plan which day I'm going to do what chore, and I always plan what we are going to have for supper. I try to get as much as possible done before I go to work in the morning.

What annoys me is that when I leave I pick up everything, but whenever I come home there is a mess in the kitchen, butter on the shelf, and dirty dishes in the sink. The kids are supposed to make their own beds and put away their laundry. Amy is more cooperative than Brian, but she's around more. He's usually out at work or with his girlfriend.

My husband, Jay, and I took over a small store from my parents recently. I do everything from stocking the shelves to selling, office work and even some of the heavy work. I worked there for about ten years before my parents retired. They just walked out and shut the door, and I was unprepared to take over. My father never doled out responsibility, and I didn't know how to assume it. I didn't have a lot of confidence at first.

My work schedule is flexible. In the spring I work six days, fifty hours per week, and in the summer I work three days a week because the kids are home. Brian is seventeen, and he works there after school and in the summer. My daughter, Amy, is eleven.

I love being a boss. I probably have more authority than my husband because he is out on the road. We're trying to get Jay off the road and back into the store so I don't have so much responsibility at this point. Being a boss is easy for me with the women, but with the men it is much more difficult because the men don't respect me as an authority. The two men have been at the store longer than I have, and they don't feel that I know as much as they do. One of them is seventy years old and really doesn't care to have a younger woman telling him what to do.

It bothers me that they won't accept me; they just don't feel I ought to be telling them what to do. The general manager is younger than I but has been there longer than I have and this created problems. If I say anything to him, he becomes very upset. However, things are improving a little because he has come to the conclusion that I am the boss.

All of this has made me grow as a person more than I realize. I'm more receptive to others. When my parents first retired it was very difficult because the responsibility was very great. When I didn't like something, even if it was a small matter, I became a little upset; whereas now I'm a little calmer. Basically I'm pretty satisfied with things at the store.

Maybe one of the things about being in charge is that I can run in and out of the store to take care of my family's needs. Amy had a doctor's appointment this morning. I opened and took care of some things. I ran out for a few minutes to take Amy to the doctor. I think that's one of the things I like best about being my own boss. As long as somebody's there to take care of things for a few minutes I can do the things that have to be done, during the day. I don't have to check with anybody.

Since I am working full-time, I would like Jay to assume more responsibility around the house, but I don't think it's going to happen. He travels a lot and spends a lot of time on his hobby, which is horses. I'd also like him to take more responsibility with the children to see they are helping to do things around the house rather than leaving it all up to me—for instance, if he assumed the responsibility of seeing that the kids mowed rather than my overseeing it. He doesn't see a lot of what has to be done. Before we left for vacation, for instance, the lawn had to be mowed, the peas had to be picked, and the garden had to be dusted and weeded. He had no idea these things had to be done because I'd always handled them.

I go through periods when I get very upset about this and say something has to be done, but usually I don't, I'm not strong enough. I think it's something I should have established a good many years ago rather than now. One thing I don't do anymore is split the wood. I used to do it. Jay knows it has to be done, but he's the type who will put it off. I won't leave things. I'm very independent, and he does appreciate what I do. That makes our relationship work. For instance, I split practically all the wood we have in the woodshed. We use wood for heat and we have two stoves. In the winter when the stoves are going I use them to cook on. The fact is, though, I'm finding it hard finding time to split the wood and I need him to help me with more things.

I should have been more forceful about my husband sharing more equally from the beginning, but I wasn't. I was the one who knitted and crocheted and made my own Christmas presents. I've gone into something different now. Work has taken the time I used to give to the other things. I feel better as a person, more knowledgeable and more confident.

Arlene Jacobsen

Working from Home

Arlene lives with her husband, Bob, in the middle of a large California city. She has four children, and had worked full-time, but now she works part-time.

I work at home as an engraver. My husband and I have a manufacturing company; we manufacture items out of brass and then I engrave people's names or their logos on the items. I use a Panagraph machine in the den, and I also do electrical engraving.

Each day, I have to decide what has to be done with the house and the kids; whatever time is left is when I get my work done. The bulk of it usually gets done early—anywhere from eight until twelve noon. I probably work three, three and one-half hours a day. Sometimes I work until one in the morning, maybe from ten until one or ten until twelve.

I like what I'm doing because it's for *my* company. It fills just enough time. It allows me to work, make some money, feel somewhat productive, and still be a mother at home. I can do as much as I want or as little. It's a nice setup. If I ever wanted to increase it though, I could start my own business without question.

Until a year ago I worked with my husband at the company downtown, which I did for about five years. Things were not working well at that time because I was frantic and my attitude was sour. Although we really complemented each other and my strengths were in different areas from his, just hearing each other and seeing each other seven days a week, twenty-four hours a day, for five years was a little tough. If he blew up at somebody and I felt it was unreasonable, I couldn't be a part of it and yet I was a part of it. And sometimes it would spark off things that would happen at home. We started having real problems. There was no separation between home and work. It just became one. The dinner table was nothing but an extension of work. The kids were subjected to it every single night.

So he bought the Panagraph and engraving machines special so I could continue to work at home and I could feel connected that way. It was difficult leaving. I built that business with him from nothing. I made the first two thousand dollars the company ever made; it was hard. To me it was like giving birth to children and then somebody just taking them away overnight. That's how connected I was to the business.

Now, for the first time in about eight years, I feel that there is a real good balance around here. Nothing feels overbearing. One of the things I found, after many years of doing it all wrong, was that *I* must set myself as a priority, because if I'm not feeling right, nothing is right. My family is important, too. I used to go to bed most nights feeling very guilty, feeling like I didn't attend to someone in the family; at the same time, feeling very cheated myself; feeling very tired, very drained, and not very happy.

Working full-time didn't work for me at all. And my work became a self-imposed prison. Now that I'm engraving at home, I'm just doing a job. I'm not there to see what goes on. What I don't know doesn't hurt me. What I hear from my husband are important things. I am still connected to the business. That's very important to me. I like to know what's going on.

A good day for me is a day when nobody is here. I am lucky enough to have a free day, say, for instance, when there aren't any appointments—like doctors' appointments. I get up in the morning and exercise, give everybody breakfast, get them off, and I can sit down at the machine. If I can sit down there from ten until three, that is a good workday for me, not being interrupted. I only get one of those a week.

A bad day would be a day that I have to car pool. It's not so much the school car-pooling, it's the after-school activities. It's enough to drive you crazy, it really is. It all happens from three until seven at night. Car-pooling plus a doctor's appointment destroys my day. It doesn't give me the time I need to accomplish anything. So when I have a half-hour here and forty-five minutes there, it's a bad day. Then there's my involvement in the community. I do counseling a few times a week. If I didn't have the community involvement, I would have no problem at all.

All the things I do, I want to do, although they make me anxious at times. Sometimes you would like to be able to do them all and you can't.

I'm extremely organized. I've never had live-in help. I have four children, a girl, eighteen, a girl, fifteen, and twins who are ten now, and I have never had anything more than day help, one or two days a week. The latest around here is that everybody except my husband has specific jobs. I do the wash for my husband and myself, my boys are responsible for theirs, and my daughters are responsible for theirs. I know the night before what's happening at dinnertime the next day usually, so it makes it much easier to gauge my work time, makes it easier on the kids because they know ahead what is happening.

As I said, there's only so much you can get done in a day, and the world doesn't fall apart if it doesn't get done. I think I've been able to develop that feeling far better now, working the way I am working now. When I was working all day, there was so much that it was impossible to even think that. My oldest daughter once said to me, "You know, you're really a joke, Mom. What you do between the hours of six and nine at night is what most mothers do in a week," and it's true. That's how I functioned, but I was a mess.

There's more of me now that I work at home. I have more to share. There's more depth to me. I have, I think, more compassion and understanding. I think also that the kids learned to deal with more things than they normally would have if I were always available. It's very easy just to unload and not to filter—not to think about what you're unloading—and now that I'm not always available, or if they come in and I'm here, but I'm tied up with something, I'll say, "I'll be through in an hour." I demand my time when it's necessary, and they have to accept it just as I don't intrude on them and their friends, and they respect me for it. I'd rather be honest and say, "I don't have the time now," than try to be that wonderful parent that's always available and, as they're unloading, getting angry inside because they are taking my time that's important at that moment. So I just say it right out and then I'll say, "Can it wait?" Chances are they won't even bring it up again because it wasn't all that important and they'll solve it themselves. It only makes them better human beings. They rely on their own resources.

Since I began working at home, there's definitely more time for my husband and me. We just joined a sailing club for adults only so that we wouldn't be tempted to take the kids. We pay a fee every month and we can go sailing Saturdays and Sundays. So far we've only sailed once a month because we've tried to make everyone happy. It's our time alone, but we're willing to settle for once a month. We just went away this weekend with the club on a river raft trip without the children. They took care of themselves. No problem. The wash was all done when I came home. I didn't ask who they had over. All I know was there were no problems. I left plenty of food. And the girls worked it out so that neither one of them was tied down a whole weekend. One stayed home one night while the other one went out and then they reversed it and everybody was happy.

My husband and I also have our own hi-fi and television in the bedroom; when we close the door, nobody comes in. Most of the time, though, either I'll be sitting in the den engraving or reading or whatever I'm doing and Bob will be in here in the living room with the kids. We're home a lot in the evenings, and usually on the weekends, we never plan anything big. Sometimes Bob and I go out alone on a week night; we have a nice dinner, something that we never used to do.

My husband has also changed. He chips in because he recognizes the fact that I work hard. I put in hours at that machine, and the stuff that I do around the house and the hours with the kids are hard work. It means something when he comes home and there's a nice meal on the table. I think he feels better about himself because he now takes an active role with the kids rather than a passive one. He feels more responsible for things.

Working makes me feel more independent. I get so much money a month, a salary my husband and I felt would be adequate. When I worked at the business my money went directly into the checkbook and I never saw it. I give some toward food and I pay for clothing, religious school, haircuts, and so forth for the kids. I have some control over my money.

I tell my daughters that as wonderful as it is to have children, don't do it to make me a grandparent. It's okay to have kids and to work. I think they'll best understand this when they get to that point. They've seen me work plus they've had the responsibility of taking care of the boys. They've had the advantage of doing that, and I think if nothing else, it has prolonged their desire, their need to have children. I think that they will wait longer to have them. I think their needs have been met. I think that they see that there are burdens attached to having children, that there is a cramping of life-style. There is a giving-up that takes place, and it doesn't have to happen when you're twenty years old.

Betsy, the older one, will definitely be a professional person, whether it be physical therapy or counseling or some type of law. She's got a great lawyer's mind. She likes to be around stimulating people. I hope all of them—I mean if they have kids, great, but I hope none of them stop what it is that they're doing—I hope all of them keep themselves involved in some way in their work, even if it is part-time. When the time comes, and they have kids, I will push them to be out of that house, to take every dime that they have to get someone to come in, even if it's twice a week.

The boys are better off than both of my daughters. They learned to be self-sufficient, independent, and get their needs met far sooner than my daughters did, because I was at home for my daughters. One daughter was nine and the other one was eleven when I went to work, and the boys were about three. When I was at work, sometimes I would get a call from one of the boys. They planned to ride their bikes over a distance my daughters never would have thought to do, or they're going to stay after school late. They would call me and ask, "Can we stay after school? Betsy will pick us up at five, or if you're coming, can you pick us up?" My daughters never did things like that. I think the boys' lives are much fuller.

I hope that my children work, even though as a child I was angry about my mother working. She taught school. She never took a day off, not even when I was sick, or to hear me in chorus; however, she did manage to take off for luncheons where they played cards. But I'm a very different mother to my children than my mother was to me. I guess working full-time wouldn't be good because I couldn't get my kids to their special activities, like my son to tutoring, and if I did, it would really take a lot of effort to do it. When I was working full-time I gave up my family goals, but not now.

I don't think during the day is quality time at all. Even when I'm here, they're out playing. But dinner time is important to me. And in the evenings—it seems that when my kids are troubled with anything, that's when they come to me, especially before they go to bed.

Right now I am at a happy middle. I've come to terms with myself. I guess I've learned who I really am and I know what I can do. I know what I've done and I know what I can do. So I'm here by choice.

Laurie Kelly

Tapping Resources

Laurie is a thirty-four-year-old divorced mother of two. She's just published her first magazine article and is looking forward to a career as a writer. However, right now she's doing part-time work as a secretary. Laurie and her two children, who are eight and two, live in California with a man who is also a writer. Laurie's former husband lives nearby, and he also helps with the children. In addition to the two men in her life, Laurie has her parents to share in the parenting.

I'm committed to being a writer and just sold my first piece about a month ago. It's been a long haul, and I'm not making a living at it. I've taken a job two days a week as a "go-fer" in a law firm. I Xerox thick briefs and documents and wash out everyone's coffee cup and run a lot of errands; I cover the phones when the receptionist is not in, and that kind of thing.

It was great when I sold my first piece. I hit the ceiling. It was to a woman's magazine. That was probably one of the best days in my life. It was a total shock and wonderful.

During the last year, it hasn't been too difficult to work on my writing and take care of the kids. Robert, he's eight, had to be at his bus by seven-thirty in the morning, so I would drop him off and then I would drop my little one, Ari, who is two, off at her day care center. Sometimes, I'd go grocery shopping, and then I'd get home and start working early in the morning. I decided to send Robert to a sports club after school, three days a week. That way, we'd have an afternoon together, and every other week his dad would pick him up on Thursdays. It worked out real well.

I don't like the fact that Ari has had to be in full-time care from the age of two. She's done very well, but I sometimes wonder if she will have a problem with emotional attachment later. She's been in two different preschools, and now she's leaving the camp she's at and going to kindergarten, and I just wonder: Are the children who are in this kind of care going to be the ones who have trouble making a real permanent attachment? Are they going to be afraid of long-term relationships?

I don't know if I give my kids enough time. Sometimes they have a rough time adjusting to change. Robert will say, "Well, I'm just not used to this!" And I say, "Well, why are you acting like this?" He'll say, "Well, I'm just not used to this schedule!" Then I see what's happening. We've gotten to the point where he can express himself, and I really feel like it's a two-way street now, so I can hear what he's saying, and then he listens to me when I get upset, too, I think.

The kids really participate in the family. We had a couple of rough years. In the beginning when we moved here, we didn't have roots, even though I'm from here originally and their grandparents are here. Both sets of grandparents are here. But emotionally we were all just a wreck, and it took us two years to really feel okay about being here.

My parents are real involved with the kids; my mother is especially, which I'm just loving. She still works full-time but sometimes she'll take them on the weekends. She'll take a day off to spend with them, and she has a real special relationship with them. In an emergency I can count on her, and I was thinking of asking my dad if he would like to take a regular day next year in the fall. He's retired, and since Ari's going to be off at twelve, I thought maybe he'd like to pick her up on Tuesday. Just so she wouldn't be at activities all the time. I think he would enjoy her company; she's a good kid and she's a lot of fun.

One of the things I've done is that I only look for work near here. I work only two blocks away from here. There's a slew of office buildings and I can walk to work. That relieves a lot of strain. I don't know if I'm going to have that choice in the future. This new job as story editor (if I get it) is only about twenty minutes from here. It's a horrible drive, but I think the trade-off might be worth it. It might be an exciting enough job.

If somebody wanted to hire me as a writer, I'd be ready. It

might be real exciting. Almost anything else wouldn't be worth it to me, and I know I would come home with a lot of resentment. If I didn't have writing as a choice, I would probably just choose to keep working at menial part-time jobs and write three days a week at home and just sort of scrape along until something else came up. I hope I don't have to wait too many years until I can support myself as a writer. I'm thirty-four, but I feel like I'm just starting out, so I want to give myself enough of a chance so I won't resent it in my later years and think what might have been.

There are certain kinds of jobs that require a big commitment. My ex-husband moved here a year ago. It's good that he is here. He takes them every other week from Thursday through Sunday, and we've made an arrangement so that I take them to school on Thursday morning and he picks them up. Then on Monday morning, he'll bring them over to school and then they'll be dropped off at my house or I'll pick them up. I think that transition has worked real well. It's been great on an emotional level for them; it's really nice that he's here. They call him up on the telephone and they talk. Sometimes he'll get tickets to special events and he'll take them.

Starting next month, my ex-husband will have the kids for a month and I'm going to have them every other weekend. Whenever he needs help, my dad will take the kids for a day. Then we wouldn't have to get any baby-sitters during that time and we could have time just to be with the kids. I think it's going to work out okay.

It's just been amazing what my ex-husband has learned. He cooks now and he relates to the kids and he's really there for them. We have a good relationship as far as the kids are concerned. If something did come up—if I had to go on location for two months, he would take the kids.

Along with my ex-husband, I have Ross, the guy I live with. Sometimes when I've been gone, he takes over. I don't know if he's ever had them alone overnight, but I'm not sure that it would make that much difference. He's really done it all as far as they're concerned, so I think that he could handle them. If I got this job I'm interviewing for, he said that he would probably take care of the children and the grocery shopping and he would be the "wife." And he would have dinner for the kids and be here when they came home every night, although he might want to alternate that with a babysitter every other day.

I get worried that it might be asking too much, but he's been very good about saying when it's too much. He says, "Get a baby-sitter," and I do.

It would be an adjustment for the kids, but I think they would accept it. In the beginning, I didn't want to ask him to do anything, and he didn't want to have anything at all to do with the kids. As time went on, he was willing to babysit at night if I wanted to go to a movie or out to dinner with a girlfriend or something. He never had any problem with babysitting, and he always said, "Oh, the kids are so much better when you're not around." It was easier for him if I wasn't there.

Ross helps out a lot in the morning. I've been running for about three years, and I couldn't figure out any way to fit it in. I decided the only way was to set the alarm for five-fifty in the morning and I'd be out running at six and it was a great comfort to me to know that Ross was here asleep in the bed. Before he moved in I tried running a couple of times, just leaving the kids alone. Even though they were asleep, I absolutely couldn't do it. I kept thinking, "This is the moment there's going to be an earthquake, a fire, something." I would be two minutes away from home, but I couldn't relax.

This afternoon when I have the job interview, Ross will be here and maybe they'll make pizza. Robert chops the mushrooms and Ari ends up with flour all over her from head to foot! She helps make the crust, and they love it. I think it's great that he likes to participate in cooking. They even make cannoli!

He plays ball sometimes with Robert, and writes songs and plays the piano quite well. Sometimes after dinner he'll sit down at the piano and make up songs about the kids. They love it. They dance; they have a ball, and he plinks away.

One of the conflicts for me with Ross now is that he talks about wanting to get married and have children. Even though I don't have a problem with having children, I have a problem with feeling like I'm doing the same thing to myself again. I don't really have a career yet, and it wouldn't be too difficult for me to have kids if I felt confident that I could make a living as a writer. Since we're both writers, we could end up jockeying roles so that I'm on assignment and he's fathering, and then he's on assignment and I'm mothering. But I feel like the burden's probably going to fall on me and then what's going to happen? Probably he would look to me because I've already done it twice. Maybe I would just start taking over as women tend to do anyway. I don't know. It will be an interesting situation. We haven't arrived at that point yet.

The kids see me as a working person, and I think it's good for them. I don't think Ari's going to grow up thinking that any man owes her a living. The other thing that happens when a mother works is that her children don't depend on her for every little thing. Sometimes, Robert will take the trash out for me, and Ari was helping me fold laundry the other night. I really do expect them to help me. I want them to be self-sufficient in real practical ways. I don't think it's asking too much, and it gives them a good sense of accomplishment and independence.

One of the main reasons why I haven't pushed for getting a full-time job is "you can't have it all," as Katharine Hepburn said. I think she's right. I'm hoping that things will work out. For instance, if I got this new job—I think it's going to put a big strain on everyone and I don't know if it'll be worth it. That's something I will have to assess. I will have to decide and see what the price is that I'm paying. I hope it works out. I don't know. Maybe I could even find someone to share a full-time job with.

If I were at home all day with my kids, perhaps I'd be screaming at them. You don't know whether time is going to be well spent just because you have it together. But then I get scared about taking a full-time job. Sometimes it's hard to know who you are and what you need. In fact maybe that's why I got married when I did. I didn't think that there was any other alternative. I didn't think of who I was and what I needed. I just did what was expected of me.

If I could do it again, I would try to follow my own script. But the reality is that I have Robert and Ari, and I wouldn't give them up for anything, even though they've made everything so difficult. When things work right it's just so much sweeter. I can't imagine life without them.

Nancy Straus

Going It Alone

Nancy devoted most of her married life to her husband and four children until five years ago, when her husband died suddenly. Although he had left her with some insurance, the costs of raising and educating four children were such that Nancy had to work. She is now forty-seven and lives in the South.

It's been five years since Al died. We were married twenty-one years and had a very traditional marriage. My husband earned the living, and I stayed home with the children. I was very much a full-time mother; as a volunteer in the community, I was involved in things that were directly related to my children. I'd been PTA president, and I was involved in school board elections and charity work. I cooked a balanced meal every single night for twenty-one years; that was my job. I don't think I resented it; I knew that was what I was supposed to do. Al was never threatened by me. He was happy when I was home, and he would have been happy if I'd gone to work.

A couple of years before he died, I was beginning to think about what I'd do when the children were out of the nest. We were having—not that Al would articulate it, but I felt we were having—some financial problems. He was a traditional husband who protected his wife, and this subject was never discussed, but I knew things were very tight, so I was already looking toward working when he got sick.

Al became ill and died within a six-month period. My children were eighteen, sixteen, fourteen, and ten. It was totally catastrophic. For the six months that he was ill, I never could tell the children he might die. I think I handled that poorly, but people handle things however they can. They knew he was very ill, but death was never discussed. My husband couldn't accept it either. The whole time Al was ill his parents were here, and my mother and mother-in-law would cook. I was totally devoted to Al; everything I did was for him. I don't know how everything else got done, but it did.

I was devastated when he died. I stayed in bed all the time. I do remember getting out of bed to fix meals and then I'd get back into bed. I was in a heavy depression, crying a lot. I'm sure my children were terrified and felt things would never be right again.

I had lots of people coming to see me the first month. My brother, who lives on the East Coast, called me two to three times a week. I had another dear friend who called me every day. But most people run away from this sort of thing. My brother and my mother and a friend in California kept calling me, and one close friend here. They were really devoted. My brother would call me and listen to me cry.

My mother was incredible. I cannot say enough about my mother's strength. Al's death took a tremendous amount out of her, but she's hung in there with me. She'd been through this a couple of years ago when my father died. She listened to me, and she was there financially as much as possible. I don't cook anymore and she's always there to cook. Yet when I don't want her around she's not here. I have my own life; I'm not depending on her, but she is just incredible. This has taken a lot out of my mother; it was just as hard on her as it was when she lost my father. She adored Al. Not only did she lose somebody she loved very much, but she saw me suffering. It was devastating to her to see the children lose their father, and she rose to the occasion.

I started to think I needed help; a month after Al died I was still in bed. My rabbi insisted I go to a psychiatrist. The psychiatrist listened to me cry and tell my story, and then he said to me, "That's life," and gave me antidepression pills. I took one pill and threw the rest in the toilet. There's an immature part of you that thinks somebody is going to make it right; you think, "I'm going to go somewhere and talk it all out and I'm going to feel better." I even went to a Christian death counselor that one of my friends told me to go to. That was a horrible experience, too. One thing I did know was that I would have to go to work; reality was beginning to creep in.

One of my friends paid me a condolence call, and I asked her to let me know if any part-time job opened in her office. One day she called and said, "Nancy, we need you. It's just answering the telephone—do you want to do it?" I said, "Yes." I looked like a skeleton; I had lost twenty pounds when Al was sick, and there I was, the receptionist. I looked like a zombie. Everybody who walked in looked at me and wanted to walk back out! But I worked every day from nine to one.

That was the beginning. I'd go home from work and cry. At that point I called someone I knew who has a master's in social work, and I started going to talk to him when I needed him, not on a weekly basis, just whenever I felt I was losing control. I'd call him and he'd see me right away. He's been the best counselor I've come across.

In the meantime I had a friend who gathered the records of my teaching credentials, which I'd been trying to do for a while. My job as receptionist lasted only for a couple of months. I had to find something permanent. My training was as a teacher. I got a job interview and was accepted for a teaching position. Then I waited for my assignment, which didn't come for several months.

During that time I was still crying but surviving, feeling heavy and depressed. Friends were taking me out with them and I would go. About nine to ten months after Al died, a friend wanted to fix me up with somebody. The man called me and I accepted, and then I went to pieces because I didn't know what to say to the children. I didn't know how to handle it. I decided to talk to each one individually after school. And every one of them was thrilled. When I told my fourteen-year-old, he looked me straight in the eye and he said, "Mom, when somebody dies you have to start living again. You're not supposed to die with that person." So I went out and enjoyed myself. The whole night I talked about what had happened to me. But it was nice to be with a man and feel like a woman again. I didn't go out again for a while.

That fall I started teaching. Al died in January, and I started teaching that August. I hadn't taught in nineteen years, and I realize now I was not a good teacher when I was young. I put in an incredible year of teaching. I was really sensitive to the children's needs. But I wasn't in such good condition. I'd be in a reading circle, and something would happen that upset me, and I'd leave the kids and go to the back of the room and cry. Then I'd wipe my eyes, and go back to the kids and continue. That went on for a whole year. I had a special feeling for those kids and they responded. At the end of the year I got transferred, which was a tremendous blow to me; I broke down in the principal's office.

I ended up teaching English as a second language in a high school. The first day there I knew this was bad for me. These were kids who didn't want to learn English, and they had no respect for teachers. They treated me like dirt. I had two sections of sophomores and juniors who were reading on third- and fourth-grade levels. I was there one week and knew there was no way I could teach them anything; so I babysat for a year, which was depressing to me because I had no commitment. It was now two years since Al had died, and I was still crying every morning on the way to work. One thing I learned from this experience is that from every negative experience you can pull something positive out. What came out of that high school was that it made me look for another job, and by December of that year I started working on my résumé. By that time I was going out with two men. Around that time I also went to an all-day seminar at the Women's Center. It was on career changes for teachers, and it really made me feel better. I sat in a room with other teachers who were looking for career changes. I wasn't alone.

I held on to my job that whole year, even though I wanted to quit. Then I heard about an opening at the Jewish Community Center. A friend of mine made me go; my friends were unbelievably supportive, and that helped.

I was interviewed and didn't hear anything for a while. Then in May they called me with a job working with senior citizens.

It's the perfect job for me. The pay is good. It probably would have taken me another five years of teaching to make what I'm making at the center now—although social workers don't make great pay. I've gotten substantial raises every year, which makes me feel rewarded. The main reason it's such a great job is that it's ten minutes from my home. My kids can pop in on me anytime they want. They can come in here to play basketball, and they stop to say, "Hi, Mom." Friends of mine stop by on their way to exercise class.

I really enjoy working with senior citizens; it is very gratifying. I do not deal with their problems; I am not a counselor. I plan things that will be fun for them. We take trips together, and we plan parties. We are trying to get performing arts going in the center, and I'm very involved in that. My job is expanding, so it's not only working with senior citizens, but doing mass programming at the center. I feel very professional; I've learned a lot in the last three years. Everyone is so supportive; and I could leave immediately if the kids needed me.

I have four wonderful kids that have not given me a day of

real worry. They're not wild or into drugs. If they are going to be late, they call me because they know I'll worry. They're wonderful kids and have never been a problem. My concerns have been to support them and to be there when they need me. But the kids have been extraordinary.

One of the hardest things for me has been all the financial responsibility. I had never been involved with our finances; I paid department store bills, but that was it. I had college expenses and not many resources. I had to sell my house. I don't think I asked enough for it. I thought I knew what I was doing, but I didn't. When I sold the house, I had to buy a smaller house. My younger child still misses the other house, but the day I moved out of it I started feeling better. We had built it together. Al was everywhere. It was a huge house. When he died the house seemed so dark, drab, depressing. The whole house changed character after he died, and financially there was no way I could keep that house.

I feel very good about myself because I'm independent and I've learned to take care of myself. It would be nice to depend on somebody at times, though, and I do miss that. I'm sad that Al is missing out on so much, and we'll never share grandchildren together and have the life that my mother and dad had. I'm in a different life; I get a lot of satisfaction out of my career and being a mother. My children have a lot of respect for me because of what I've done since Al died. Their admiration makes me feel good. I don't know if I'll ever be able to remarry. I've got my life together finally, and I wonder if I want to shake it up again and make all those accommodations.

I'm going out with a man now who's twelve years older than I. He's a terrific human being, an incredible person. I don't need him to take care of me, but he does enrich my life. It's been difficult, but when something terrible happens you have to survive. You can't just give up. I've been left with some very deep scars; if something happens to the kids and I'm not sure what's the matter, I go to pieces. But when you are left with the choice of living or dying, you have to choose life. I was up against the wall and there was only one way to go. I kept saying to myself, "It's either sink or swim, and I don't want to sink."

Ellen Diamond

Living in Different Cities

Ellen and Michael Diamond moved from Chicago to the Southwest with their two children over a year ago for business reasons. When Michael's partner couldn't sell his house and move to join them, Michael began to commute between Chicago and his family.

I'm thirty-eight years old. I was born in Chicago and lived there until eighteen months ago when we moved to Texas because my husband's company was supposed to move down here. The company hasn't moved because my husband's partner has not been able to sell his house in the Chicago area. We have two children, a nine-year-old son, Josh, and a thirteen-year-old daughter, Kasey. They had a difficult time adjusting to life here because they were told their father's business was moving here and we'd have a beautiful life together, but it's turned out that their father visits here on weekends primarily and is in Chicago during the week on business.

I applied for a teaching job as soon as I got here, but there were no jobs available at that time. I got a job three months later, and I've been at the same school since then. I was able to get the job because the school was overcrowded and they gave me what the teachers referred to as their "rejects." I realized it when out of a class of twenty-four students, nineteen were retained in the grade the next June.

The school was so overcrowded that I was out in a portable classroom. Since I wasn't in the main building, the other teachers never thought I was part of the team and they ignored us when they planned activities. The children knew this, which made it very difficult at first until I realized, "I'm self-contained and there are things I can do that they can't," and we had a lot of fun. It was a frustrating year, but I wanted to do the best I could with the children as well as with the home situation I was faced with.

This year I have a lovely group, and we're inside the building. The teachers are working more as a team. We have a new teacher again this year, and they tried to do the same thing to her they did to me. Having been on the receiving end, I've tried to include her in every possible way.

Six months after we moved down we realized that my husband's partner's house wasn't going to sell. Mortgage rates had skyrocketed, and the market seemed to have come to a standstill in the Chicago area. The hope is that within the next two years they will be able to sell their house and come here. The question is whether our family can survive another two years of separation. I figure, we've done it for over a year. Why not try it for another year? Take one day at a time.

In the morning I get the kids up and put breakfast on the table for them, or they can handle it themselves if they need to. Josh has a key, and knows what his schedule and responsibilities are. The kids leave for school at the same time. Kasey is bused to and from her school. Since Josh walks, he comes home before any of us. When he gets home, he gets a snack and does homework.

Often I cook double on weekends and ask Kasey to take something out of the freezer so we can have a hot meal. One day per week when I car pool for religious school, she does the cooking. Usually she cooks something easy like Shake 'n Bake chicken, which she can handle. I trust her in the kitchen. The only thing she is not allowed to touch is something like the food processor. I have cleaning help one-half day per week, but her job is not to straighten up after the children. She is there to do the dusting and washing that I can't do or don't want to do when I come home.

Sometimes there are days when one of the kids has gotten up and said, "I don't have a clean pair of jeans to wear," and I say, "Go to the dirty laundry," and they look at me and I say, "There are moments in life. . . ." It's amazing what you can do when you have to. For instance there's nothing wrong with pizza for dinner. Our meals aren't always as balanced as when Michael is here, but the kids haven't suffered.

This past summer, when my husband was not around, Kasey had to take a lot of responsibility on her shoulders that she might not have wanted, but she managed beautifully. I asked her afterward, "How much did you really hate?" and she said, "I guess I have to learn to do these things eventually."

The independence I have now is new to me. I'm an only child, and I spent thirty-six and a half years of my life within ten minutes of my parents. I even lived at home and commuted to college. I had a full tuition scholarship offered to me at an Ivy League school, and my mother took me aside and told me if I went away it would kill my father and my father took me aside and said if I went away it would kill my mother. I look back at it now and don't think it was the best situation in the world. Any ideas and opinions I had were basically those of my parents. Even if I was going to buy a new dress, I used to take my mother with me. I have clothes in my closet that I never wore because my mother purchased them for me and I didn't like them. I'm talking about when I was in my thirties—that's pathetic!

Now I'm really on my own. For example, when the automobile decides to die: I used to say, "Michael, what do I do next?"; instead I say to myself, "Ellen, you do it." I had a bad tire blowout on the expressway going to work one morning, and when I finally got to school, one of the young married teachers said to me, "Didn't you call your husband?" and I said, "He's twelve hundred miles away, what's he going to do, hop on a plane and fix my flat tire?" Her attitude was, that's what your husband is for.

There are times when I don't hesitate to call Michael, like when our son brought home a note saying he was bad in school and I felt it was important that we talk to him about it. We also call for good things, like when our daughter made National Junior Honor Society. But a lot of the responsibilities that a woman looks at as being her husband's, I have to take on my shoulders. You learn you have to do it. I don't like taking the plunger and unplugging the toilet, but I do. It's not the most fun in the world, but it's better than having a flood in your house.

There are days when I come home and lie down. I need to get away from whatever it was that bugged me that day. Maybe it was bad traffic, maybe a kid at school, or maybe it's because my husband isn't around. I come home and want to share how I feel with someone. Who are you going to share it with, a nine-year-old?

A lot of times I feel angry and frustrated. Why can't my husband be here? How dare he be out there having a good time, eating out in restaurants, while I'm struggling with two kids and a house on my shoulders? But in saner moments I realize what he's doing is what he has to do in order to keep our family together. And I try not to unload on him when he comes in. We do discuss things more than we used to because we know it is important for us to really know what is going on in each other's lives more than it ever was.

Michael tries to come home every weekend. It's become a routine and Kasey told me once, "I'm not even sad Dad is going because I expect it." Often we'll get up extra early and the two of us leave a note on the kitchen table for the kids, "Gone out for breakfast," and we'll go out and sit and talk. A lot of our friends think there is something weird about our arrangement. Basically I think it's a lot healthier than what I see going on in some people's homes because our lines of communication are open. During the week two working people don't spend a lot of time together. Lots of times we didn't see each other in Chicago; I was out of the house before he was, and he was the one who got the kids off to school.

Sometimes we'll take the children out for lunch or go to the mall and just walk around. If he has been away for a couple of weeks, we'll spend Saturday night with the children. Basically it's not planned activities where we feel compelled to go to the zoo or go and do something—we'll just sit around the house and do things as a family, put a jigsaw puzzle together or something like that.

At first Kasey wouldn't go to a pajama party on Saturday night if Michael was coming home. Now she feels that it's not that urgent for her to be home. She's not losing him by not being with him.

There are also some power struggles between Michael and me that never used to happen. He wants to be in charge of the house and the children when he's here because that was his traditional role before, and I resent it. When he comes home I don't want to give up the routine that I've managed during the week, and I don't want him to take over control of the children, because when he leaves on Sunday night, it falls on my shoulders. He gives in on a lot of things with them that I wouldn't give in on. If our son wants to stay up till midnight, he says fine. I say it isn't okay because I can't get him up the next day.

But at the same time he needs to feel that he is still in control of some part of our lives. On Saturday when we get back from breakfast we usually sit down and go through the checkbook together. Although I have the checkbook and there is no problem in handling the bills, I feel that he needs to know exactly how our money is being spent. That way when he decides to go on an austerity kick he can't tell me, "What are you wasting money on?" I can say, "Look, this is where the money is going and nothing is being wasted."

He changes the filters on the furnace. That's his responsibility, and he knows it has to be done regularly. He goes grocery shopping with me. The first time he said, "How can you spend so much money on so little?" I said, "Honey, next week you'll find out," and we went shopping together.

On Saturday nights we go out with friends. The people we've made friends with are basically my friends that he either fits in with or he doesn't. The friends we have made are people who have been transferred; they are people who have gone through much the same thing that we have. The relationships are much more intense. You get close to someone in a shorter period of time because you need someone that you can confide in, especially when you have no family down here. We came without knowing anyone.

When I'm asked if I would consider moving back to Chicago, I say no. My relationship with my parents and my husband's parents has changed tremendously. The kids love it when their grandparents come.

My husband and I have discussed the change in me, and he sees it as positive. It's a trade-off, however. It's lonely, very lonely for me. And he feels frustrated. There are times when he says he sort of likes it not having all the burden on his shoulders. I originally went back to work in Chicago to share some of the financial burden because he was going through business setbacks. I don't really mind the responsibilities. I hope that the end result will be worth it; the business will grow and prosper and in the long run will benefit us. I hope it's worth it. I think it is.

I've realized life is short. I don't mind some of the things I have to put up with. I was in the hospital this summer. I had a mass in my lung and they didn't know what it was. The doctor said it could be cancer. He asked me if I wanted to know without my husband's being with me, and I said, "It's not going to change, whether he's here or not." When you're faced with something like that, nothing else is important. Maybe because I was alone it made a very deep impression on me, and my attitude about lots of things has changed. At one time if a dish got broken, you would have thought my whole life was destroyed, and now, big deal!

A few months ago, I went back to Chicago. My friends said

they couldn't put their finger on it, but something was different about me. I guess I am a different person. Even though my husband isn't around during the week, I don't feel I have to be with him or the children every minute of the day when we're all home. I don't feel they need that, nor do I in order to be who I am.

Kathy Hassan

When Money Is the Issue

Kathy Hassan is the assistant to a department head at a large university in the East. She's twenty-seven years old, and met her husband Ahmed when they were both university students. They lived in his native country in the Middle East for a few years, where Kathy taught retarded children. They now have an infant daughter and live in a city.

For us, money has always been a problem. My husband just started a business, so we live on my salary right now.

Our baby is eight months old; I had two months' maternity leave and then when she was two months old the two of us went back to work together. My office was all female. My boss was a fantastic lady who loves babies, and she couldn't wait for me to bring Eila to work.

At the office everybody'd play with her, and when she got crabby, I'd nurse her. She'd fall asleep, and I'd put her down and get all my work done. However, after six weeks she wasn't ready to go back to sleep when we were through playing with her, and that was the end of her being in the office. We then found a woman who took care of children in her home, and I dropped Eila off at her house each day. It was fifty dollars a week. I've always been someone who's had to conserve money and now that skill comes in handy.

My husband, Ahmed, is from the Middle East, and we lived there for a while. I came back alone because he couldn't leave for political reasons. I got a job as a secretary in a university and I thought I could get a teaching job the next September. However, when September came, I couldn't get one. I didn't want to be a secretary, and when I was asked if I wanted to become a program coordinator for $12,000 a year, I thought that sounded like a good deal. I thought I'd get myself established in a job paying a decent salary and then, after a year, use that as a springboard to get something else. In the meantime, my husband came back, and I got pregnant. I now make $15,000 a year, but with a B.A. in education, I really have no salable skills. So I have to work in small places where I can be a jack-of-all-trades. I know you have to specialize in something to make more than $15,000 a year, so I'm going to be here another three years and get a master's degree part-time. I get tuition as a university employee, and I plan to take advantage of that.

My master's program is Career and Training Development. I can do it in two and a half years part-time. It's a multi-disciplinary degree, but basically a master's that combines business and education. I think the master's degree is an effective, long-term way of solving the money issue. But right now, time has almost become a bigger problem than money.

I try not to waste money: my family was lower-middle class but comfortable. I always had an after-school job in high school and helped put myself through college. But I don't have any creative ways to economize. There are just basic needs. We could save on rent, but I want a place where I'm not afraid to unlock the door. I feel paying for rent is basic. Since we moved here, we've had to get a car so we could get back and forth to work. We're paying for the car and car insurance and health insurance. Those things are bottom line. It's marginal things we cut out. We feel we have to have a phone, but we try to keep long distance calls down to one a month. You have to eat, but we eat a lot of Middle Eastern food, rice flavored with seasonings and onions—only a little bit of meat. Or a lot of potatoes and a little bit of vegetables. Those kinds of meals that are really delicious but cheap. No dessert.

I don't buy baby food. If you buy baby applesauce, it's eighty-two cents a pound. If you buy supermarket unsweetened applesauce, it's forty-two cents a pound. It's the same thing. I buy real bananas and mash them. All Eila's clothes are gifts or secondhand loan, so I haven't bought clothes for her. People bought her toys and other things for gifts, and I give her plastic measuring spoons, empty yogurt containers, and that sort of plaything. She'll get hold of a newspaper and play with that for an hour; she loves boxes, too. And there is always doing without! Eila chewed on my watch, for instance, and got her spit in it, and it stopped. I didn't have twenty dollars to buy a new one, so I now have my brother's old watch. We just do without some of the things we need.

My husband was an art professor in the Mideast, but now he has just opened up a little print shop. It's doing well for a new business; it's paying all its own expenses, but it's not making a profit yet. It'll be another year or so before we can expect a decent profit, so my salary has to cover everything. Right now it's hard. I feel like I'm carrying all the responsibility; I don't think that's fair.

Ahmed does not share child care equally, but I wouldn't mind that so much if I didn't have to do the housework. The house, job, and child care are a lot. I want him to think of all this as his equal responsibility, but I don't know how to do it. He agrees with me logically, but he doesn't do anything, and I don't know how to go about straightening that out. It might be less stressful if I just gave up and did everything myself, which is what my mother did, but I guess I can't do that. The pressure has definitely increased since we had the baby. Before she was born, I just did everything; I didn't complain. But now sometimes I end up sounding like a shrew. Then I drop the whole subject, we make friends with each other, but then we go through the whole thing again. Ahmed tries to be supportive, but he doesn't really understand what I mean about sharing responsibilities.

Luckily my dearest friend had a baby four months after I did, so she is a real good person for support. Then I met a woman in Lamaze class; we discovered we lived in the same building, and we've been friends ever since. Her boy is just six weeks older than Eila. My old boss remembers very clearly the problems and headaches and time-juggling of having a baby, so she was a source of comfort also. I'm somebody who feels better after I talk about something, if I'm sure that the person I've talked to isn't going to tell everybody else in town. I feel much better when I talk.

Sometimes, though, I think this whole thing is unfair, and I wonder why I should be stuck in this situation. It seems to me there will be a number of years of hard work before it gets any easier. Even if three years from now I finish my master's and get a marvelous job at $50,000, I'll have to put in so much time and bring home work at night, and there will be a whole conflict all over again. The money problem may not be there, but you still want to give time and effort to your child and husband.

The whole thing bothers me a little; it bothers me that when she's older, she'll come home from school and go to a sitter's house. And then, I'd like to do more comfy, homey things, like sew some clothes. I just feel I have so little time for my family. And it bothers me. Someone once said to me, "You know, Eila definitely knows who you are; I thought since she spends so much time with a sitter, she wouldn't feel attached to you. But I can see that she does." It was supposed to be a nice comment, but I thought, "Is that what people are saying? that the kid doesn't know who her mother is?" I thought of nothing else for a few days.

After Eila was born, I cried all day and night for weeks at the idea of leaving her to go back to work, but in the morning when I dropped her off, she was happy to see the sitter. I wouldn't have let her out of my arms otherwise. She was content to be where she was. But when I came home at the end of the day, she'd throw her arms up in the air for me to pick her up. She had a big smile. She knew who I was.

One of my husband's theories is that Eila's better off in this situation. If Ahmed sat down and cried with me, we'd be in bad shape. But he really does believe that children should be with lots of different people so that they are more well rounded and more tolerant. He thinks she'll be less spoiled and that it's a marvelous experience. I think he's got a point.

Randee Pierson

Corporate Career and a Baby

Randee is in her early thirties. She and her husband, David, a lawyer, live in the suburbs of a large midwestern city and they have a four-month-old son, Zachary. She has worked for a major corporation for several years. Recently, she completed her Master of Business Administration, after attending school at night for a few years.

I've been with my company for ten years, and I'm now Compensation Planning Manager. That entails the development of our compensation plans for salaried employees throughout the corporation. I report directly to the Vice President of Human Resources, and I have a staff of seven.

I worked right up until my baby was born; I took six weeks' maternity leave. My husband and I talked to a number of people who were working mothers and fathers, and it seemed like six weeks was enough time from a standpoint of spending time with the baby and getting used to the idea of what we'd be going through. Physically six weeks is good for the mother, and I think we developed good bonding. It was difficult for me, especially the first couple of weeks. You can't walk very fast, and then the second week I was trying to do too much. I'm not good at sitting around and having people wait on me.

I started working out child-care arrangements six months before he was born. I talked to people we knew who were working parents about how they felt about the adequacy of child care, if it was better to have somebody in the home or better to take them to a child-care place. Then I called county services to find out names of individuals who have day-care homes as well as day-care centers, and who are licensed. I also called an agency that would supply live-in domestic help. But they did a very poor job in screening people. I gave them requirements and said I didn't want to talk to anybody unless they met those requirements. They had to speak English well, had to have their own car, because if something happened to him during the day I wanted them to be able to drive him to a hospital or doctor. It was the old employment agency game—we'll send you bodies; you interview the people, and if we happen to come along with somebody who meets your requirements, we'll be real happy because then we can charge you a fee.

I interviewed three day-care centers in the vicinity of my office and found they had good care but not the care I wanted him to have when he was just a baby. I decided a day-care center was not the kind of thing I wanted, and so that meant it had to be somebody to come into my house or it would have to be a day-care home.

My day-care woman, Sandy, charges seventy-five dollars. She initially charged fifty dollars. She used to be a pediatric nurse and loves kids. She started out by taking care of other nurses' children, and now she watches five kids full-time. She is a unique individual; I feel very comfortable with her. I don't think I would have felt comfortable going back to work if I didn't have someone like her.

I don't feel guilty about not being with Zach all day. Even nonworking mothers don't spend all their time with their kids; my sister has four kids and my sister-in-law has three kids and I have friends with kids and I know they don't spend every waking moment with them. They have other responsibilities, too. Maybe I have no guilt because I've seen Sandy work with kids. I feel she does a better job than I would in certain situations because of her experience; she's raised two kids of her own, and she has been doing this for five years.

Adding a new person to our family changed our lifestyle. We're very comfortable with each other. If we have a problem or feel we're not spending enough time with each other, we take care of it. We don't get as much time together as we'd like to, but it's the difference between being a family and just being two of us. I might not spend as much personal time with David as I'd like to, but we try to set aside time where we can be together and sit down and talk. As Zach gets more independent, David and I are not going to have the kind of time we had before. That's a problem. Since we leave him during the day, I don't want to leave him with a sitter at night. That's the time I want to spend with him.

I'm a very compulsive person, a perfectionist; things have to be a certain way. If I'm having somebody for dinner, everything we serve must be right. That means from 6:00 A.M. to 6:00 P.M. on a Saturday all I'm doing is getting ready. David says I'm nuts; he says if something is not right, people will realize we have a baby and are both working, and they don't expect to come here and see everything in perfect shape. I do have cleaning help once every three weeks.

Everything I do I want to do as well as I possibly can, and sometimes it gets a little ridiculous. I'm getting to be more realistic about things, though. Before I had Zach, I had no idea how much time a baby takes. When I went on maternity leave I had one of the people at the office bring work home for me during that six weeks. I had no idea that I wouldn't be able to get it all done. I couldn't imagine what a baby could do from 6:00 A.M. to 10:00 P.M.; what could take up that much time? I thought I'd probably have eight hours during the day to devote to other things. But I found out. One day at 3:00 P.M., I called a friend; I was still in my bathrobe and had not taken a shower or washed my hair or brushed my teeth. I hadn't done anything. I said, "I think there is something wrong with me; I've not done anything—not eaten breakfast."

I thought, "This is incredible!" How was it possible I could stand there at 3:00 P.M. and not have done anything? I was breast-feeding; nobody told me how long it would take a baby to eat and how many times he would eat! When I was in the hospital, I thought, "This is the easiest thing in the world; they bring the baby to you and take him away," and I thought, "This isn't too bad." Then I got home, and that first weekend!

I had no idea I would react the way I did. I remember needing some things from the grocery store. David had said he'd be home by 6:30, and it was already 7:00 P.M. and he wasn't home. I thought, "I'm going to go to the grocery store—this is ridiculous." The baby was six days old and I left him with my mom. I was in the store, standing in the line, crying. I didn't know why. I came home, and I was upset because my husband was an hour late. Any other time it would not have bothered me at all, but this was a whole side of me I couldn't control.

I can usually go on six hours of sleep a night, but it's the interrupted sleep that is unbelievable. It's like no sleep at all. I remember one night after Zach spent every one and a half to two hours getting up, crying—I thought that if he didn't shut up, I'd hit him. My God, why would you ever hit a little baby? But I was so tired I couldn't cope. After the first two weeks, I was getting more sleep and things got better, but I still didn't know how I could go back to work. I'm a list person, and every day I'd make a list, and by 4:00 P.M. not one thing on that list was done. I didn't know how I could go back to work if I couldn't even write thank-you notes or pick up something at a store. I couldn't even do small dumb things that would normally take ten minutes or an hour. David would come home, and I couldn't believe I hadn't done anything all day! I didn't realize that babies took so much time.

After six weeks, though, I did go back to work. I'm still nursing in the morning and at night. In the morning, I get up at 5:00 and nurse from 5:00 to 6:00, and then get ready. David takes him to the sitter. During the day, Zach gets bottles; he takes from three to four bottles a day.

I don't feel the baby has impinged on my career development at all. If anything, he's probably made me more aware of time, more efficient than before. I make sure I don't waste time. I think you have control over situations. If, for example, a program were being implemented at work that was requiring an inordinate amount of time to the point that I was not devoting the kind of time I wanted to my family, it would be up to me to say to my boss, "I'm committed to getting this done, but here is what I'm going to need in resources to get it done. I can't do it all myself. If you're not willing to give me those resources, then prioritize the projects, because we can't do everything." I try to manage the best I can, I try to work out a time schedule, and alleviate some of the problems ahead of time or at least talk about them. I have the ability to put things together, to define objectives, to know what I want to get done, and when I want to get it done. I've always had initiative, to get involved with more than one thing at once, primarily because I have a high energy level. I don't get tired.

But I know you can't be everything to everybody all at once; there are going to be times you do well in your career, and there will be times you do things well with your husband or partner; there will be times when things click with everything. And then there are times when things go wrong with everything; but I think that's life. I think there are cycles you go through on an ongoing basis.

If people are looking at whether or not to have a family, there are many things to look at. How committed are they to a child, to a career? What kind of career do they have? Is it something just starting? Is it a career that will require much time and emotional involvement? I was at a point in my career development where I felt fairly secure about my company. I knew I had a lot of support; I had been with the company long enough for the managers to know me and what I'm like and to trust me. It wasn't a problem of my having to build up relationships and trust. I knew the political environment, and I'd spent time and energy learning how the organization works and how I fit in. Who I could trust or not trust. I don't have to spend that energy now because I know where the problems are. I know the political atmosphere, I know what's good and not good, what's accepted and not accepted. It's not a matter of me just starting out and needing to put a lot of effort in it. And David's at the same point. We're not just starting out changing careers. I had my M.B.A. and a good position.

I feel confident that Zach is getting the care he should be getting. I feel good about the time we spend with him; I think we're instilling values in him. He knows who his mother and father are, there's no doubt in my mind about that. That's who you get your values from. I don't think he's going to feel we hated him because we sent him off to have somebody else take care of him during the day.

Heather Gardner

An Alternative Lifestyle

Heather is a social worker with a fifteen-year-old daughter and a twelve-year-old son.

She recently moved into New York City after living in the suburbs for years. She is juggling three jobs and, as a lesbian mother, is raising her children alone.

Years ago, I moved to a development on Long Island as a married woman with no children. All the houses were just going up. There was lots of friendliness, block parties, people planting their bushes together; there were many other women in the same boat with me. We had our babies, stayed home and drank coffee together. I knew those people for a long time. I must have been living in that house for eight or nine years before my marriage broke up. My relationships there were based on my role as wife and mother.

When my marriage broke up, I made no secret about being a lesbian. It was common knowledge in the neighborhood, and to anybody who was a friend of mine, I would talk about it.

I found out, though, that a lot of people, even though we had socialized, weren't my friends. For instance, I had a babysitter, a very responsible teenager on the block, and one time one of the neighbors whom I had many coffee klatches with called her up, invited her over with another neighbor on the block, and started grilling her about my life and what was going on in the house. When her parents heard I was a lesbian, they put pressure on her not to sit anymore. That's the kind of thing I have to deal with a lot. This fear of, or prejudice toward, homosexuals is pervasive in our culture. It affects gay men and women in the work place, in graduate school, in the PTA, in their role as parents. Homophobia is the main difference between being a lesbian working mother and just a working mother.

My kids at first didn't think anything of my being a lesbian. Then they learned the social taboo on homosexuality, and they didn't want to tell anybody. As adolescents, my kids are sensitive about issues of conformity, but we've had a dialogue for years about judging people who are different. Different isn't necessarily worse, it's just different. I think that realization has opened them up so they will be better equipped to be who they are as they get out into the world. So, while there have been some uncomfortable moments for them, I feel in the long run my lesbianism has been a positive factor in their lives. But still they feel embarrassed sometimes, and they don't like that.

There's also the fact that we went through a major life transition, and all of our old support systems failed us. At first I didn't feel free to say I was a lesbian when my marriage broke up because I was in the middle of a divorce, and custody is always an issue for lesbian mothers. I wasn't going to take any chances. I wasn't going to tell anybody because I didn't want to lose custody of the kids. When you go through a major life transition, you're shaking, and I was shaking. Everything was new. I didn't know how to support my family. I didn't have connections with the lesbian community. I was pretty messed up and very alone. I was not at that time the most available mother. So a lot of my kids' anger comes from things like that more than from my being a lesbian. I think any mother who is divorced goes through that to a certain degree. My divorce was very dramatic. My support systems disappeared, and it was like moving into a foreign country, except the language was very similar. All of my old friends fell away. It wasn't only that they didn't want to be friends with me, but it was also that I was changing and wasn't so interested in them. So it took me a few years to work these things out.

Shortly after I "came out," I knew I didn't want to stay in the suburbs. There is a level of conformity and conventionality that exists in the suburbs, and if you are different—different race, different sexual orientation, different lifestyle—there are social pressures.

I stayed in the suburbs for seven years after my divorce. Although money was tight then, I did get my master's degree in social work. After I got my degree and started to work, I felt that I could move to the city. I had a lot of friends and social activities here, and a friend of mine owned this house and had space to rent. It was as if the Red Sea had opened up and I just walked through! Although I am somewhat rent-poor, I do have a place where I can see clients, and the kids and I aren't on top of each other. There are other lesbians in the community, too. There is a women's restaurant, for instance, and on back-to-school nights, I can walk down the hall and meet three lesbian mothers that I know socially.

There is anonymity in the city. Neighbors don't look out their windows to watch to see who's coming to visit. In the city people are used to differences; they welcome them. It's just a mix—racially, sexually, economically, socially. Nobody stands out, and in that respect the children are more comfortable.

The neighbors help each other. The woman in the building has helped my kids when they're sick a couple of times; she's brought soup or something like that. Basically, though, I'm the person who is needed all the time. My ex-husband is also involved to some extent, but he just takes the kids on his scheduled weekends. He's remarried and has two other children. He doesn't pitch in to do any more than he has to for my kids. I had a cancer operation and I asked him to take them an extra weekend—it wasn't his weekend—and he said no. He only does what the letter of the separation agreement calls for. Period. We also have financial disagreements, and money is a problem.

I'm middle-class, and it's very expensive to live that way in the city. My kids want to go to camp, and my daughter needs orthodontia. I definitely feel economic pressure. At this point I have three different jobs. I work in a gay clinic in Manhattan, as well as in a nursing home. I also have a private practice here at home. Because I'm working in so many places, it takes me forever to commute. I feel conflicted at this point about how to work things out. The kids like it when I'm home. If I had a few more clients at home, I could be with them more often. There'd be more communication, and I wouldn't be so exhausted. A therapist's main hours to see working clients are at night. Right now I can either see more clients at night at home or make less money. At some point, I'd like an office in the neighborhood rather than having it in the house, because now I hear the noises from the kids and I have to tell them to be quiet, or the phone rings. It's a strain, but it's better economically.

I like to work with adults. At the nursing home, I work with the staff. I do in-service training of staff on things like the effects of a stroke on the emotions of the person. I show them how to work with patients who have certain problems, like speech defects or perceptual deficiencies. I love working with old people. I've learned a lot from them. I like to work with people who are living an introspective life, people who want to grow and develop psychologically and spiritually.

I have stripped away the nonessentials in my life. A lot of the props that I had went—money and certain kinds of superficial social relationships. I really had to figure out what was important. If I could take the step of acknowledging to both myself and the world that I was a lesbian, there wasn't anything else I couldn't say about myself. It was a liberating experience.

I'm not a closet lesbian. I am known as a lesbian in all of my jobs, and that hasn't held me back. I may be fortunate because by the time I came out I'd had so many years of self-denial that I wasn't in the mood to continue denying myself. So I'm pretty much willing to take the consequences for the freedom of being myself. It has not gotten me fired. People who want to move a little further away, move further away, and the people who are interested in getting close, move a little closer.

I think I used to feel driven; I had to produce, and sometimes it was at the expense of the kids. I'm sure most working mothers do that. But now if they really need me, if my physical presence is necessary, I take time off, even if I don't get paid. In some ways I have a very easy life now, and one of the reasons I have been able to combine working and having kids is that I don't expect myself to be Superwoman.

Audrey Rosseli

Living in a Group

Audrey, a woman in her early thirties, lives with Philip, who is the father of their three-year-old daughter, Kira. A nurse administrator in the Pacific Northwest, Audrey works with city and hospital administrations.

Philip and I are not married. We have a three-year-old daughter, and we live with two other adults in a house we own. Being married is not something we really desire, although we are committed partners. No question about that; we have a house and a daughter, we have things in common, and we've been together for about six years. I envision being together for a long time. As a result of having property and a child together, we have had to consciously make contracts and deliberately establish how we are going to do things. A friend said, "Why don't you just get married? It's much easier." I said, "That's why I don't want to get married. I don't want to assume we can take things for granted." Philip and I grew up in families that didn't have good marriages. So we don't see marriage as easier.

In the group I used to live in, unlike this one, we all felt we were equally responsible for the children. We shared total responsibility whether we were family or close friends of the child. What we found was that the expectations of the non-parent were too great and were a hardship on the parent. There was a struggle for loyalty on the part of the child. Before Kira got very old, we decided to clarify the relationships. I am THE mother—Philip is THE father. The others are not surrogate parents.

Group living helps with expenses. Philip and I have lived alone together once. It was not a situation that we particularly wanted. We don't want an insular kind of household. There are disadvantages to living with other people, however. When we want time alone it's difficult to find. Another problem is that once you become a mother it's hard to draw the line, and sometimes I find myself being the mother of the house. This happens with things like meals and cleaning the house. I have always assumed that adults can see and will take the initiative, and they don't always.

When things are working well, they're working in all ways. We have a fairly straightforward financial situation—Philip takes care of it and pretty much everything is divided equally. He and I take special financial responsibility for household repairs, since we are the landlords of the house. Having other adult bodies around to share work is wonderful. I have friends doing it by themselves, and it's a terrifying ordeal. However, sometimes I feel that if I don't oversee everything, it won't get done—taking care of Kira or taking care of the house. It makes me crazy. Sometimes I can't tell whether it's me doing it to myself or if it's people that expect it of me—I suspect it's a combination of both.

Even when everybody's here I feel Kira is my responsibility. For instance sometimes I say, "I'm going to my room, I'd like to read." Philip gets irritated with me and would like me just to leave. The reason I ask is to protect myself, because if I leave and don't feel like somebody is actively taking care of her, she'll follow me and I'll have to take care of her. I resent that.

I would like to tally up how many hours I do what, because even Philip and I get into discussions about this. Because he works later hours, that doesn't mean he works longer hours; in fact we work equally. I think sometimes he feels put upon, and I'd like to emphasize that we work equally. Philip has always worked on weekends. The only arrangement we have is that he would take care of Kira in the daytime while I worked and I'd take care of her in the evenings. He'd awake with me in the morning before I went to work, and I would try to get up in the middle of the night when he came home so we'd see one another. This arrangement has created a strain. He doesn't want to get up in the morning and I don't want to get up in the middle of the night. We've had to make a special effort to have time together. Sometimes we leave Kira with friends for a weekend. One of the compromises we made was I felt it was too much for Philip to work full-time in the evenings and have total child-care responsibility, so when she was about fourteen months old we put her in day care two and a half days a week. That provides some free time for him and the company of other children for her; we still have a half-day a week when neither of us works and we have time together.

The day care is associated with a university program, but we pay as private members. It's a cooperative, and since we don't have the time to spend at the school, we pay a substantial amount. Since we both work and therefore have money, we've been able to get good care.

I work as a health educator. I currently run the pediatric and obstetric program at a community clinic and basically keep together the program for two other clinics as well. I do administrative work, and I spend a lot of time negotiating with the hospital where our obstetric cases go to make sure things run smoothly.

Our clinic is suffering from federal budget cuts. I'm under more pressure now because there are more and more people in need and we anticipate that this need will grow. I work nine to five and one evening a week, and since that's when Philip has off, he is usually at home.

My work environment is very supportive. The office is crowded, but I like everybody. As the head person, I supervise men as well as women. The men have always felt a little slighted. Initially we preferred hiring women, but recently we actually hired two male doctors, one works full-time and one works part-time in our clinic and part-time in another clinic. It's hard to be a doctor's boss and most of the time we work jointly. I'm rarely in a position of strong conflict with them, and if I really think something is important, they'll do it.

It's much easier to supervise men if the roles are clear. It's much more difficult for me in a place where it is casual and friendly and the roles are not clearly defined. Though I seem aggressive to many people, I am really not. I'm really kind of a coward, but when I have to assert myself, it is almost like acting and it is a role that I am comfortable with. It's not easy to know what to do. I know in the past when I've been aggressive I have gotten less, and when I fell back on more traditional ways, I've gotten more. I've always been diplomatic, much more so than I needed to be. I've been criticized by other women because I wear makeup and try to look too feminine. However, I was doing what I was comfortable with.

Basically, this is a good place. If it is necessary, we bring children to the office. We have staff meetings and occasionally children are there. If your child is ill, you can leave in the middle of the day to take care of him and not be penalized. The clinic has excellent maternity benefits, which are helpful to those of us who've taken time out to have children. For instance, they will hold your job for you for a limited period of time.

Basically I feel good about my life. I believe a communal situation can work if you are with people who like children and are committed to the idea of shared responsibility for the children.

We're doing okay. We're well cared for, we have everything we need physically; we're all healthy, strong people, and we have one little girl who is really keeping us on our toes. It's a lot of work; I think if there is anything we're all learning about home and family, it's how much work it really is. As much as our mothers and mother-figures complain, I don't think they ever really explain that there is a difference between complaining all the time about what you have to do and clearly outlining how much work and responsibility you have. That's why I think you need others to share—it's hard to keep it all together by yourself.

Joyce Lindstrom

Single Mother

Joyce is a divorced mother of two sons, ages nine and twelve. She moved to a large Texas city from a rural area outside a small town because she needed to earn more money to support her family.

I'm thirty-five years old, and I am an executive secretary; in a couple of months, I'll also become office manager, supervising five new people. I work for an engineering company, and I like what I'm doing. It's what I was trained to do and what I enjoy doing. I'm not satisfied as a housewife. There's nothing wrong with being a housewife, but I'm just not satisfied with that. I like being out in the working field and gaining knowledge and insight into people. I think if I can bring that knowledge home with me, it will help on the home front. I've never felt I neglected my family because I've always worked. They were born into it, and we've always adjusted to it and made arrangements as far as the children's activities and things. I've always managed.

I was raised very conservatively in Indiana where when you graduate from high school you work for a year and then get married and raise a family. The husband does the work and provides for the family. That was instilled in me. But when I got out into the world, I saw things weren't as they seemed to be.

I was divorced two years ago. We had been living in a small Texas town where income opportunities are few and far between, especially if you are a woman. I had to pay for rent, car notes, groceries, education, and clothing, like every other single parent, and when it came time to get an increase in pay, I got a small raise. I went to my employer and pleaded my case with him. He said, "Joyce, the other two people who have the same title you do are men who have families to support." I said, "What do you think I have?" Two weeks later, I was looking for a job in a big city of my own volition. He did not fire me, and when he found out I was taking a job in the city, he offered me more money, but it was too late. There is no alimony in Texas. I do get some child support, but I am the primary provider.

I had three interviews before I accepted my present job. I felt with this position I had more job security, a better chance for advancement, and better salary. Finding an apartment was a problem. I wanted something near the office, and something in a good school area, something convenient to supermarkets and shopping malls, but I also wanted something that was decent, not trashy. Many apartments were nice, but they were for adults or older children. I wanted something where there was a family environment and family activities.

I found something very nice. This place has a pool, playground, and recreation room. Right next door to my apartment is a big, open grassy range where the kids can go out and walk the dog or play baseball or whatever, and not bother other people. Sometimes I have to work late and the city is large and sometimes dangerous, so the children are sort of confined until I get home. I don't allow them out unless I'm there.

The "Y" and other places do have after-school activities, but they are few and far between, which is very surprising. My boys usually end up doing homework, watching TV, reading. The youngest one is an outdoor person, but here he is confined. The farthest they can go is next door to play with the children there, or down the street to a little playground. We used to live out in the country, and they had plenty of room to roam and we had animals. They could ride bikes, and I didn't worry about them, but here in the city it's more difficult for them and I feel guilty to a certain extent.

Right after my divorce, I went into seclusion. I didn't have much of a social life for the first three months. It started getting the best of me. I think the worst part of divorce is the first six months of being a single parent—all the adjustments. I didn't know how my children would react to my going out with a man other than their father. I was surprised that they accepted it quite well, because they understood the man was no threat to them. I've always tried to talk to them on a level which made them feel included. So I think they accepted the fact that Mama is going to go out and Daddy is going to go out and they're not going to be neglected. I see no resentment on their part—not yet anyway. My ex-husband is now remarried, and the boys spend every other weekend with him.

I dated someone for approximately eight months. The boys

became quite attached to him, and the question of marriage came up. I asked what they thought, and they were both quite agreeable to the idea. When I told them that we had decided it wouldn't work out, and he would no longer be coming around, they were disappointed. He was good to the children, on the surface, at least; I don't know what would have happened if we married. I'm very adamant about the fact that I will not remarry just for my children's sake. That I won't do.

I find that divorced women are stereotyped. It's not difficult to meet people. It's difficult to meet people with whom you can become good friends. My mother is so worried I won't get married again. I'm not concerned with that at the moment, but sometimes you come home in the afternoon and you face four walls and sit there and wonder, "Is this all there is to life?" And, "Why don't I have a husband like Jane Doe down the street that I can spend weekends and holidays with?" Then again, twenty-four hours later I'm probably thanking the good Lord I don't have that situation.

I still have a family; I may not have four members of a family, but I have three members of a family. Nothing has changed that drastically. You have to understand that in my particular situation, my husband was gone away from home a lot the last two years of my marriage, so there wasn't that much of a change. My responsibilities remained the same; I was mother and father to the children even before my divorce. I used to lie awake at night thinking, "How am I going to handle such and such if it should arise?" I was always pessimistic and worried about something happening rather than crossing that bridge when we had to. I've gotten to the point now where you do what you have to do. You just do it, I don't know if it is instilled in you or what. It's not always easy, and there are times when you wonder if you made the right decision, but I don't think it's that hard.

Once in a while I feel overwhelmed. Not too long ago I was working Saturdays and a couple of Sundays, and I felt if I had to work another extra day, I was going to run away from it. When you get to that point you have to do something. So I told my boss I had to have time off. He's a workaholic, and he lets that come over into my job. He had no idea of my workload; I was physically and mentally spent, and I told him at that point you don't do your job to the best of your ability. I said if there is a deadline that is impossible to meet during the regular work hours, fine, I'll work on a Saturday, but it was becoming a habit.

I have two of the best employers in the world. They are so understanding, but lots of times they don't realize what you are doing or how much of it you are doing unless you show them. They didn't realize how much was on my shoulders.

I expect a lot from people. I supervise people, and I expect quite a lot from them, but no more from them than I would of myself; I'm very hard on myself. If you're going to get paid, you should do your work to the best of your ability. I even expect a lot from my children, and they know it. I am a disciplinarian; I give them a lot of freedom for their age, but I also expect a lot from them, and it has worked thus far.

My father and mother taught me to be an independent person from the time I was a little girl. Since I was thirteen years old, I've worked. I left my parents' home the day after I graduated from high school. I had an offer of a scholarship for college, which I refused. I wasn't ready to continue my education then. Now, maybe I regret that, but I wasn't ready then. I walked out into the world and went to work. I think people who start out being independent can handle a lot. It depends how you are raised when you are young; if you are raised to be dependent on someone for everything, then that's how you go through life. I depend on people for certain things, because you can't do it all yourself. After my divorce, I was scared at first; I was thirty-two years old and on my own with two kids. But you get out there and do it because you know you have to. It's not going to be given to you, and you don't have that husband to help support you. You've got to do it yourself.

Kate Tcholakian

When the Going Gets Tough

Kate and her husband, Aram, met when he was a foreign exchange student at the college she attended; their son, Yuri, was born two and a half years ago. They live in California.

I have worked in data processing for about thirteen or fourteen years; for the past few years I've worked for an airline, so Aram and I did a great deal of traveling. We were married eight years before Yuri was born, and we had been very independent. I assumed we could continue to travel after the baby. But that hasn't really worked out.

We took a family vacation last year in Hawaii. Yuri's a good traveler; he sleeps anywhere and eats anything. The problem is we stayed in a condominium and it was no vacation. I had to cook all the time and I hated it, even though I love to cook at home. And then Yuri was active and demanding. He is cute and is bright and has a lot of personality, but he didn't turn out to be exactly my idea of what a child would be like. Maybe I just didn't know how a child changes your routine, your whole life. I'd love to get up in the morning and eat a decent breakfast and get dressed without somebody hanging on me. I'd like to go out without toothpaste on my skirt!

When I'm alone with Yuri for long periods, I end up screaming at him. I'm normally very quiet and I remember calling my friend and saying, "I'm a madwoman—I'm screaming at this child." My husband has never made me scream like that. I have found consolation only in other mothers, but there's no doubt this pressure is very great. Sometimes my husband and I look at each other and say, "Did you ever think it would be like this—did you know this and not tell me?"

For instance, after work, when I pick Yuri up at the sitter's, I have to chase him three times around the neighborhood. "I want to stay here, I don't want to go home," he says. He's busy doing something just then, he wants to stay and play. He is glad to see me, but just for one minute. I think it's because when I get home, I have intentions of changing clothes and going to the park with him. But what happens is I watch the clock so we can get to the park and home for an early dinner. I feel if we horse around, we won't get to the park till late and then we won't eat till eight, and the whole night will become a disaster. We end up in confrontations, and his temper tantrums drive me bananas. It also hurts me because I see him such a limited amount of time.

I'm particularly thankful that my husband is the way he is; he does everything for Yuri except take him to the doctor or buy his clothes, things like that. But the problem is that he has begun to travel a great deal in his work. When he first left, I thought it was wonderful; I could really spend time with Yuri. I thought I'd visit my mom in Michigan. I figured I could fly anywhere with him. It turned out Yuri was at a difficult age, just turning two, and he was so unpredictable it was hard to control him. I was so tired that I couldn't handle it very well, and I felt I couldn't risk having him go through one of his fits on the plane.

Normally Aram travels twenty percent of the time, but this year he was gone ninety percent of the time during the first six months. He took two trips to Bangkok for four weeks at a stretch—that was crazy. The thing that frustrated me was that when he traveled before, I never minded. In fact, I enjoyed the time to myself. But now I feel very frustrated and trapped. It's unfortunate because I know he likes his work, and I believe he is doing what he thinks is right in accepting these assignments, but I have a great deal of resentment.

I think our communication has broken down since the baby was born. It was easier to talk to each other when we didn't have constant distractions. I don't think we have enough time for ourselves. I feel it's really important for working people to spend time together and then some time with the child. My husband's from a more child-oriented culture, and he disagrees. We had a secure relationship before our child was born; we knew each other well and were good friends. It has been a shock for me to see that changing; we just don't share things like we used to. I knew it would be difficult when we had a baby, but the one thing I took for granted was that our relationship wouldn't change.

With a small child, so much affection goes toward the child; affection you would have given your husband goes to your child. I remember when Yuri was very small, my husband said, "You hardly kiss me anymore," and I said, "Your face is too big!" That was my reaction. I was home night and day, staring at this little sweet, innocent, helpless face, and that's what I felt!

In addition, when Yuri was small, I didn't have the energy I would have had normally. I had a serious blood clot in my eighth month of pregnancy and I became critically ill. It was very serious; I almost died. So there I was, taking care of a new child, not knowing much about babies, and taking injections every eight hours around the clock for eight months to control my blood. I had a health problem plus a demanding little boy.

I had planned to take a short maternity leave, but ended up staying home a year. My job was secure because I was on sick leave, but I was apprehensive about going back to work. I didn't want to leave my child, yet I felt locked up and lonely at home. When I went back, it was half-days. But even now I can work whatever eight-hour stretch I want to, and what I try to do is to go in very early and be finished at three or three-thirty. In data processing, people can come and go at odd hours because of the availability of machines. People even work at night. I can go in early and leave early if I choose.

I'm fortunate to work in a big company. As grueling as it can be in a bureaucracy, I have a really good time and I have nice friends. I have a good friend at work; she's a manager, and she has a child one year old. She can't relate to half the problems I have because she doesn't know them. She has a girl who does all laundry and housework, and my friend doesn't know what it's like in the morning to get the child dressed and ready to take to a sitter. She pays this woman two hundred seventy dollars a month, and I pay my sitter three hundred dollars a month. Of course, her girl has full room and board. I'm thinking maybe that's what I should do. These live-ins come in from Europe and we have a friend advertising for us now. This might be an answer for me. I found when my in-laws stayed with us, I was much happier when I had a helping hand and when I knew somebody would be home when I walked into the house with Yuri at 5:00 P.M. I also think that would relieve some of the pressure I feel when Aram's traveling. For instance, Yuri's been ill the last two days, and when I dropped him off at the sitter, he cried and cried. That depressed me all morning. When a child is sick and we need to take time off from work, we can take vacation time or make up the time. We are not supposed to use sick time. We have unlimited sick days, and I guess because I don't feel working mothers should get special treatment, I try to be honest about it. What happens is that they deducted five days' pay for last year; I ran out of vacation. I get a sense of reproach from the men I work with, especially the ones who have wives at home.

Sometimes I wonder what we're doing. I look at Aram at times—I know he's not happy. I go through spells of asking, "What is it all for, both of us working?"

To me the alternative is not my quitting my job. But we are looking at options. One thing we're investigating is the possibility of buying a business. In the beginning, I was somewhat opposed to it because I knew we'd have to give up our jobs. But my husband's sister has moved here and she'll manage the place. I've noticed a change in Aram since we've begun talking about it. I don't think he intends to give up his work, but he is very creative and this is an outlet for him. I don't need to work eight hours a day to be satisfied; I would gladly work four days a week for a six-hour day. So this could be an answer. We do have some choices.

Cheryl Kotsera

The Second Time Around

Cheryl Kotsera is married for the second time. She and her husband, Steve, live in New York City. Cheryl is an executive for a nonprofit organization, and she is the mother of two children, Tim and Rebecca.

My first husband and I were married in graduate school. He got a Fulbright and I got a teaching fellowship. It was a student marriage, a simple life, where I assumed the role of learning to cook and making some sort of a household, and we moved a lot. He got his degree and started doing research, and I finished all the exams for my Ph.D. in art history.

At that point I got a grant to write my dissertation. I was the first woman at my university to get a President's Fellowship. That was accidental; I happened to be there at the right time and they had to give it to a woman. I had no idea I was pregnant when I applied, and when I got it I went to my advisor and told him. He was delighted and said, "Serves them right that the first woman that gets it is pregnant." I was willing to turn it back, that's how traditional I was. We decided I could write my dissertation and have the baby. It wasn't that easy. I had the wrong expectations; I thought the baby would sleep all the time. I was teaching pretty much to the very end, and my dissertation wasn't going very well at all.

I was still working, teaching part-time. I could arrange my hours; I usually taught in the evenings or at times when my husband was home. What was interesting was that he called it babysitting. After all, they were his kids, but he would "babysit" for me so I could go teach. Parenthetically, he's in a second marriage and he's started another family. His wife is a lawyer and his second child was born a month ago and from what I hear he's apparently very much committed to sharing the responsibility. In our marriage it must have been my attitude, too, that contributed to his attitude. I simply assumed the traditional role.

When my daughter was born, the marriage didn't seem to be so good. I decided I'd better get my dissertation going. It's a rather poignant story. One day I was taking a cake out of the oven and I looked at the cake and said to myself, "If I put all the cakes together that I cooked, it probably would equal the Great Wall of China," and it suddenly dawned on me that men build the Wall of China and women bake cakes. At the same time I must say I truly enjoyed my children and I still do. My children are the most important part of my life. My relationship with them is wonderful and has made me who I am in a way. I have learned a great deal from them.

My first husband then got what seemed a fairly good offer in California—in no-man's land. What became clear is he had given no thought to what would happen to my career. I had given many, many years to it and was close to getting my dissertation done. There was no possibility for me to do any of my work there—nothing, it was barren as far as the humanities or history were concerned. That pointed out something to both of us, that his career was primary and mine secondary. It was primary for me to take care of the household. And that was really the beginning of the end of our marriage. It lasted until my daughter was four years old and my son six, which was about three more years.

We never went to California. He decided to stay and has never left New York. During the last years of the marriage, I went to see a woman psychologist to figure out why I was so miserable. At that point I had my Ph.D. and I was teaching. It became clear that I needed to become a full entity by myself, and that we really didn't interact well with the children and probably would be better parents if we separated.

I spent ten years divorced and alone with the kids, the critical years from six to sixteen and four to fourteen. For three of those years I had family and friends, but no men. Those were the most important in terms of my children. We really got cemented together. I had no interest in getting remarried because I had been disappointed in various relationships many times. Before my second marriage I was in relationships that seemed very draining. There never seemed to be any balance. In my first marriage I was dependent emotionally; in my other relationships, when I became happy with myself, men seemed to want to move in and be taken care of, almost like another child. While it seemed wonderful to be needed, it wasn't wonderful for me in the long run. It seemed great to be the inspiration for a poet or a writer, but it was emotionally draining for me. So I had come to the point where I said to myself, "I have everything in life that is meaningful—wonderful children, a great job, a sense of myself—I do creative things. A meaningful relationship with a man is just one aspect of life," and I stopped looking.

I married my second husband Steve two years ago. We really seemed to have nothing in common except an attitude toward life. He's a stockbroker and he doesn't know much about art, but he convinced me it was worth giving it a try. We dated for about a half-year before getting married.

The kids have continued to see their father every weekend, but it has been very difficult for them and still is; I have tried to make it better. It's been particularly difficult for Tim, but I think he has finally accepted his father. Sadly, he has come to what most of us come to when we are thirty, accepting our parents for the people they are and not expecting any parenting. Tim said, "It's nice for Dad that he has a second family." He doesn't expect anything anymore. But there were times during those early years when he did.

The second time around my husband knew who I was. Usually I cook dinner because he doesn't like to and he can't do it well; I love to do it. He does the chores I hate most—washing windows, for example—without being asked. There are intangible ways he shows that he knows who I am. Before our wedding we were trying to figure out how to get married because it's a mixed marriage. Steve said, "Since your church is a very important part of your life, and you had a lot to do with having it built, we should get married there. I'll see if I can get a rabbi, and we can get married by your minister and a rabbi." That was his idea, affirming our separateness. And it's important that we did that. I wouldn't have thought of it. I suspect that even at that point I would have compromised. My basic model of what a woman does has to do with the way my mother related to my father. My mother's role was one of devotion to a scholar. He was a great scholar and she doted on him.

My daughter would never do a thing like that. My daughter can't imagine not having a career and children and having a wonderful husband and being happy with it. She assumes that's what she will have. She could not imagine not being engaged in the outside world, not just to earn a living but to be creatively engaged. I think that's a generational difference as much as a personal difference.

Steve has three adult children. His was a very traditional marriage. He lived in the suburbs and commuted to Wall Street. The children went to private school, and his wife worked in charities. When they separated, part of his separation agreement was that he paid for her to go to graduate school. He said he always wanted her to have her own life. I think it has to do with how secure a man is.

One of the clues that he is secure is that he wants to listen. He's not just a passive listener but a contributor. It's the kind of listening that women have been doing with each other a lot. He seemed right to me. I could imagine myself being old with him. It wasn't a young infatuation kind of love. I will share my life with my children for only a few more years. So I knew I would very soon be alone with whoever I married. The hardest part was giving up my aloneness, which I had come to love.

There are still times when I need to be alone. I go away twice a year for a weekend by myself, and while he is not enormously thrilled, he understands. I've been able to do that without him resenting it. There are some husbands that let you go, and in their voice and tone they look like hurt little boys. He does not do that.

The kinds of things I found I had to fight for in my first marriage—who's in control, who does what—aren't issues anymore. I think it's a matter of age. I'm forty-seven, he's fifty-two. I think when we're young we see things very much in black and white. I've accepted gray and have learned to live with contradictions. I don't need absolutes. I can accept that Steve can contradict himself, and he does.

I have accepted that I have contradictions in myself too; I can be the person that appeases, that makes life together easier, that finds ways of making peace. The children were much more mature than my second husband when we first got married, and because I loved them all, I could accept that. It didn't seem threatening to me. I knew that things could be worked out with caring and understanding and listening. Right now the relationship is extraordinary between my husband and the two kids. They have wonderful conversations.

Tim went to college last year in the city. He just got his own apartment. We see each other a lot. In fact this summer I have taken off every Monday because I have lots of vacation time, and I'm spending every other Monday with one of my children, the whole day, which I've never had in my whole life. I've never had a vacation with them that I remember, and that's very precious.

I have essentially two careers, one of which earns me a living. I'm a director of a nonprofit organization. I handle all the publications. I do quite a bit of writing, but I'm in charge of all the production—anything that comes out in print comes over my desk. It operates like a little publishing house—about $350,000 income for the organization per year. It's a wonderful job—I love it—it's perfect.

I'm also very much engaged in art and art history. I organize shows here and there, and I teach one course at a college. That's very important for me. I also have a job that isn't paid but takes a lot of time. I handle the exhibitions for a church.

Steve and I try consciously to make time for each other. We need to. We talk about it, we plan. We have time at home together because when you have teenage children they are out a lot. On Saturday I don't do the shopping and the laundry; we go out for a walk or something, just find a separate space, a sense of leisure, of being together. I used to think that when there is a disagreement, or maybe justified or unjustified gripes or anger, it had to be talked out right away. Now, I know you have to create a comfortable situation before you can talk constructively.

I think that had a lot to do with the fact that I'm not threatened by being alone. If Steve disappeared out of my life tomorrow, I wouldn't fall apart, although I love him very much. I've acquired a sense of self I don't think I ever had before and which I might never have developed if I had stayed in that first marriage. I probably would have had a similar career, but I wouldn't have felt the same way about it. It has nothing to do with the external. It has to do with who I am.

Cindy Voight

Dealing with Stepchildren

Cindy Voight lives in the Midwest. She and her husband, Norman, have been married for about fifteen years. He had children from a previous marriage, and they have a fourteen-year-old daughter from their marriage. Cindy works in a university near her home.

When I married Norman he already had three children from his first marriage. We also have one daughter who is a child of this marriage. His youngest child, Seth, was twelve when we were married, and the oldest was seventeen. The only one who lived with us was Seth. He was thirteen when my own daughter was born. The kids were very excited about this new sister, and Seth was so excited he ran up a phone bill calling out-of-state relatives to tell them she was born. That was his role in feeling a part of things.

Even though there is almost thirteen years difference, the younger two children are very close, although there is some sibling rivalry. Seth used to be somewhat quiet and depressed when Nina's special days came—birthdays, for example—and would wonder why he hadn't gotten a present when she did, even though it was her birthday. When she was four or five he would say, "Why do you always say yes to her? She has to learn what no means," or "Don't give in to her all the time." I was sad for him that he thought life had to be so unhappy.

Norman's daughter, who is in her twenties and married with children, came to visit one time and she saw the things Nina was doing, dancing, and synchronized swimming and all the things you want to give your child. She said, "She's swimming like that? I can't even do that and I'm much older," not in a resentful way but rather, "My God, what a good life Nina's had!" When we got married, the age difference of the children was so great there was no way to make up for any of those things. I was able to give our daughter things because I was working and we had two incomes. She's on her way home now from Europe. She's been playing with a special orchestra for which she was chosen, but she wouldn't have been able to have music lessons if I hadn't been working. She's had a much fuller life than either my husband or I had.

One of the difficult things that happened in my life was Norman's long absences in Viet Nam. I had to handle things as sole parent.

It's kind of hard to explain, but sometimes I have a feeling that I've gotten myself into a secondhand marriage because of the stepparenting part. For the first couple of years I found myself not really acknowledging the existence of the children to other people. For example, someone would say, "Is this your only child?" and I would say, "Yes," not that I lied about it, but I never owned up to it even though Nina would often say, "Mommy, I'm not the only one," and she'd tell people about her two brothers and sister.

Seth is the only one of Norman's three children that finished college, so he benefited from the model of my being there, from our life together. I think the other two compared me with their mother much more than he did. The mother lived hundreds of miles from here; she died about five years ago. I think divorced parents who live close to each other have to be very mature and struggle a lot not to ask the children what's going on in the other house. You ask a question of concern, and they interpret it another way and feel guilty about what they say. I never lived near the mother so I never was with her, but I do remember one time when we were in the same room together because of a death in the family and I was very anxious. I remember my husband wanting to walk her to the bus and I felt they didn't need any time together so I went with them.

There have been many times when the children needed help and we wouldn't have been able to help them if I hadn't been working. I remember feeling angry about my stepdaughter because we were sending her money. She was home taking care of her child, and we were helping support her while I had to go to work every day and couldn't stay home with my child. Even though in every way, socially, economically, emotionally, my life is more satisfying than hers, I still found myself resenting the fact that she could be at home with her child every day while I was going to work and sending her money. She could nurture her baby in a way that I couldn't.

In fact, it was probably my decision to send her the money.

I was the one who carried it through. I was the one who wrote the checks. It's funny that we do this to ourselves. We bring these kinds of responsibilities on ourselves.

I think it's difficult when you have a stepchild and a natural child for instance, and the natural child gets deprived of something that the stepchild can do because the mother is working, like Nina's going to a day care center while we sent a check to Norman's daughter who was staying home with her baby. I've done a lot of growing in this regard, but I have felt this resentment. My situation is a little different perhaps, because I had more adult stepchildren. If the children were close in age, they would all be at the day care center when I was working, not just my own child.

I work for the university and I wear two hats. In one of my capacities I am the assistant to the chancellor of the university and an affirmative action officer; my other responsibility is as an instructor in the school of social work. It is my job to urge and assist search committees to get women and minorities in the positions that are being filled. I also deal in a more indirect way with professors in their relations with students. Ideally these things can be addressed in an informal way. For instance, I might go to a faculty member and say, "Are you aware that your student Mary Smith has consistently raised her hand in class and isn't being called upon?" It can be very difficult bringing this to the attention of professional people, who are probably unaware they are discriminating. It doesn't happen very much, but as an affirmative action officer I'm also involved in any sexual harassment situations. I might have a department meeting and deal with the entire department so that I can go on record as having informed the department of a situation dealing with sexual harassment.

I have the option to go full-time administration or full-time faculty in the future. The work is exciting and demanding, and it's a highly visible position. I've only been with the university five years, but I've worked for seventeen years and I had been involved in social work before that.

I think the knowledge I have as a social worker has helped me in my personal life as well. I think I would not be married today if I had not been able to distance myself from some of the things that have been going on in my family life. For example, one of the stepchildren lived with us for a year. The goal was to help him get himself on his feet. If I hadn't had my professional knowledge, I think there would have been times when I would have said, "Get him out of here!" There have been times in the past when I would yell and scream; I'm human too. Now when I get angry I get physical. I wash baseboards and cupboards—I wash a lot of things that don't normally get washed.

I find that I cope better if I am physically fit. I run now and I find I can cope with more. The things I get upset or angry about I still get upset about, but the intensity isn't there because my body can tolerate it better. I find if I don't run, my ability to say, "I'll do that for you," or "I'll handle that," in a calm way isn't as good. My goal is to run at least five days a week, in the winter too. I even run in subfreezing weather, and I think it may be healthier for you. I also watch my diet and I am careful about what I eat.

I would like to share one other thing about coping. I either separate from my family or have them separate from me—they go away or I go away. I've learned not to feel guilty about that. I think of it as a preventive; otherwise I'd end up yelling. I just walk out of the room; it's much healthier to get away and then let it subside. There are times when, for instance, someone will say, "But . . ." and I'll say, "No buts—later, okay?" I'm glad I've learned to do that. I find it's better to cut it off before we get to the point of yelling.

I think you can have a career and a husband and a child and do all of them successfully. The one thing that's suffering is my house, my house physically. I have a personal hang-up about hiring help. As I get older it intensifies. Three people, all over thirteen years of age, ought to be able to maintain a house, but that's not true. I think I'd deal with that better if I got some help with the house.

It does mean that I've motored my child around and that I've gone to the office while she had her lessons. It means that I've had to use other kinds of support (even the public library) as a babysitter. The public library was near the school. My daughter was too young to come home alone and I was unable to pick her up, so I told her to go to the library after school and I'd pick her up there. The library has never been alien to her.

Sometimes I'll call the swimming coach and ask him to bring her home. (He doesn't live too far from us.) I've shared carpooling with other parents. For instance, I'll ask them to take the kids and I'll pick them up.

My office is only two miles from my home, and I have negotiated for more flexible hours. I try to be at home when Nina gets home from school, even if I have to go back to work at 7:00 P.M. The main thing is getting the job done; so if I have to, I'll go in very early in the morning or late in the afternoon to accomplish a task. I am available by telephone. Sometimes I go in on weekends; Norman's busy very often too, so he understands that.

I think the trade-off for me has been personal time. I'm not one to shop for clothing, but I think my wardrobe suffers because I don't take time. There are times when I look around my house and I get upset because it's not as clean as I'd like it to be. I don't have time with friends either.

I have a high level of energy. I'm currently serving on four community boards. One of my goals is to decrease that because, although it meets my social needs in a productive way, it's not really fun time as such.

We all have so many outside activities it's really not healthy for family life. All that extra scheduling helps one to deal with the guilt, I suppose; probably programming my child so much has been my way of compensating for not being there all the time.

There are times now when Norman, Nina, and I just look at each other and say, "We're never home, we only use this place to sleep." In fact, as a family we've decided we're going to spend more time together.

Gail Gordon

Not Afraid of Risks

Gail is forty-three, divorced, and lives with her ten-year-old son, Matthew, and her friend Joe, an engineer, in Massachusetts. She recently went into her own real estate business.

I have always been very independent. I went away to college at seventeen, graduated with honors after only three years, and went on for my master's. I got married and divorced within nine months, one of those dumb things that should never have happened. After I got divorced, I left Kansas and came to New York in 1961. Then I married a traditional, upper-middle-class professional and had a baby.

We owned a brownstone in New York City. He was a law professor, and I was a volunteer—Junior League, Botanical Gardens, Neighborhood City Council, political parties of the Upper West Side Liberal stripe, 1960s variety. I had a full-time maid, the whole works. My husband's family had a good bit of money, so if I wanted something, I could have it. That is not to say I wasn't always hard-working; I'm a high energy person.

By all traditional standards I guess it was a very good marriage. We got along well, never argued. He was a good provider; he didn't cheat and he never drank. But at some point we stopped talking to each other.

We had a summer place and twenty-five acres of land in the Berkshires. The idea was we'd use the cottage as a temporary place while we decided what to build on the land. The longer we kept coming up the more I wanted to be here all the time. It got to the point where Friday until Sunday was not enough.

In 1975, he took a sabbatical. Even though we owned a place in the city, we spent the time in the Berkshires. We lived here for four or five months. When he had to go back to work, I said, "I'm not going back to the city—I don't want to." He said, "Okay, no problem." So he commuted. He went down on Monday and came back on Thursday. We discovered it didn't work. I didn't look forward to his coming back. I was happy when he left on Monday and did not look forward to Thursday. I finally said, "It's no good." At that time there was an opening in a deanship in a nearby law school. He let it be known he was available, and he got it. So he moved up full-time. Then what we did, and this is what wrecked the marriage, is we built the house.

We had very different notions about what we wanted in a house. We ended up with a $175,000 monstrosity. I was the general contractor. It took two years to build. There are lots of people who think it's a beautiful house. I personally don't like it. He loves it and is living in it now with his new wife.

When we got divorced, we split everything fifty-fifty. He pays alimony and child support. I bought another house here in town for myself and my son. My ex-husband takes Matthew on weekends. The weekend situation was arrived at because I work in the real estate business and weekends are my busy times. My ex-husband is supportive of my business. We have an amicable relationship, with Matthew at the center. Matthew can ride his bike from one house to the other, and his father's house is always open to him.

After having been the general contractor for the house that my ex-husband and I built, I was told that I ought to go into real estate, that it would suit me; so that's what I did when I got divorced. I became a broker associate with a large firm in this area. I was trained by one of the large franchises and was extremely successful. The first year in business I made over $20,000.

My boss felt very comfortable about me and my ability to be professional, but she did not feel so comfortable that I was living with a man who owned another real estate company. She insisted that I leave. Joe, the man I was living with, enjoys the engineering aspect, but he doesn't enjoy buyers and sellers. He suggested that I buy the business from him, and I did. He has been absolutely sensational, supportive without interfering. Joe is not my partner; I own it strictly on my own. I have three people working for me; one just works in the summer.

I'm making a living in the business. In spite of the bad market this first six months I'm more than breaking even. Two to three years down the road, I expect it will be a very good business. Even though I have people working for me, I have to list and sell property myself. If you've got $5,000 commission, and half goes to the firm and half to the lister/seller, then I'm a lot better off if I'm both.

My goal is to have a good reputation. I want to be at the point where ninety-five percent of my business is personal referrals from satisfied buyers and sellers. I'd like to build a business—but slowly. Land development is what I like; I have a couple of big projects—seven hundred acres—that I'm starting to work on. I have one that's going to come up in the spring that could easily make me a millionaire in a couple of years. But the work involved is going to be tremendous. Sometimes I think, "I can't do it," then I think that's not really true. I'm brighter than ninety-five percent of them out there. And I work harder than most, so why shouldn't I be able to do it?

It isn't as though I don't have anxiety attacks in the middle of the night. I do. There are days when I don't want to get up. I say to myself, "Wouldn't it be nice if somebody could take care of me?" I've had a bad throat for two weeks, but I haven't stopped. I don't give in to that sort of stuff, but there are times when I want to and I have to fight myself. There are times when I say, "I can't make it through this cup of tea—I don't have the strength." Generally speaking, that passes.

The last six months have been very intense because of the new business. When I was working before, I could take two days off mid-week, especially in the winter. Now because I am out on a limb in my own business, I feel I have to be there. People have to know you're available.

I'm on a tight schedule. I have breakfast with my son and then drive to his school thirty-five minutes away. I'm home by nine, do exercises, change into business clothes, and get to the office by nine-thirty or ten. My associate is there at nine-thirty three mornings a week. The rest of the time I have to be sure to be there.

In the afternoon Matthew is picked up by another mother. Her son and Matthew are best friends, so they are comfortable together. If she wants to go shopping or go to the library or they want to spend the afternoon together, no big deal. Otherwise she brings him home at approximately three-thirty. He calls me immediately; that's the rule. Depending on my schedule, I either go right home or I tell him I have a client. He is not a self-starter. He would never make himself dinner, but he will get his own snack and clean up after himself. He is very responsible.

If I don't have a client, I get home at four or four-thirty. Joe usually works longer and will come home at six. I generally make dinner, and after we eat Joe often goes back to the office. Right now he is rebuilding the Victorian house that houses both our offices. We don't usually see each other during the day, but we set aside Sunday night to be together. On Sunday nights, we drive Joe's kids home to Connecticut, which is a forty-five-minute drive, and we go out to dinner after.

Joe and I share the household chores. He has taken over doing the laundry. He does the world's worst job, but I finally decided I have to stay out of the laundry room. It's very hard because my clothes come back shrunk and the whites aren't white. I do the cooking. We are beginning to get the kids to help. They have to fill the woodbox, clean their own rooms, and dust and mop. Joe cleans up the dishes after dinner most nights. If there is any reason I'm not there, he will make dinner. He's wonderful for all sorts of repairs around the house too.

I own the house. At this point he does not contribute. We've only been in the house for a couple of months. Right now he owns a house that even I cannot sell. I think it's unsalable. We once talked about burning it down, but unfortunately we're not arsonists! We're going to have to sort out the money issue soon. It's not as casual as it might sound. I have a little book that has the insurance, mortgage payments, taxes, electric bill, telephone bill, listed. We're going to wait three months and find out how much it's costing us and then figure out how to split it.

Right now financially I'm quite comfortable. I get alimony and child support. My ex-husband is very generous and I don't feel guilty about accepting payments from him because I am providing his son with a lovely home. If I get married, I lose the alimony.

What's the advantage of being married? If Joe stops loving me or decides he wants somebody else, then legal bonds are not going to keep us together. If he decided he didn't like living with me anymore, I don't want him staying just because we have papers. Even in a small community like this, the little old ladies know I live with Joe and it's not a problem. We're nice people.

As far as my son is concerned, he's proud of me, especially when I make sales. And I'm proud of him. He says, "My mom has her own company." He's very supportive for a ten-year-old. If I say, "Somebody has just come in and I have an appointment and won't be home till six," he says, "That's okay, Mom, I'll be fine. Don't worry," every time. He is not a totally altruistic child. He knows if Mommy gets more listings and more sales, he gets more toys. He likes the new car and the new house, the things that come with my business.

The last few years it's been tough. We've been in four different houses in eighteen months, and that's a lot for a kid. His things were in storage for over a year and he was very good about it.

I think I'm a fun mom and a good mother. I am not a projective mother; I don't get my identity from being a mother or from being a wife or a girlfriend. I see myself as successful; I can support myself. But there is no question in my mind that I am more comfortable and happier with myself when I am connected with a man. Joe touches something special in me. I feel more me with him than anybody else I've ever been with. That doesn't mean I want to marry him. That just means I want to be with him.

I take one day at a time. I want to be the best me for the people in my life and for myself. I don't have any major goals. Joe and I were talking about this, and we said, "If we figure we want to be rich in five years, we'd better figure out how rich and how much per year and we'd better write it down and figure out how to go after it." If you don't have specific goals, you're not going to get there, because you're not going to know where you're going. I don't see any reason why I shouldn't have whatever it is I want to have. It's just a question of defining whatever it is, and I don't think I've done that completely.

I do know I can't define myself in terms of anyone else; children grow up and go away; men come and go; parents die. I'm an orphan, the oldest living member of my family, and have been for nine years. And there is no home where I can go and they have to take me in—I'm it.

Marjorie Kennedy

Owning a Business with Your Husband

Marjorie's always worked. She's in her forties now, and she didn't get married until she was nearly thirty. She had three boys soon after that, and they're now fourteen, thirteen, and eleven. Her business partner in her California company is her husband, Murray.

Before we were married, my husband and I worked together in an advertising agency. About a year after we got married, Murray decided to go into business for himself. At that time, I'd just had a baby; I stayed home and had three children in a span of four years. When I was pregnant with the third child, one of Murray's partners left. In the back of my mind I believed that ultimately we would be in our own business together. Neither of us is the corporate type, and I knew that *eventually* we'd be in business together. But there I was with three children, the youngest of whom was three months old, and I was given a choice: "Are you going to be a partner or not? If you are, there's no playing games." So I went back to work three days a week. That's all the business could afford then.

The first year I took them out to a sitter down the street (we lived in a flat at the time). That presented enormous problems for us. It was hard in the morning—to get up, get them dressed and change the diapers and gather the bottles and to carry them all down the street. And they felt displaced. They didn't know what belonged to them and what belonged to the sitter. At that point I made a decision and have stuck to it since: I would have somebody come to our house.

I hired students. They were not housekeepers, strictly sitters. The first two years I only worked three days a week, so I had one person. I then went to work five days a week, and the child-care person was required to be there by nine, and had to stay till six-thirty. It was too long for one person, so at that point I decided to have one student on Monday, Wednesday, and Friday, and one on Tuesday and Thursday. The children would be exposed to two different people. I'd have them at least one semester, and maybe they would carry over to another semester, but it usually meant new arrangements every five to six months. I did all my hiring through a local college, and I only hired people who had a specific talent. I didn't care what that talent was; it could be cake-decorating or puppet-making or drama, but I wanted somebody creative, and I never kept anybody who wasn't innovative. If they didn't talk to the kids, and do something the first day, then I got somebody else. I felt the children got a lot more than they would have gotten from me. I don't think this is overcoming a guilt complex, either. I'm not cut out to be a full-time mother; I'm kind of a nasty, neat person who doesn't get into finger-painting or teaching kids to make chocolate chip cookies—it's not me. So I wanted someone who could do that better than I did.

They developed close relationships with the people who took care of them too. I had a lot of men as sitters, by the way. I tried to find men. I thought they were a calming influence; both Murray and I are hyper, and we're in a hyper business. I thought it was better to have a calm person during the day and then us at night.

The type of child care I had for the boys was very positive;

they learned lots of things they never would have learned from me. They had exposure to things that made them more independent. For example, they are starting to make some meals now, on their own. But I don't take up their offers as much as I should. I become Supermom and say, "I can do it better than you can." I think it's my nature; it would probably be worse if I were home. I'd constantly be badgering them. Murray's involvement, or lack of it, is due to my strong personality; he doesn't have to do much. He knows everything's in good hands. He's not interested in sports, for instance, and so I'm the cheerleader at all the games while he's at home making supper.

Right now I'm trying to make myself more available to the boys because there are some specific problems. One of my sons is having trouble with Spanish, and I told him I'd get home early or get up early in the morning to help him. Greg, the oldest, is fourteen, and I'm just beginning to realize I may be missing opportunities of communication by not being here all the time. Sometimes a working mother doesn't know when there's a problem; I think we're quick to blame ourselves because we're not around a lot. Perhaps I overreact to things concerning the children. For instance, I worry about "Why is he so quiet?" or "Why does he look unhappy today?"

Maybe that's guilt. I suppose every working mother feels it, at least the women in my generaiton do. Perhaps if the husband takes more of an equal share than mine does in school activities and other duties, there's less guilt. But on school holidays when I know they're going to be alone, I feel I'd like to be able to take them on a picnic. And then when I get home late at night and realize somebody hasn't done homework because I've been too tired to watch over him, or I go out of town on a business trip and come back home and get a report card with grades that dropped from B to C and think it happened because I wasn't here, I feel guilty.

One of the things I did do, though, was to take six weeks off last summer to take the boys on a 10,000-mile camping tour across the country. Somehow it's hard to find enough time for everybody.

For instance, I sometimes feel Murray and I have no time for tender loving care. During the school year, I have an abominable schedule: getting up at 5:00 A.M. and making sure everybody has a hot breakfast and their lunch. We don't have time in bed for a last hug before getting up. I guess my husband takes a back seat. He comes home at night after working from 7:00 A.M. to 8:00 P.M. and doesn't have a hot dinner waiting for him because I've just fed the kids, and instead of being greeted with dinner, he's at the kitchen table with homework and a Swiss cheese sandwich.

I barely have time in the morning to say hello to Murray, and he's working late at night, when *I* need some tender loving care. So where do you meet? On weekends, when there's a soccer game at 10:00 A.M., another in a different field at 1:00 P.M. and both kids want you to go to the game? And the groceries have to be bought, the dry cleaning picked up and Saturday night you want to spend some time as a family, so you go to a movie. Sunday morning is Mass, and we're lucky if we can have a family breakfast. Sunday afternoon is spent getting ready to start the treadmill again.

We make our lives easier in one important way. We don't commute. We live twenty minutes from the office. We felt the city had more opportunities and is more well rounded for our children, and I would rather fight the battle of private or parochial schools in the city than public schools in suburbia. We talked about buying a Victorian house when we first went into business, and living upstairs and having the office downstairs. But I didn't want the office that close, because you never get away from it then.

Murray and I don't come to work together, and we never have; if we come to work together, we automatically get into a fight because he wants to talk business and I'm not ready until I walk through the office door. He leaves early, and I stay home and get my act together. I make lunches and breakfast, clean the kitchen, and make beds if the kids haven't; so maybe I don't get in till nine or nine-thirty. I turn the house off when I'm at the office; I don't want to hear from the kids who spilled orange juice on the kitchen floor or that the teacher was mean to them. By the same token, when I get home, I don't want to discuss business. Once I walk into the house I don't want to think about business. I resent it when anybody calls me from the office with a problem.

The business is set up so Murray has his area and I have mine. We're partners; I am never in a secondary position. We both have our own clients, and financially we have equal responsibility for the books and the decisions. Occasionally when people come to work here, they have difficulty trying to figure out who really runs the show, but that's their problem, not mine. People who have worked here three to four years have said that when they first came they thought it was my business and Murray worked for me, and then other people will say that it's clear that Murray runs the show and without him there'd be no business.

Murray always introduces me as his partner who happens to be his wife; I've never heard him say, "This is my wife." It clears the air right away.

Our business has grown quite a bit in the last four years; we have a large staff. And there are real advantages to having your own business. You don't have to kowtow to a corporate structure; you can have a company car. You don't have to keep a client you don't like; my income will go down that month without that person's business, but I'll go out and get somebody else's business. The hours are flexible and you can take as much vacation as you want. The disadvantage is you can never be gone very long. In fact, we've gone on four vacations in fifteen years, just the two of us.

It's never a nine-to-five job. There's no clear separation between business and private lives. You don't have a personnel department at your beck and call, either. You train people and they want to go somewhere else, so you have to find new people and start over again. In a small business, that responsibility falls directly on your shoulders; that's the situation I'm in now. I have to replace a key person, and I'm going back to base one, where I was five years ago. That means I have to stay here later at night, and I should be at home helping with homework or at professional association meetings or at Mothers' Club meetings.

The Mothers' Club is really important to the parochial schools around here, and now so many mothers work that there's nobody to volunteer because they say they don't have time. I remember standing up at one meeting and saying, "I've done a survey and seventy-five percent of our members are working mothers, and we can no longer use that as an excuse for not being involved in a child's education." The board of the Mothers' Club sits and complains about the fact there are only twenty women involved, and I keep saying you have to look at the other women out there waiting to be tapped, but you can't tap them for monthly board meetings. Tap them for their resources. An executive knows how to run a business, use her. They say, "She hasn't volunteered for anything." I say, "She doesn't have time to volunteer—you call her." It's the same way you allocate positions in management.

They can't see that as an avenue to go; I can give them all the help and support they want in printing. Give me the stuff, and I'll reproduce five hundred to a thousand, whatever they need, in half the time. But they want me to go to board meetings to discuss if we should make coffee for the district principals. They have to readjust their thinking to account for the fact that women are working women, and they need to utilize their resources. Don't think of somebody as a cookie maker or chairman of the fund-raiser. The Mothers' Club is not going with the times. There are two frustrations: one is that working mothers don't do anything; the other is that the management of the Mothers' Club cannot see how times are changing, and how they have to address their thinking to the working mother.

I'm a pragmatic person. I was educated to be strong and resourceful. I went to a small women's college that taught that women were a valuable commodity, no door was closed to you because you were a woman. I remember that we had a nun for a professor and we were terrified of her. One of the girls was so terrified that when the nun asked her a question, the girl fainted and fell down. Two other girls tried to help her up, and the nun said, "Leave her alone—leave her on the floor—our women don't faint." I've taken that through life, and I've lived my life as if no door were ever closed to me.

I think business will always come first in my life because it's economically necessary. But I go through periods when I'm not sure I love working that much. The business provides me with a lifestyle and an outlet I need, but when there's an expansion of the business, it generates from Murray rather than from me. I have a guilt complex about working, and it manifests itself mostly because I don't have time to talk to my kids, time to really communicate with them. Maybe I was better off when they were little, and I could say I didn't have much time, but they were getting quality time. As they get older, though, I wonder about not being there at the precise moment they may need to communicate, and that moment may never come again.

Joanna Altman

Working in a Humane Place

Joanna Altman is a lawyer in her early thirties. She has two children—Timmy, who's four, and Julie, one. Joanna and her husband, Rick, were married when she was 21 and still in school. They waited six years before starting a family, and now they live and work in a California suburb.

I used to work in the city for a large law firm. Out of two hundred fifty lawyers, there were two women partners. When I decided I wanted to move into a suburban environment, I looked at a list of law firms, and this was the only one with more than one woman partner. I wanted to find a law firm where I would not be the only, the first, or even the second woman. This was the only firm I interviewed. It was the only one where I felt I would not be a test case.

I began to work part-time after my second child was born. This firm does have a prorated partnership, although I'm not familiar with the compensation arrangement. I'm now supposed to be working four days a week and I'm paid an eighty percent salary of somebody my level. I get a bonus; my whole compensation is based on eighty percent. That does not mean that I work four days a week; what it does mean is that when I can get away nobody begrudges me that. I'd rather feel they felt they were getting a good deal because I was putting in extra effort than to be a hundred-percent person and try to take some time off. It's worked out very well.

For instance, today is supposed to be my day off. I'm working, but I'll go to my daughter's nursery school class today at two. I'll leave and nobody will ask any questions. I need that flexibility to have time with my kids. One thing I learned, especially in our practice where we so often work nights and weekends, being full-time means no time for your family. Somebody that works one hundred percent here is the same as working one hundred fifty percent. That is not acceptable to me. I couldn't continue to do that and feel like I was doing justice to my children.

After my first child was born I was real frustrated for the first year or two. I went back to work full-time right away and didn't feel like I had time with him. I wasn't sure what came first, my career or my child. I had a terrible time. I was torn and depressed. That was the worst time in my life; there was a lot of pressure, and finally I went and talked to a psychologist. I saw him two to three times, and for me that was a real turning point. At that time I started to understand that I wanted to get out of everything I was involved in.

There was a lot of tension between my husband and me at the time. I blamed him for my unhappiness; I used him as a focal point—I tend to do that. I felt at the time that one of the problems was that I didn't feel his commitment to the family was as great as mine. In fact, it is not. We have a very conventional relationship in terms of roles at home. Rick works around the house but still is very traditional in terms of how we relate to kids. I'm the primary caretaker in our family.

I tried to figure out how I felt about my whole life, and what my priorities were. Before I established priorities, I just responded to things; I didn't feel I had an understanding of what I wanted to get out of my life. I didn't know what was important to me.

One of my decisions was that I couldn't continue in litigation. As a litigator, you have little control over your hours. The litigation group was not supportive, either. The person I worked with was not supportive of me; he didn't feel I was pulling my share and was very negative about trying to work through timing problems. Any time I left the office, he would ask where I was; that was when I felt a lot of pressure. I made a conscious decision to get out of litigation; now I'm in corporate law and I like it better. I didn't know I would. I decided to do it because of other considerations, but I like it much better. You have more control of your schedule in corporate law. There is a lot of acceptance of personal scheduling problems in the corporate group. We've been working day and night on a particular deal right now. We were here until about eight-thirty one night, and the man I was working with in the office had to go home and babysit. So I stayed here until nine-thirty with the client. Sometimes in a client situation, I feel uncomfortable if I have to try to make child care arrangements, but within the group of lawyers, I never feel uncomfortable saying, "I have to go and do this with my child." Almost everyone here has children; everybody has common scheduling problems, and there's a lot of understanding.

Last year I was up for partner, the last thing I should have done professionally was get pregnant and have a baby. Rick and I had to make a decision; we wanted our children spaced about three years apart. Did we wait another year in the hopes that I'd make partner, or go on and have another baby and say forget about the partnership now? My changing groups might have postponed my partnership anyway, but it didn't seem to me that I should structure my personal life around professional life, but rather the other way around.

The only way I've found to resolve the problems of career and family is to retrench on my career. My children are more important than my career right now. I love what I do, and that's why I'm still doing it, but if at any point I felt my children were suffering, I would stop working. After my second baby was born, I went from working full-time to three days a week. Now I've increased it to four days.

I live within two miles of my office. That was our criteria when we looked for a house. I had to have flexibility in traveling back and forth between office and home. My husband has a very demanding career, and one problem with two careers is that sometimes you have to be at the office at 6:00 A.M. and don't get home until 11:00 P.M. We need something beyond ordinary day care, and we recognized our need for live-in help. We were very lucky to have had the same person for four years, but she left about four months ago. She got too expensive; when I cut back my days, I was paying more for the help than I was netting. That just made no sense, no matter how good she was.

I paid a lot of money for the sitter we had for four years because I thought she was very good. Since I wasn't home, I thought the most important thing I could spend my money on was child care because that woman would have a lot of influence on my child's development. I had some fears about having a sitter: that Timmy and Julie would think she was their mother, and that they wouldn't develop normally or would be slow in language skills because I wasn't around. Those were my primary concerns; they really never happened. As time went on, I felt my sitter gave them everything they wanted. She even began to spoil them, and that was another reason that after four years I felt it was time to make a different arrangement. She would not be firm, and they could do anything they wanted. She was loving and warm and good; I never felt they suffered by my not being there. I used to try to go home for lunch every day, and I tried to spend at least an hour there, especially when I worked full-time.

With Timmy, one of my concerns about the sitter was that she was putting on a good act and wasn't as nice to him as I thought, and one of the ways I tried to resolve that was to have friends drop in at the house at odd times and see what she was doing with my child. I did the same thing. I spent a number of days taking funny times off and checking the house until I felt sure she was as good a caretaker as I thought she was.

So much depends on the health of your kids. If your kids are healthy and progressing normally and you have good sitters, you can really do what you want. But if kids are not healthy, or need you because they are not developing correctly, or if you start having babysitting problems, it's tough. That's when a day care situation is harder than having your own sitter at home.

If something's wrong at home, it's easy to reach me. Everyone here knows that if my babysitter calls, they can interrupt anything to get a message to me.

Having a housekeeper at home gives me flexibility with car pools too. The housekeeper can pick Timmy up at his nursery school if I can't. In addition, I have car pool arrangements with several other people in the same situation. We switch off; the way we have it now is one of the other lawyers in the office whose wife is nearby and my husband, who works about fifteen minutes away, all share the driving. The car pool is between two families, with access to four cars. Whoever is available drives. Sometimes I leave meetings for thirty minutes to pick up the children, take them home, and then come back here.

Rick and I try to arrange our lives so that when we're not working and are at home, we're with the kids. We don't socialize that much. We see friends with children. The friends we are closest to are those who have children our kids' ages. If I have a dinner party, children usually come too. We also hire a sitter so the kids are with us, but when the adults sit down for dinner, somebody else takes care of them. That costs money, but we feel that gives us time to socialize and to be with the children. We also have someone who helps with gardening and cleaning once a week. That frees us more for the kids.

We devote mornings to our family. That's when the kids are in the best mood. I don't go to work till nine or nine-thirty; we get up at six or six-thirty and spend an hour or two with them in the morning. We have breakfast and dress them. That's the best time for us to spend together. It's hard at night, the kids are tired and want you. My daughter doesn't want to be with anyone but me when I'm home; she screams when I'm busy. So Rick has taken over most of the cooking.

The kids do not compete for time and attention as long as we are giving them both attention. Tim will play with his sister if I'm playing with them both. When we're in the house, one of us has to give attention to the kids a good part of the time without anything else getting in the way. After dinner, I clean up and Rick tries to spend time with the kids. We don't turn on television. If the news is on, the kids compete for attention, and arguments start between them. The hardest thing is for us to have a conversation together. That's the other time the children compete.

I don't work at home; it puts everybody on edge if I try to work. I also try to leave the office by 6:00 P.M. If I have to, I will go back to the office at 9:00 P.M. and work after they've gone to bed.

Rick has always been very helpful and steps in when I've been pushed on certain days. He works about fifteen minutes away from home, but he's about to start working in the city and commute by train. He will travel quite a bit, and we will be in a much more difficult situation. For him it's a career move he really wanted. I'm ambivalent; I think he needed to do it career-wise, but it will be very difficult for us to handle.

I had to travel a lot this summer, for instance. I was gone four weeks, and I'll have to go again for three to four days next week. Rick is very supportive, and I don't know how this career change will affect us. Both of us are committed to make time for kids, and when something suffers, it's our relationship. It's important to us to work on our relationship, so we try to find time for each other. If you didn't have a good relationship, you couldn't live like we live. Rick is the biggest support I have, and I think I am for him too.

One of the reasons I cut back on my work was so I would feel I could go away for the weekend or out at night. If you only spend a couple of hours a day with your kids, how can you walk out of the house at night without feeling guilty? Since I've been working part-time, we've been able to spend a bit more time together.

At one point, two years ago, I really wanted to quit and not work at all. I couldn't figure out how I felt about working and having kids. What I finally said was, I know I love my kids and would never consider not having kids. Children have been the most significant thing I've ever done. They have to be my priority, but I also love my work. I find it stimulating and exciting. I wouldn't put in the hours I do if I didn't enjoy my job. But it has to come second. There are times when, if a choice has to be made, I feel I can make it in favor of my children.

Risa Zimmerman

Creating a Successful Business

Risa Zimmerman lives in the suburbs of a large midwestern city. Risa's in the needlepoint business. She designs needlepoint kits and ships them all over the country from her home.

I'm from Philadelphia. Needlepoint was a big thing out East. My mother bought me a kit thirteen years ago, and I finished it in two days. I decided to get some canvas and paint them for myself and for friends, and I've ended up with a $300,000-a-year business from my basement! My first order was $2,000. I went to a department store here; they ordered and I called a lady in New York that I knew sold the canvas and told her the order. She then took over the distribution. My original investment was literally $100—just the canvas and paint—I was just selling painted canvases. Later I went into making kits and then I had to come up with $1,000.

The woman in New York was a distributor; for twenty percent, she did all the billing and guaranteed I got paid at the end of thirty days. My contact with her gave me credibility, got me in stores all over the country, and into mail-order houses.

Some big department stores have a policy that if you make something that you want to sell to them, they have to see you. I knew one here would see me.

Now I have a full-time manager and a woman here three days a week who helps ship the prepackaged kits. All out of my basement! When this thing first took off, it took off real big; I had an order for $25,000 worth of one kit. They had showed it in the biggest needlework mail-order catalog in the country.

You know, I found myself in a big business, but I didn't go looking for it at all. I guess I have intuitive business sense, though. I put in a computer billing system when there were companies doing three million dollars a year that didn't switch over to computer. I rented space on somebody else's computer. I've never had a bookkeeper. People pay a computer statement a lot quicker than a letter on flowery stationery saying, "Dear Sir, you owe fifteen dollars."

Wherever the business went I wanted to go, but I would not let it take me out of the house. Wherever it went, my husband and I went with it; if it meant doing trade shows, we'd do trade shows. We had a wonderful time at first because it was secondary; he was working. We would go to a show and would stay at the hotel where the show was. It was our vacation! We really enjoyed it in that respect.

I started out doing everything in the business. I was the shipper, designer, and packer; I did it all. As the business grew I found other people. I'd put ads in the paper, and I took people according to how badly they needed the money. I learned right away, don't use your friends. When the original canvas painting order came and I found myself with this enormous order, I took the six or seven painters I had and told them I would pay each of them seventy-five dollars for any painter that they trained who stayed with me for six months. So it became important for them to train other people rather than to hold onto what they could do, because they figured if somebody else contacted me, there'd be less work for them. They knew I'd always eliminate by a seniority method; there would always be enough work for all of them.

I sold to stores all over the country. The problem was that there was big volume in four weeks' time. I had no problem getting materials, because the source of the material also made a commission on the order; so she wanted to find me canvas and yarn to fill it. Then I also had the yarn-counting done by students in the educable handicap program at the high school. Everybody related to me counted out yarn, too! It didn't matter if I didn't make money on that first big order; I had to fill it. I did, and business has been enormous ever since.

My children are three, nine, thirteen, and sixteen, and even if I didn't work, I wouldn't have enough time for all those children. You can't imagine the age spread; at the dinner table one wants to talk about the fact that he's in love or something about college, and the one who's thirteen is sensitive, and the one who's nine talks even though you tell him, "Be quiet; it's not your turn." The three-year-old doesn't want to eat, and he's crying and has left the table! You can't work cohesively as a family; you have to take each kid separately. There were times my big one was in the mood to talk at midnight, and at 3:00 A.M. I was up nursing the baby.

The business really took off when my older children were four and a half and one and a half. I had to learn to delegate. But you don't just delegate, you pay royally. I have someone now who works for me, she's been with me for a lot of years, because she's never going to make that kind of money with anybody else. But I think she should make money, even if I get nothing, because if she doesn't come in tomorrow, I'm tied with a chain to that basement.

My housekeeper does all the marketing, and she's marvelous with the children, but she makes more mess as she goes along than she cleans up; so my kids know they have to do a certain amount of straightening. I won't come down till I've given the bathrooms a once-over; if the bed is unmade, I can't work. So I will do that. Two kids come home for lunch, so I'm out there with them. That breaks up that part of the day. I'll get a few more hours' worth of work done in the afternoon, but always with interruption. Something is going on after school that somebody wants you to be involved in. It's not carpooling because of where we live, but they want you to see what they're doing.

If I move the business out of the house, I'm absolutely tied to help to go to work. If I had an office outside the house, I'd have no option. I'd either have to be home and eat my heart out because I wasn't there, or I'd have to be there and worried because I wasn't home. I can't put the kids out of mind and out of sight. I have the old guilt. I think when a kid throws up, they want their mother; I don't think it counts if somebody else, no matter how wonderful, is there. I have this wonderful woman, and do you know what my kids want? They want us both. They walk in the door from school and the first thing they say is, "Where is my mother?" Now they *know* where I am, I'm in the basement. They don't necessarily say hello to me or talk to me, but that's always the first question. I think most kids are like that.

I've never had problems finding help, because I've always paid more money than anybody else. There were years I didn't make money with what I paid for help. When the children were small, I'd find somebody who advertised for babysitting and if they got two dollars an hour, I would say, "I will pay you four dollars an hour if you'll do the laundry and make the salad and set the table." That's what made me nervous about dinner—anybody can put a piece of chicken or steak on the stove—it was the stuff you had to do at the same time that made me nervous. Get the table set; slice up the lettuce. If all I had to deal with was a vegetable and piece of meat, I felt better. If the kids were really hungry, they could have their salad.

If you are afraid to spend the money on your household—invest in yourself—then you don't belong in your own business. It is a terrifying thing, though. I'm dealing with it now. I'm separated from my husband. I think in some ways the only thing I could have done worse for my marriage than succeed would have been to do nothing. That would have been just as bad as to have become the success. I don't know what the future holds for us; I do know we're going to be apart for at least a year. We have a very good relationship. I can call him any time and talk about my business and the kids, but I am not essentially married.

When my husband and I separated, one of my sons had real difficulties. Finally I found out he was afraid we'd have to move. It never occurred to me to tell them we didn't have to move. We weren't like everybody else in the neighborhood—first the husband goes, then the house and whatever. We could afford to stay here. I own this house. They didn't know that, and I guess that's because I never felt the need to say it. I wanted them to see their father as the financial head of the family. They knew when he bought things he talked it over with me; it wasn't just he who made the decision. But I always played down my financial success. It's very hard to tell your children you're financially successful without in some way lessening their father. We didn't start out as two working people who had children, so the kids didn't always hear talk about what I was contributing. I didn't say, "We're going to do this; *I* can afford it." So how do you tell the children, "Look at what I made!" How do you express to them you make as much money as your husband? It's very hard.

I'm in the generation of women in their late thirties and forties, and I don't know women who own their own businesses. It's hard on friendships too. The women I know might do *something,* but we came from a tradition where the man wouldn't let his wife work. When we were out with friends, the husband might be the first one to turn around and say to his wife, "Why don't you do something, and buy *yourself* a car?" And then maybe he'd try to sell me life insurance. It's not very nice for a woman to sit at a table and listen to her husband try to make a business deal with the lady sitting next to her. So the women I had babies with are hard to stay friendly with now.

I think I'm intimidating to those women. I'm very comfortable around men and not in a coming-on type of way. I'm just comfortable among men. You know, I keep finding out that people who are really successful know they don't know a whole lot, and they pay somebody else who does know; that's most of the trick.

My big area of insecurity after my first success was, "Now what do I do?" I found myself with a successful business, and I had a need to say, "I'm not a fluke; I didn't just get lucky." When I deal with other people I have to *make* myself remember that I really have a business that is substantial, not because I was in the right place at the right time with the right idea. The hardest problem after you're successful is staying successful. If your last thing was phenomenally successful, like the woman who is afraid and goes out and sells a million dollars worth of real estate, what's she going to do next year? It's very hard to learn to sit back and relax and enjoy it. I don't think men have it either; that may be why they lose their marbles when they're forty, fifty, sixty.

I'm on the board of education. All I had to do was say I went to Wharton. Nobody asked what degree I had. I only went for a little over a year. I never graduated. My husband said I never would have been successful if I'd graduated, because I would have had parameters about making a certain amount of profit margin, having a certain amount for overhead, and so forth. I would have known what to do. I didn't know what to do, so I came up with prices that didn't include anything for me. I saw profit, but I didn't see my labor. It gave me a certain naïveté. I could always say, "Can I ask you a question?" If you come across as naïve, men will stand on their heads to help you. They'll send you to the next guy who will help you. If you come across as knowing as much as they do, but you want to know something else too, they catch on and you don't get the help.

I like the board of education because there's no bullshit. When the superintendent has a problem and calls, he states his business and hangs up. He doesn't give you a list of ten women to call like the Parent-Teacher Association or room-mother type of thing. You go to meetings with prior information about what will be discussed, most of the pros and cons. Even though the board has not made a decision when you get there, you have all the tools to have made a tentative decision prior to board discussion. There's only one meeting a month. I'm on it because I think public education stinks, and I have a lot of kids who'll go through a lot of school and if I'm going to complain all the time, I at least ought to try to do something about it.

I think my kids are most important to me; the time you need to be home with the kids is when they're big. That's when they want you to set up the rules; it's harder for them if you're not home. I've always worked from home, and my kids are always here and so are all their friends. I have a parade of teenagers coming through the house; their friends' mothers are all teachers or nurses, their mothers are doing things, but they're not home. If you make the decision that what *you* need is most important, then all this saying, "I'm worried about my husband and kids," is a bunch of crap. Stop worrying about it; you decided *you're* more important. Accept it, that's the way you are, and learn to live with it. Women can't say that, it's a terrible thing to say; but if you can pose the problem, you're really saying, "I have this feeling that my needs are really more important"—my need to be in business, for example. Then you have to deal with your guilt.

If my kids need me at school, I'll be there. I feel really bad for kids whose mothers aren't there for the things they want them there for; maybe because I was an insecure child and wanted my mother there.

Part of life is sacrifice; I do think kids recognize when something is necessary and when not. I think if a mother finds herself in a divorce situation and has to go out there and earn that buck, kids know the difference between that and when mother says, "I have to find myself." Kids recognize when you are doing something for yourself regardless of them. I think they resent that. They also resent your being home because "you're making me be at home."

I don't know, but it's hard to be married today under the best of circumstances. Maybe I lost my husband as my self-confidence grew. It might have been a factor. But this is who I am, and I love what I do!

Barbara Matthies

Getting to the Top

Barbara Matthies lives in the South, where she is an actuary (she statistically calculates risks, premiums, and other insurance information) and vice-president of a large insurance company. She has worked throughout her marriage, even during the years when she was in college and had already started her family. Barbara and her husband, Shel, have three teenagers.

I am vice-president and associate actuary for a life insurance company. This profession requires ten very rigorous examinations, and it takes eight years after college to successfully complete all the examinations. But you're working at the same time and you're given a certain amount of study time off from work. You receive large increases in salary for passing the examinations, and it's encouraged within the profession to take them because there aren't very many actuaries. When I finished my examinations in 1969, there were only thirty-five women actuaries in the United States and Canada out of about three thousand total.

I have a small staff of eleven or twelve people, and I am responsible for the corporate actuarial area, about $800 million of liability. I'm also responsible for the administration of corporate planning—comparing the progress of corporate plans with actual financial progress as we go along. In other words, I furnish management information that helps senior management run the company, determine where they are, and where they want to be.

I've been with this company almost nineteen years. Before I finished college I worked as a technical research assistant. It was a dead-end career. I had gotten as far as I could go, and I hadn't even finished college. That was more than twenty-two years ago. In those days, for a woman in the South there weren't a whole lot of opportunities—especially for me, since my particular talent was mathematics. I was replaced by a man who was automatically paid more and given twice as much vacation. It was a different world then.

I attended a professional meeting in New York last year, and based on that I think the South is far behind New York. But women in the South have definitely made progress. I see women excelling in lots of ways, but it's more difficult here. In a lot of businesses there have never been any women at the top, and the men don't think of women in those roles. At this company I am the only woman vice-president; I was the first woman officer, but now we have three other women officers and another woman actuary who is an assistant vice-president out of a total of sixty officers.

I have been successful because of my professional specialization and the automatic respect that gives you in the insurance industry. The actuaries are involved with almost all the other departments in some way. So that gives an actuary a tremendous advantage. With passing the exams, a female is automatically respected in her profession without much discrimination.

One thing that helped me was that I had a mentor. I think almost everyone who moves up rapidly in an organization has a mentor. But when he left, I had to go through a couple of reorganizations. Now I'm on my own a lot more, and at my current level, I have had more trouble "networking" with the vice-presidents whom I naturally come in conflict with. This has been a very difficult thing for me to learn. I guess I've muddled through it now, and I've decided if you're going to be in a lot of adversarial roles (my particular responsibilities naturally put me in those roles; I have to be the company's conscience a lot), then you're going to have to feel friendship with those men and make them respect you. You can't sit back and say, "They're doing this to me because I'm a woman." You've got to get out there, not be too aggressive, but be firm and make them respect you. It's really the only way to fulfill your responsibilities and not be that token woman.

In my professional role there is a certain danger of my coming across too strong. If I'm confident about something, I let people know, and since I was only meeting those people in situations where we were at odds, I decided it was creating some degree of antagonism. Maybe I can't overcome my own personality, but what I can do is cultivate their friendship when we are not in adversarial roles. Maybe I could try to look at things from their point of view.

We had a program called "Managing Personal Growth," which allowed me to communicate more with my immediate superior, discuss lots of concerns out in the open. We've also been very aware that communication could be improved, so one of our corporate planning projects has been retreats. The first time I and nineteen guys went away for a retreat together, and this year I and twenty-two guys went off, my level VP and above. These have provided more opportunities for us to get together as a group where I felt accepted, and able to get to know them better.

My husband and I have been married a long time, and my going away doesn't bother him. We're very close friends, and besides it would be inappropriate for a business woman to have anything but very proper relationships at this level and my husband knows that. It would hurt my career. The insurance industry is very conservative, and the South is superconservative.

Shel owns a manufacturing company, and even though he's in a different business, he has some of the same concerns. We can share observations and be sounding boards for each other.

We have three kids, aged twenty-two, sixteen, and fifteen. The oldest one just finished college but hasn't found a job yet. My mother spends the week with us and goes home on weekends. One of my children is a diabetic and needs lots of supervision. My mom has been here for several years, but I've used child care facilities, too.

My kids have certain assigned chores. Ordinarily they keep their own rooms clean, and very often they clean up the kitchen. My son always cuts the lawn and takes care of the yard. I'm here lots of the time, and my husband pitches in even though he's working very long hours. Last winter I worked long hours. We shift to accommodate family needs. As a family we communicate fairly openly and frequently.

I expect a lot from the kids, especially the girls, and Shel expects a lot from our son, interestingly enough. I think you want your kids to be perfect and not make all the same mistakes you did. However, I personally don't think the house is the most important thing. If the kids honestly try to do it, I try not to go behind their backs and do it over again because it's not the way I would have done it. But sometimes it's tempting.

I am very different at work than I am at home. There is a definite emotional involvement at home. My daughter worked in my office for a while, and she was surprised at the difference. At work I'm the wonderful person who always smiles. I would never personally attack anyone on my staff. I always try to be very understanding and bend over backward not to hurt their feelings. Yet sometimes I'll come home and directly attack one of my family.

I think there's a difference between work and family, although I use some of the same executive skills at home. I delegate a lot. I think that I do not do as good a job of managing at home as I do at the office. My kids depend on me to be the mover and shaker at home, and Shel's the good guy that everybody loves and who never loses his temper. He never really feels he has to do the disciplining.

I used to feel more guilt, but I feel very comfortable with my role now. I'm a good cook. I can sew. I can do all those domestic things if I want to, so I don't have to feel I'm a domestic failure. But at the same time it's not something that I feel takes all of a person's time. I think if I were a full-time mother, when my kids hit the teenage years and began to rebel, I would have gone out of my mind. I guess I've come to grips with all this.

When we first moved into this neighborhood I was the only woman who worked outside of the home. At that time lots of women said, "Are you really in such difficult financial straits that you have to work?" That came across loud and clear. I used to say to them, "I studied eight years beyond college. I put in the equivalent of a Ph.D. or medical doctor. I've invested time in my career, and I'd be a fool not to pursue it." I enjoy it and that's the way I feel about it. It's given me an extra dimension.

However, it's also true that I don't ever feel free to stop thinking about my home and family. It's a responsibility that's always there.

Since I have a high position, I can leave if I need to take care of kids. No matter what I'm doing, a phone call can get through. At the office I'm very open that my responsibilities at home are important, and the people with whom I work understand that. I think my colleagues admire the fact that I'm able to work efficiently and run a family, because most of the men have kids the same age as mine. Last month I came back from a trip, my mother didn't happen to be here, and all three of them came down with something and were sick as dogs for a week. I had a very important meeting with the auditor that had been changed three times. I knew it would be at least another month before we could see him again. I also knew it was a crisis situation. I called up my boss and said, "Listen, my kids are sick. Do you want me to come to your house and bring all this material and you cover for me or what?" He said, "No—change your appointment."

Actually the men have a lot of the same problems with their families that I have with mine. Most of their wives are full-time homemakers and are able to assume more of the responsibility so they don't have to do a lot of things I have to do. But I think they're just as worried about their children as I am, and I think that has strengthened my relationship with them. I think they admire me because I can handle not only all the things they delegate to their wives but also a full-time responsibility at work, and I don't shirk my responsibility at work. I have the same responsibilities as they, and I sometimes bring them home with me. I worked at home while the kids were sick. They probably have to do things like that too, but they aren't as open about it as I am.

I've always commuted, but I don't have to be at the office on the dot. We have variable work hours, and I think that's helpful in my not feeling I should be here on the dot. I shift my schedule to best accommodate my family. When the kids are in school I see the kids off to school and leave when they do. It would be better in terms of the traffic if I went in earlier, but I enjoy seeing that they have a good breakfast and that my diabetic child gets her shot and gets herself together. I take that luxury and leave a little later in the afternoon. I use the time to plan, think, and relax. I leave work about 5:30, 6:00, and get in about 9:00 A.M.

I have some problems in scheduling things for my children. For example, with my diabetic child I talk to the doctor fairly frequently. I call him, he calls me. It's a challenge for him to get me within half a day. I'm trying my best to make it as convenient for him as I can. At the same time it's hard to get through to him as well, so we're both working on the problem.

All my doctors have been super about understanding that I have responsibilities, and they work around my schedule as much as I work around theirs. I'll leave the office and home numbers, and lots of time they'll call me at night at home. When I was pregnant, the nurses in the obstetrician's office would call me when I had an appointment if the doctor was going to be late so I would be away from my office a minimum amount of time. If people understand your situation, they do try to help you the best they can.

These days it's easier to handle emergencies. The system is set up better to handle that. My younger child broke her foot in gymnastics. The school called me. I was in the middle of a very important meeting; people had flown in from all over for it. They couldn't get her grandmother, and she needed to go to the hospital. I excused myself from the meeting, called my doctor, and asked him what needed to be done. He said she should come to his office first so he could check it out. He would stay and wait until she got there. Then I called until I found someone who was in the neighborhood who could take her to the doctor's office for me. There have been lots of times when I had to rush home from the office to take care of one of my children or I couldn't go in because of a sick child.

With my son, I took six months of maternity leave and I got pregnant the day I came back. Within fifteen months I was on maternity leave for nine months. This is part of life. I have lots of friends who are professional women who have chosen not to have children. And a lot of women who are ambitious make that choice these days because they don't feel they can cope with all these problems. I think every woman has the right to make that decision. I could not have been happy with myself if I hadn't had kids. I would have felt incomplete; I would have hated to face my old age without having had children. I always wanted to have three children, even though mine weren't really planned all that well.

What I see now are very interested, career-minded young women coming in. To me they are so refreshing, so bright, and so sure of themselves. Some are not doing it for money. They're doing it because they have grown up wanting that career. Also most girls realize that divorce is fairly common and they better have something they can fall back on. The younger men coming along now are more accustomed to competing with women, and I think it's going to be a lot easier for them.

I think there will be just as many women moving up as there will be men.

I like to participate in all aspects of my profession. I'm president of several organizations. I tend to get involved in too many things. I often say to myself, "You would be better off if you limited the number of things you do."

I came from a very domestic mother and from a fairly rural line of people who were not particularly educated. I never saw career women as role models, but I was good at what I was good at. I enjoyed competing with the guys. When I got married I really intended to quit work and stay home the way all the women did. I went on to college and I loved going to school and I loved learning. I thought I wanted to be a teacher. When I was pregnant with my first child I quit my job because I felt that was what I was supposed to do. I was still going to school full-time, but I was miserable not doing the work I loved so much and getting the recognition that I seemed to crave.

At this point I'm involved in women's networking, and I try to spend a lot of time supporting the other women I see coming along. At least now people around me see things somewhat differently, whereas I had nobody up there pulling for me or even thinking about me. Political action by women has been very helpful. But my particular position is in a conservative company, and I guess I've always thought it would be damaging to me to be involved in a political movement that was perceived as radical. I've always steered away from that and tried to work from within because I've always felt that was the most practical way for me to work. The group I'm involved in, a nonpolitical support group where executive women can meet together and discuss items of mutual interest, acts as a sounding board but actually helps with business transactions to try to gain a power base.

The woman who is the top corporate woman in the state and who is, I suppose, my model, has always worked from within, but even working from within, she can inspire young women. She can support a women's issue without having a radical image to high-level men. They respect her because she is a competent corporate woman. I guess we need this type, maybe more than we need the people without the credentials out there lobbying. You need the competent women there to prove that it can be done.

At a recent executive management seminar there was a lecture on balancing your life, spending more time with your spouse, spending more time with your children, getting involved in community activities. I guess I do balance my life; I don't think I'd do a better job if I spent more time at home with my family. I think I would be bored. I don't think it's the amount of time you spend, I think it's the quality of time. Same thing with my husband. My husband works long hours, but he and I spend a lot of time talking together. I think we have a lot of togetherness. He would probably say he would like it better if he had a wife at his beck and call. But in reality he would get tired of it after about a week. I wouldn't be happy and I would make him miserable. On the other hand, I don't want to be president of the company either.

Alice Wilkins

Making Your Mark

Alice is a state legislator. She lives, most of the time, in a large metropolitan area with her husband, Alan, who is a lawyer, and their four-year-old son, Geoffrey. When she's not living with them, she stays in a small apartment in the state capital.

My job as a legislator has a varied schedule. Some times of the year there are not many days away from home; other times, I'm away from home most of the time. Sometimes the job calls for daytime and morning meetings and conferences; other times it takes up evenings. It took a while for my family to understand that parties, receptions, and dinners are work for me. I'm not going to have a good time; I have to be there.

At first I wasn't prepared for what's involved. It's a seven-day-a-week, twenty-four-hour-a-day job. But this is now my second two-year term. I had practiced law; I was working for the Justice Department. That wasn't nine to five either, but closer to that than what I have now. I worked through my pregnancy; I worked through Friday, and Geoffrey was born on Monday afternoon. Then I stayed home because my husband had a fantasy of a wife who keeps a nice house, makes nice dinners, and makes sure his socks match. He really did like the idea of my being a lawyer (we met in law school), but we were both getting into the swing of things of my being home when the legislator in this district retired. I had been at home with Geoff for four months at that time. People said, "Why don't you run?" At first I wasn't inclined to run, and then some people said I couldn't win. That was enough for me to say "Phooey on them! I'm getting out there and I'm going to try it." So I did. I ran, and I came in first in a field of nine candidates. It was a tremendous victory, and I've been going at it ever since.

The job involves essentially three different roles. There is the role of the legislator, the role of community ombudsman dealing with community issues and problems, and then the role of politician. All of those things obviously affect one another, but they make different demands on your time. I schedule fewer perfunctory appearances where you just come out and wave your hand; I concentrate on those things where I have some reason to be there.

I've had situations where I've called home, and my four-year-old said, "Mommy, come home. I don't want you to be away." He wants me to pick him up from school.

"Nana will pick you up or Mrs. King (the sitter)."

"No, no, Mommy. I want you to pick me up."

I said, "Geoffrey, I can't because I've got to go to work," and he said, "Johnny and Debra's mothers pick them up from school every day, and I want you to pick me up from school."

"I've got to go to work and you know I go out of town to go to work, and that's why I can't pick you up from school."

"Their mommy comes, why can't you?"

I said, "Their mommy doesn't have an apartment in the state capital and their mommy can't take them to the Capitol Building, and their mommy can't take them to rallies and things." He thought about that for a second, and he said, "I suppose that's right, but I still want you to pick me up from school every day."

I have a curious child-care arrangement. In the morning, my husband takes Geoff to nursery school right across the street. In the afternoon, he is picked up by the sitter, who keeps him until early evening. The sitter collects these little kids in the neighborhood and takes them places. Alan picks him up at night; if he is delayed, my mother comes from down the street and she stays.

Geoff sees me as a glamorous character who comes flying in and takes him off someplace and introduces him to everybody. He's a very sociable child and likes getting out. He plays well with other kids—he can strike up conversations with anyone. The other side of it is that I sometimes feel that not having Mom around upsets him, and it upsets me twice as much, not being able to pick him up from school.

Alan and I haven't done any traveling, just the two of us. Geoff is so small, and I guess I feel I'm away from him so much I haven't really wanted to take a vacation without him, so we travel with him. He's cute, four years old, and he says, "Mommy, I want to go back to San Francisco,"—he can't even pronounce it—or, "When are we taking an airplane again? I want to go on an airplane." The kid zips all over the country!

Geoff's a healthy, happy, bright kid, presumably well adjusted. I think it's working out, but I don't know, and that really does concern me.

One thing I do, come hell or high water, is cook dinner on Sunday night. That's the one time a week that I know we'll be at the same table together. That is the only structured thing, although we do a lot of things together as a family. We have a summer place where we go on weekends. When I'm in the capital seven days a week, Alan tries to take off a weekend and come in on Friday night with Geoff to spend the weekend with me. I try to get home as much as I can; sometimes I just can't because I'm in session.

I generally drive back and forth, which adds to the time problem. The flight is an hour and the drive is almost four, but I'm terrified of flying, especially in those tiny airplanes. The car gives me a kind of flexibility I don't have in a plane.

But I'm away from home so much in such a high-powered, high-stakes, fast-moving kind of game, functioning on a level that doesn't lend itself to openness and warmth, nurturing and sharing. So then I'm this high-powered person coming back home. First, I have to go through the whole shifting of gears.

Although Alan's a lawyer, too, he doesn't concern himself with all the tedious interplay and games that are now part of my life—the power plays, for instance—and so we have some difficulty in sharing. He makes more money, and a lot of men equate money with power; so in his own mind I think he feels dominant. But I'm more visible. I don't think he minds; I think he's kind of tickled by it. He has his ego intact. That's his strength. But the tension comes, I think, from my relating to high-powered, fast-moving, sometimes Machiavellian kinds of dealings that are not part of what he does. At times that's caused a kind of strain on our marriage, but I think we've worked it through.

When I'm away, Alan runs the whole ship at home. That's one of the conflicts for me; I feel sometimes I should have more responsibility here than I do. That's odd, too, because my mother worked. Historically, most mothers worked in this country, within certain social strata. We have an idealized vision of what THE FAMILY has been about and *should* be about, but the fact is that in American families, women have always worked. Rich women probably did stay at home, didn't work, and had housekeepers. Upper middle-class women got to stay home without going out to work or taking in laundry or working in a factory or whatever. But most women in this country have always worked one way or another, at one time or another, outside the home.

I come from a family, even a whole culture, in which working mothers were not a new phenomenon. My background implies I wouldn't have those kinds of conflicts. But I do, in part, because this is my first time doing it. I do have ambivalent feelings about working. I had lived through my mother always working, and one of her messages was, "What I'd give to be able to sit down and have a house and children and not *have* to go to work!" So this was the message I got: "Prepare yourself to work, prepare yourself to be totally self-sufficient, but the better world is to find a fireside-and-slippers-husband, somebody who will take care of you and give you the material things you want, take you traveling, and that sort of thing." When I was in law school, that was the prepare-yourself part, and then I got married, and that was the wouldn't-it-be-nice-to-sit-at-home-and-clean-my-bookshelves part. Once I had my baby, I fully expected to stay home through his younger childhood. That lasted all of four months.

There's still some part of me wanting to be protected and taken care of and secure, while there's also part of me wanting to be aggressive, adventurous, ambitious, and constantly discovering. Adventure and discovery are the opposite of security; you can't have it both ways. There are times I feel overwhelmed, when somebody just pulled off some fantastic move that I never thought existed before, some politician just quadruple-dealt somebody out of something, and it came—not from left field—but from another ballpark altogether; things like that. That's when I say, "My God, what am I doing this for? I'm aging myself, working my tail off for $28,000 a year, my kid saying, 'I want you home,' my husband having cornflakes for dinner." I don't have an answer; I just work it through. I just tell myself to get back to what it is I really want to do; I tell myself I'm committed; I believe in what I'm doing. I tell myself I believe in it for myself, as well as for the greater good.

I started off wanting to save the world; obviously my expectations of what I can and cannot do have been greatly changed by this experience. I think that if I have made a contribution, it's been in being honest and faithful to my constituents. I haven't been afraid to speak out on issues, irrespective of political consequences.

Right now, I'm going through the throes of asking myself why I'm killing myself, but it's a wonderful job for having a sense that you can do something. That's a very strong impetus to stay in this. The impetus to get out of it is that I'm not making enough money. It's one thing to rely on your husband, and another to feel like you're self-sufficient. The fact of the matter is, financially I could not support myself. If Alan left tomorrow, had a heart attack or something, I could not take care of myself financially. That's kind of scary—I don't like that.

I try to organize and budget my time to the best of my ability. You can juggle a lot more if you are organized about what you're doing. If you don't have to send out for a loaf of bread every time you make dinner, or if your laundry is done at a certain time, then you don't run around with your husband's nose out of joint because he doesn't have any clean underwear.

I have a cleaning lady who comes in once a week. I do laundry when I'm around. Marketing is the worst. That is my responsibility regardless. So I've worked out something. I have a butcher up the street and a vegetable man, and every two weeks I go to the grocery store and load up and go to the freezer, open it up, throw it in, and hope it lasts. What bothers me is when I come back home Friday night and discover all the zucchini and all the vegetables I bought still in the refrigerator, while the potpies and hot dogs are gone. Nutrition really concerns me. When I'm here, I go heavy on vegetables when I make meals, because when I'm not around, their diet is less nutritious than I would like it to be.

I can't always prepare meals, but I compensate. For certain, Sunday dinner is there. Other nights of the week I will either prepare something in advance and leave it frozen for them, or, another element of expense, I probably spend more money on groceries because I buy things, steak, for instance, that take no skill to fix but that are expensive. So we manage. I would say we have a prepared meal for dinner as much as most families do, assuming it's not a family where the husband comes home on the same train every day, to dinner every night, and there mother and children sit with scrubbed faces waiting for him every day. Obviously, this is light years away from that, but it works. Nobody around here is underweight, and I do care about nutrition. We've struck a rough balance with that; again that's a function of making it coordinate.

I choose what I do carefully. I don't take classes. I don't belong to any bridge clubs. We don't go to the movies as much as we used to because of the time. That's something you wipe off. I don't wash the walls as often as I want, my closets are not quite as clean as I would want them to be, I'm not as organized as I could be, but I manage to get those things taken care of that have to be done.

I take time for myself. Sometimes I get physically worn down; I need to recharge my batteries. When that happens, I just go off to my corner and rest. I call those my sleep spells. I'm a high energy person and I'm constantly on the go. If I showed you my schedule for today, you'd go AHHH! So when I get tired, I retreat and sleep.

I haven't got it all figured out. I try to coordinate the different aspects of my life; to coordinate my career and intellectual development with my relationship with my husband, and my development as a parent with my relationship with my child and my home. The fact that they all work, to the extent that they do, is a function of coordinating and meshing those functions and deciding what's important to me and what I cannot do.

In terms of my relationship with Alan, we've had to work at it. I have had to submerge my ego sometimes in dealings with Alan. When he says something annoying, instead of my snapping back, sometimes I'll let it go. I go a bit further in reconciling differences than I might otherwise, because he's taken on a lot of additional responsibilities. In order to make this work, we've had to coordinate, to give a little more on other levels.

I have a good friend who's a child psychologist and she has helped me gain some perspective. Things were getting to me at one point. When I came home, "the pots were cold and the house was dark." Alan was retreating more and more into himself. He was becoming more and more of a stranger. I resented that because it was aggressive. People can be very aggressive by their withdrawal. I'd get back and find this person I would exchange a few words with, and then get snapped at—not really snapped at but kind of a left-handed remark. We were getting really ugly; it couldn't go on like that, so we both started making a conscious effort to work it through.

If I didn't have a supportive husband, I couldn't do it; there's no question about it. Alan is more than supportive to me. He does the things that make the house run, and he also doesn't throw it back in my face.

The fact is, you have to pay the price somewhere. Either you're willing to devote tremendous amounts of financial and personal resources, or you just suffer the guilt. Marxian analysis holds that the initial division of labor was between men and women with women relegated to housekeeping and nurturing kinds of functions. Probably one of the reasons why that division of labor has persisted so long is that it's easy. You take this segment of society and say this is your job, and take the other segment and say that is their job, and never the twain shall meet. That way you don't have to explore who gets to do what. Now people are reexamining who gets to do what. And you can work a resolution so that the tasks get divided up between two people in a way that is not gender-based. The idea is to split them up to make them work. That's the hopeful part.

I'd like to think we have made it work, but again you pay the price. Housekeeping expenses, by virtue of my absence, are tremendously high. I'm certain if I sat down and figured the cost of running this household in my absence against my $28,000 a year, not to mention the tax consequences of my working, I probably would not come out ahead financially. But there are other gains, benefits. I'm fulfilling myself as a person, and given the fact I only live once, I feel I'm kind of important too. But the money is something you've got to sacrifice. Or, if you can't sacrifice the money, then you've got to reconcile yourself to the guilt that your closets are not clean, or dinner wasn't made, or the children had to get it themselves. Or yes, I cooked dinner and I went to work, came home and did the laundry, and when I went to bed tonight, I was not interested in sex. Those are the kinds of adjustments you have to make. Being a working mother complicates that division of labor that in another kind of world was simple.

We've been married nine years, and we've had to work at making the marriage work. I think it's paid off. I'm pretty comfortable that now we can give it another nine, at least!

I don't know if I'm doing the right thing. In my panicky moments, I can't really see Alan going off with some young chickie, but I do see Geoff growing up being a man who can't make commitments or can't really get involved in a loving relationship because his mother was so distant; that scares me. I don't know enough about the workings of the mind to know that if I had been there when he fell down at four, it would have made a difference. There's no way to know. There is a real difference in the psychological dynamics of a woman who *has* to work and one who *wants* to work because of her choice. I'm going around tearing my hair out, concerned about things my mother wasn't concerned about—she couldn't be. I hope that Geoff winds up normal and sane; if that happens, and if Alan and I aren't divorced before the year is out, we'll have made it!

Alexandra Hitchcock

Taking Charge of Your Life

After teaching for several years, Alexandra Hitchcock decided that she would leave the security and convenience of her suburban job and head for the challenge and excitement of a career in the city. She is now with a large communications company, and she commutes daily from her home in the suburbs to her position in New York. She and her husband, Russell, are the parents of three children.

I was a high school English teacher. I chose to leave teaching after seven years and get a job in New York City for a number of reasons, one of which was burnout. It hadn't happened yet, but I recognized the signs. I had gone into teaching very idealistically, thinking I could change the world, and I found out quickly that I was one against far more giants than I had thought were out there. I thought I'd only have to fight the board of education and the administration, but I found I had to fight students, parents, and colleagues as well. When I left teaching, I was fortunate in the sense that I probably had more nerve than I should have; having always done things the hard way and having survived, it never occurred to me I might fail. My attitude was, "I'm going to do this and it's going to work and I'm going to show them all I can do something with my life other than teach high school English."

I was trying to make a natural transition. When I talked to people about leaving teaching, most of them said to me, "You're crazy, you'll lose the security and summer vacations." Others said, "There's nothing else you can do with two degrees in English, my dear." I thought about that and realized that I'd done a lot and I put my family through a lot, so I ought to have marketable skills and I'd better find out what they are. I figured out what I thought was a nice transition: to go into publishing. I thought I would publish the "great textbooks" that would turn around the minds of all the young people in the country. I was able to go in and easily sell the idea that I had a background in education and I knew what kids were interested in and I certainly knew how to use the language. I thought that would be where I could make my mark and my contribution. I found out within two months' time that that was a mistake, but I was not going to turn around and say, "I'm going back to teaching."

I had been fortunate in that when I made the move from education to publishing, I chose a company that was connected with a large corporation, and it did not take me long to look around and say, "There are lots of opportunities here. You just have to figure out what you can do." Then I worked very hard to prove that I could do it and I put out my series that was going to turn everything around. Then I made contacts to impress the right people with my competence and looked within the corporation for something to do. By that time I had figured out I wanted to get into an area where I could teach. There is no question about it; I am a teacher pure and simple, and nothing makes me happier than being before a group and finding out that they can think and that I can make a difference in their thinking. I identified this department as someplace I'd like to go, and it was just a problem of getting from there to here. I knew I could not make that leap, I had to do something in between, so I took what I knew was not the right job to give myself a certain amount of visibility. I was able to demonstrate my skills, my ability to read, write, edit, and to go before a group and make a presentation. I got the visibility and recognition I wanted, and another job opened up and was offered to me.

My husband has always been incredibly supportive. When I went to college after we'd had kids, he worked at several jobs. I think he is unique. I'm hoping that the two sons we're raising will be like him. Part of it is that he is secure in himself. His self-image is not tied up in degrees, money, or even my degree. He knows who he is and what he is about. He knows my strengths and I know his. This is a joint endeavor.

When I started working in the city I said to him, "You're used to having dinner on the table between 6:00 and 6:30. Well, if I don't get home until 6:00 or 6:30, we don't eat till maybe 8:00," and he said, "What's wrong with me—think I can't cook?" So I took him up on it. When I walk in the house, dinner is on the table. Every night he takes care of it, but I plan the menus, and on weekends I try to do some things ahead, a casserole or a roast. We have a menu calendar on the refrigerator door, and I write in the day's menu and he and the kids follow it.

We structure our lives quite a bit. One thing I found out very early when I was trying to do all the crazy things that were important in my life was that I was running out of time quickly. What I worked out for the family is a system of calendars. I have a calendar on the desk that my husband and I use. There is a similar calendar on the freezer in the kitchen, and each of the kids has his or her own individual calendar. Any event, whether a concert or a dance recital, has to be slotted onto the calendar in the kitchen and in the bedroom. If it is not put there in ample time, at least two weeks ahead, so that planning can be made for it—tough!

We've always tried to attend the kids' school activities. I was fortunate during the time they were in elementary school that I was either going to school or teaching and I would be excused. Since I've been working in the city I've been able, because I know far enough ahead of time, to schedule my time so I can go to my son's awards assembly, or whatever. To make up the time, I might, for example, work through lunch. I knew that wherever I worked I'd make sure I had that kind of discretionary time because I was willing to do what had to be done to get the job done, even if it meant taking it home and working on it that evening. When I need to adjust my schedule, I always go to my boss with a game plan, spelling out how I can get the job done. It works very well.

If necessary, my husband will pick up the slack. If all else fails, we say, "Look, we really would love to be there, but this is the way it is." We make sure we never miss any evening function, even if it means giving up one of our activities. I think that's why the kids are as decent as they are. They know they have our support and we're interested in what they're doing. We're not just saying, "Fill up your time with stuff so you're not hanging out on the street," but, "We're proud of what you do and we want to see what you've been doing with your time." I think that makes a difference.

Since Russell works near home, the kids have him available, and they know in an emergency they can reach me. We also spend a great deal of time talking about changes that affect everybody. Before I left teaching and started commuting to the city I said, "Look, my schedule is going to be different. I'm not going to be nearby. I won't be there for you to say, 'Mom—quick—I need—whatever.'" We talked about the impact the change would have on our lives.

Russell and I don't have as much time together as I would like because in addition to everything else, we're involved in church and community. However, I'm finding that now that the children are older we have more time to sit and talk. We make time for each other, but it has to be slotted in there with everything else. One thing I found happening was that by the end of the week no matter how much I tried to get rid of things, a certain amount of my work was still in my head, and the same with him. So after dinner on Friday evening we started having what we call our "debriefing sessions." He tells me about his week and I tell him about mine and we offer suggestions, just the two of us. That time we have with each other is nice.

We have been incredibly blessed. Ever since the kids were small, a retired couple in the neighborhood has taken care of them. They became like grandparents to them. They loved my kids. They were taken everywhere by these people. At the time when I was going to college and my husband was working at two jobs, there was no money, so I paid them a token amount and then we tried to do as many things around their house as we could. My husband took over the gardening and painting and whatever else we could do because they would not accept more, knowing we did not have it. They said to us all the time that the children made them feel young. My children are probably closer to these people than to their natural grandparents. I never had to worry about where they were or how they were taken care of.

I'm one of a group of training managers, and as such I do a variety of things. One thing I do is stand-up training. I conduct management seminars on a variety of topics for employees in just about every level of the company, from those working in entry-level jobs as secretaries up through and including VP's. Part of my job is to talk about such things as what makes a good manager, what is motivation, how to communicate effectively. Though it is not necessarily part of my mandate, I also talk about such things as options in life. Too many people get into the corporate world and feel there are no options. They say, "I'm stuck." You're never stuck. You don't have to live with an untenable situation. I also try to make sure I discuss how one treats another human being in the corporate world.

I also develop seminars: come up with the concept, write them, and deliver them. The third part of my job is to do informal counseling with participants who will come to me and say, "I like what you had to say and I'd like to talk about it in some more detail." A great deal of human interaction takes place, which is what I love about the job.

When I'm running a seminar I don't have any flexibility. I have to be there at a certain time. When I'm not running a seminar I am working on developing projects or materials, or interacting with people in my department or with the corporation, and time is much more flexible for me. But when I need some flexibility in my time, I make sure it happens. I don't sit there and moan and groan and say, "Why don't they let me?" I go in and present my case. The first thing I do is to make sure I'm doing my job to the best of my ability. That is the bottom line. You can't go in with a request for flexibility just to have someone say, "I'd love to do that, but it seems that you're two projects behind already." You have to make sure you can justify your request.

I've become more vocal about the stress that corporations impose on their workers. They want everything done yesterday or the day before. Now I go in and say, "Look—this is not humanly possible. If you really want it that badly, either you give me some help so I can get it done on time, or you give me more time so I can do it myself." I make sure I know what is feasible, and I present my argument as to why it is.

Many women feel that when they go in to see the boss they can smile prettily and say, "I really don't think that I can do this." Of course the boss says, "I really would appreciate it if you would, I'd be so grateful," and that's the end of it. Or they go in angry, "I can't do this and what do you expect of me?"—without any facts to back it up. So the boss says, "There's another woman who can't do the job. I don't know why they gave HER a chance." If you open your mouth and you have something to say, people will listen. As simple as that. But you have to go in with something to say, not just vague ramblings off the top of your head. If I believe in what I say, I'm going to fight for it. Sometimes my emotional response is anger, but I don't go in when I'm furious. I sit there and try to figure out why I'm furious and what to do about it.

I've always been a very nervy kind of individual, blunt to a fault sometimes. I cut through garbage to what I see as the reality of the situation. I tend to be a leader, and it never occurs to me that that isn't what women do. Not only have I never understood the shrinking violet, but I also have no patience with that kind of woman. It's beyond me. It never bothered me at all to engage in intense discussions or arguments. I think it is because I am the oldest of five children, four girls and a boy, and I was given a tremendous amount of responsibility at a very young age. I also had a father and mother who expected the boy to be born first. I should have been the boy; so when they realized what I could do, nobody ever said, "That isn't what a girl should do."

Because I'm a commuter, my day starts at 6:00 A.M.; on seminar days it starts at 5:30. I walk to the station to get an 8:00 A.M. train and then I take a bus to the office. When trains don't run well I'm late. It's as simple as that. In the wintertime the trains are worse than in the summer. The only time I have a minor fit is on a seminar day, and that's why I get up at 5:30 and catch a 7:15 train. Even if it is an hour late, I'm still okay. Everyone knows I come in on the train, and if they don't get a call from me, they know I'm sitting in a tunnel somewhere.

In the morning I read on the train. Occasionally if there is someone I know I'll spend the time talking, socializing. Going home, I usually walk from the office to the station. Walking gives me the extra exercise that I need. On the evening train, my head goes back as soon as the conductor collects the ticket and I sleep. This refreshes me, and I walk in the house ready to deal with the family.

I've operated under an incredible amount of stress for many more years than I should have; I'm driven, and over a period of years I've developed some health problems. There is not much I can do about it but keep it under control and recognize what I'm doing to myself. This is one of the reasons I stick to my time limits now. I don't know whether too many people, much less women, would want to pay the kind of price that I have in terms of trying to juggle everything and do everything equally well. I tried to be a supermom, superwife—super whatever I was working at—you name it, I was going to be THE best. I soon realized that that leads down the road to self-destruction. I have learned to monitor what strength I have and to say to people, "Look, just because I happen to be efficient does not mean I'm the only one who can do this." You get caught in the trap of thinking that you're somehow Superwoman and you're not. You're just an ordinary woman who happens to have done some additional things. It took me a long time to reach that point in looking at myself, to say, "Look, you haven't done too badly and why don't you slack up a bit, relax, and enjoy it?"

I've been fortunate that I haven't had to choose between family and career; I've been able to have both. But it has also fragmented me in many senses because I haven't been able to give any one my full attention. To be honest I probably would do it this way again because I think I have children who are going to make it and will be able to take care of themselves. I think I have a strong marriage, I think I have a good relationship with my children, and I think I've achieved a certain measure of success in the professional world.

Joanne Mayer

Working Well

Joanne Mayer is a psychiatrist living in a suburban area of California. She and her husband, also a psychiatrist, have three teenage boys.

When I was young, I didn't want to be a doctor; I wanted to be a psychologist. A friend said, "Why don't you become a psychiatrist—you could do it." I was ambitious, striving and achieving—a bright girl from the Bronx—so instead of being a psychologist, I went to medical school and became a psychiatrist. I also wanted to get married and to have children.

I made my career plans to be a mother and a career woman from the very beginning. I never considered academic psychiatry or hospital psychiatry; I could have gotten a part-time job in academia or in a hospital, but I wanted to do out-patient psychotherapy.

I was twenty-six when I had my first child; that was practically over the hill then! I was never a hundred-percent housewife, even in the years when the children were young; I worked a couple of half-days a week. Putting on high heels and a suit and going to work for three hours made a difference. I completed medical school and my internship. Then, following my internship, I had all three children in a short space of time.

I have always tailored my aspirations because I had children. I structured my residency as best I could; the university allowed me to train half-time for two years, and then, pregnant, I was able to find a half-time training program in psychiatry. I was fortunate in that I never had to do night service, and I did my emergency work during the day.

Over the years, I've had a variety of housekeepers. I've increased my working hours as the children got older. During my training, I had full-time help. Then I took two-day-a-week jobs and had a lady who came in when I was working. Once I went into private practice it was less difficult because I could make my own hours; that meant some sacrifices. There were certain patients I couldn't take, and my heart was always partly at home, but as the kids got older I became much more involved in my profession. I still get home at 5:00 P.M., I don't have to anymore, but I still want to, and I start at 8:00 A.M. I used to wait until they were all off to school and work from 9:00 to 2:00, then 9:00 to 3:00, and gradually 9:00 to 4:00, as they were able to take care of themselves.

My household arrangements have been tailored to the needs of my family. I now have a cleaning service and a young woman who does light laundry, shopping, and cooking half-days. After many years of cooking, I realized that I don't like to cook, and I finally got someone to do it for me. This whole business of household help is a tremendous problem. Your needs differ as the children grow; my children don't need sitters now, and I need somebody to do services rather than take care of the children. This happened around junior high school age, they were well able to take care of themselves, but in the afternoon it was nice to have someone around. For a long time, I had a woman two days or one half-day a week, but I really could have used more help than that.

Private practice has given me flexibility. However, I didn't want to practice in my home because I need to get out of my house. I'm the kind of person who has to do the dishes if they are in the sink. I think there are problems enough being involved in a profession and having a husband and children, without working at home.

I was fortunate enough to find an office ten minutes from home. When opportunities came to work elsewhere, I stayed in this office when others who worked here moved on. There were reasons it would have been advantageous to move, but I like being so close to home in case I'm needed there.

I manage to stay free of car pools because I don't enroll the boys in as many activities as I might. They bike a lot of places too and sometimes my housekeepers took them places. I must say that I let the boys develop their own interests; I do not intrude into their private lives. I would say that my children, and this is reiterated by people who know them, are individuals and are quite comfortable with themselves. They're also quite comfortable speaking out about their feelings and opinions; they even feel free to criticize us. They respect my husband and me, and they see me as someone with a good sense of herself.

My husband shares parenting with me. He's always been a good parent, even from the very early months when the boys were babies. He was not a father who avoided infants; he liked babies, and he'd take care of newborns. The older they got, the more involved he got. They just turned to him more and more. They admire him, and their interests are the same. I say half-kiddingly, half-resentfully, that I feel like I'm in the middle of a locker room—sometimes it's funny and sometimes it's moving, with so many large tennis shoes around!

Household work doesn't interest my husband. For a while we tried to share it, and there was even one period of time when he took over cooking and shopping for a month. But our psychological backgrounds caught up with us; neither of us was comfortable with it. He felt unmasculine doing it, and I felt unfeminine letting him. To our dismay, and in some ways to our satisfaction, we have a very typical division of labor! He takes care of cars, occasionally fixes things if he has time, or I call someone to fix them, and he makes all financial decisions, although he often consults me. I'm becoming more interested in that; now we go over various legal and monetary things. I take care of running the household—and the various children's needs, his needs, and those of the house. Other people may do the work, but I manage it. We both do a little gardening and then we have someone come in once a week to do what neither of us wants to do. We don't have a big garden or a big house, which also helps.

Our professions demand a lot from us; so do our children. We try to have time alone; our master bedroom is on the second floor away from the kids. We try to spend some time there. We also play music together; we were both musicians when we met and dropped it when we didn't have time. Now we're getting back to it; that's a source of a lot of relaxation. Our standard of marital relationship is a pretty high one; we expect a lot from each other. We try to be supportive because we're in a profession with very little praise forthcoming; a pat on the back is rare in our field. We both come home quite drained, and there is nobody here to build us up. It's a problem we both understand. Psychiatry involves a kind of extension of oneself in an ongoing way. Out of any given hour you are really working fifty minutes out of the hour if you're good. So as much as we enjoy it, our work can be draining.

I have a lot of respect for my husband and he respects me. For a long time we were in different areas of psychiatry, but my husband has changed his interests and he now has a practice very much like mine. He had been interested in community hospital work, but now we are doing the same thing. In some ways, that means we are able to talk about our work in ways that very few couples can, because we know what each other is talking about and that's very satisfying. Our patients are not coming from the same patient pool, so we don't compete as such, but I think we both feel it would be a little bit easier if our work were a little more separate in some ways. Perhaps it has to do with recognition in the professional community.

I've paid a price. My marriage could be better; on the other hand, some people look at me and say, "You've been married nineteen years, that's practically a world's record in California!" We've had some tough years, but we're very committed to staying together. I think my kids have paid some price too, and I think my work has paid some price. For example, one of the trade-offs for me was not to go to the Psychoanalytic Institute for special training. I may try it two to three years from now, but I don't know if they will take me; I'll be in my late forties, and it's not easy to get in. I may or I may not be interested then. It's very hard work, and that's a sacrifice.

You can't have it all one hundred percent. The question I raise is, Who has the notion that people who have only one or two of these things have one hundred percent of them, either? What lies at the bottom of this concern is one's personality and ability to cope. I don't think I would have been better off for not having worked. I'm not sure my kids would have been better off, either. I would have been very frustrated if I hadn't had a career, and I might have been less encouraging of their own development than I was. A frustrated mother can't be a nurturing mother, either. I suspect, too, that those of us who are concerned about whether we're nurturing mothers put in some pretty good quality time.

I'm speaking both professionally and as an individual now, but I think that such personality conflicts can't be overcome by psychotherapy. People come to me and say, "If only I could do such and such, I'd be all the better." I know they'd be somewhat better, and I hope that's what they'd settle for. Real difficulties are there no matter what one does; certain things one does make it easier, and certain things make life harder. I used to race around, and people wondered how I did it all. I didn't myself know how hard I worked, and I didn't have proper help. But I'm easier on myself now; I know what I am. I would like to think that one of the outcomes of the women's liberation movement involves some liberating of women from having to make the same mistakes that men have made. Perhaps we can all temper ambition not just because we have children, but because we would like to enjoy life, too.

Suzy and Scott Newman

Shared Parenting

Suzy and Scott Newman have shared parenting responsibilities since their children were born. Their twins, Alicia and Jonah, are now eleven.

Both Suzy and Scott are lawyers; Suzy went back to school and received her law degree when the children were five. They live and work in New York City.

SUZY: I wanted to work and have a career, and I thought I couldn't do it and have children. I thought it had to be either/or.

SCOTT: I never thought much about it; I just assumed there would come a time when we'd have children. Suzy felt negative about it, and it was *her* view that changed. I think what put us on a joint path was the fact that after Suzy decided she did want to have children, it was very difficult for her to conceive. It just didn't happen; we worked at it for a long time before the doctor isolated what the problem was. That brought us together, and maybe that working together has just continued.

SUZY: The logistics of working and having a baby just seemed to fall into place. I was teaching then; I was not a lawyer. I took three and a half weeks off when the twins were born. I went back in March. Then there was a couple of weeks of spring vacation, and then I worked two more months. I was off for the first summer after the children were born. That made it a little bit easier.

In retrospect I think I would advise people to take a few

months off. I was nursing two babies, and commuting sixty miles each way. I had someone sleep over for the first few weeks. I'd get home about four-thirty and I'd nurse them. I'd nurse them again about seven-thirty. I'd go to bed by nine. Scott would stay up and he would feed them bottles at midnight. I'd get up at six and nurse them. Scott would sleep till about eight. I'd leave for work a little after eight when the baby-sitter came.

I taught for two years and then decided to go to law school.

SCOTT: She had been in law school several years before and she had dropped out so we could go into the Peace Corps.

SUZY: We kept the routine we'd had when I was teaching. I got up real early and I'd leave, and Scott got the children up and gave them breakfast and waited for the baby-sitter. When I came home it was time for the sitter to leave.

SCOTT: I spent a lot of time alone with them on weekends then because Suzy would study the whole weekend in the library.

SUZY: The summer I took the bar exam, Scott spent every weekend with them. I was gone from 8:00 A.M. till 11:00 P.M. Scott took Jonah to Virginia for a week when he was four, and Alicia and I stayed home.

SCOTT: Then that summer I took a long weekend and Alicia and I went camping in Pennsylvania.

When the kids were two, we banded together with other parents in the neighborhood and ran a cooperative play group outside people's homes. We rented a storefront; then we rented rooms in the back of a church. We had to carpool one or two days a week. The first year the parents had to work three hours a week; we didn't even have a full-time teacher.

SUZY: The people in our cooperative knew us and knew our babysitter, and the first year, except when I was on vacation, the babysitter did our share one day a week. Our deal with her was that she got a couple of mornings off because the kids were both gone. The second year, they hired one teacher, so we only had to work once every other week. So I would work one week, and Scott would work the next time.

SCOTT: A half-day once per month wasn't so terrible to accommodate.

SUZY: The third year we hired two teachers and nobody worked, but through all the years we had to be involved in a car pool. What we did was take them in the morning.

SCOTT: Our car-pooling was always to school because we couldn't be there at one.

SUZY: When I finished law school, I took a job with Legal Services. It was close to home and Legal Services people tend to be very supportive. You can go in any Legal Services office and always find a couple of kids there. I was in court three or four days a week. I could bring the kids to the office and leave and go to court and somebody would watch them. I was a few blocks from both schools and was able to run over if a child got sick. If the after-school program was canceled, they could come to my office. Now I have a new job with a federal enforcement agency, and I've only been there a few weeks, so I don't know exactly how it's going to be. I looked carefully for this job, and in fact I knew someone who was working where I'm working now. I spent a bit of time grilling him on whether you have to stay past five-thirty and if you can bring a kid to the office. I wanted to make sure I could do the same kinds of things I'd been doing, like going to every school play.

SCOTT: My firm is small and I have a greater degree of flexibility than I would have in a major firm of one hundred or two hundred people. I bring the kids to the office all the time. I'm in midtown Manhattan. As with most parents in this situation, we're always conflicted. You feel an obligation to your profession and clients and an obligation to your family. You feel bad because somebody is always being shortchanged. Even when you accommodate one pressure or the other, you have the feeling that somebody is being shortchanged even if they're not.

SUZY: There's a balancing that we do that I think gets rid of a lot of guilt, though. We often are among the very few parents who go to school performances. We're always available for that to make up for the fact that we're not available for other things. Other things that I do include going out to breakfast with one of them. Jonah loves to go out to breakfast. We'll leave here at seven and go downtown near where his school is and have breakfast out, and he goes to school and I go off to work. It's a nice time, especially because we have two children the same age and they're usually together. So we often split up; one weekend a month Scott will take one and I'll take the other.

I don't think we could handle this if we lived in the suburbs. It would mean another couple of hours a day with them being taken care of by someone else. They need us. I want to be with them. Even with my new job, I'm home within a half-hour to forty minutes.

SCOTT: And it only takes me a half-hour to go from my office to school, so I take long lunch hours for the kids if I want to. It is very important to try to schedule things as far ahead as possible so you can treat it as any other professional appointment. I find that the school schedules things for nonworking parents; they are constantly scheduling events in the middle of the day. It is the worst possible time. Night would be easier for the working parent. I resent that. It seems to me the thing to do might even be to schedule all these performances at 9:00 A.M. For conferences, they do try to schedule some at 8:00 A.M. so we can get there before we go to work.

SUZY: The school is supportive of the kids; it's responsive to their needs.

Now that the kids are older and in school all day, it's easier. We need less help. We only have someone here all day Monday and all day Friday. Our kids go to various after-school programs on the other three days. They're just at the age now where we feel we can let them come home alone for a few hours and they've done that a few times.

SCOTT: This is a very friendly neighborhood. The kids love it. There are things here for them—an after-school program with gym and swimming pool, a church-sponsored athletic program, and a city-sponsored soccer program. The kids do have instructions about how to come home alone. We try to teach them to live defensively; don't go in the house if someone's on the steps behind you. We also put a wrought iron gate on the front door. They use only buses, not subways.

SUZY: I am kind of concerned about them; I worry. We do have a problem when they're sick. Alicia was sick this week, and I left one day at 2:00 P.M. I was really uptight about it, since I just started, but my immediate supervisor said, "Don't worry about it, it happens to me." They were really nice about it. I took work home and brought it back the next day and no one said anything.

SCOTT: I was at work and planning to leave early to spend the afternoon at home with Alicia when Suzy called and said she would go home. I think that's an example of her feeling guilty. I wanted to take care of Alicia that day, but Suzy wouldn't let me. I wish she had dealt with her own guilt feelings in a little bit more direct fashion. I think it would have been better for the children and for her. But given the results, I can't complain too much. They're pretty reasonable and responsive kids.

SUZY: They have both said they are glad I don't stay home. When we were talking about my decision to change jobs I said, "What would you think if I quit?" Jonah said he thought that would be terribly lazy of me. We kind of made them a part of my whole interview process. I told them when I was going for interviews and what I was doing.

SCOTT: The children have been part of the profession as well. I took Alicia to Albany when she was very young to be with me when I had to argue before one of the courts in Albany. She sat in back of the courtroom and drew a picture of the court. Jonah's grandfather took him to hear an argument in the U.S. Supreme Court and he took Alicia to Boston to the U.S. Court of Appeals.

SUZY: I've taken them both to court with me. They know what we do. I was representing battered women in Legal Services, and quite a few times we've housed a battered woman in our home. They've gotten involved in that way; they always know what we're doing.

SCOTT: We've involved them in a lot of things; we always travel with our children. My attitude is if they hassle you, ignore them, and they'll stop hassling you sooner or later. We've had a marvelous time.

SUZY: For the most part we take them on vacations with us. We don't make plans that exclude them on weekends during the day, and I don't go out at night during the week unless it's absolutely necessary.

SCOTT: We've not had much time alone together in the course of eleven years. We've been away by ourselves for a week each time on three occasions. We take the kids with us in the summer and then they spend the rest of the time in camp.

SUZY: They have a very long summer vacation, and they've gone to as many as four camps during the summer.

SCOTT: Jonah in particular is beginning to resent being shuffled around from one camp to another.

SUZY: That's one area of concern. Another area where we really cut corners is cooking. I don't know if what goes on in this household can really be called cooking. Every once in a while I resolve that we'll have real meals. As it is now once a week I take the children for pizza and the kids will have French toast another night. And then there's the wonderful pasta store that makes everything themselves and sells ready-made packages of stuffed shells and manicotti. There's a Chinese take-out place. We have not ever been able to organize the food shopping or the cooking very well. I do the shopping, but there's no schedule. It's usually done as I run from the subway and buy this or that. I can't organize it.

SCOTT: Of course I don't get home until eight, nine, or ten in the evening, so I just grab something to eat. We've had different kinds of approaches to it in the past. There were times when we'd try to shop once a week. A disadvantage of living in the city is that the supermarket is so much grubbier and more expensive than in the suburbs. For a while we went way out on the parkway to a supermarket every Thursday night, either with the children or we had someone stay with the children. We'd go together and we'd try to do all the marketing for a week or two weeks. After a while that system broke down, and it got to be catch as catch can. It's all very marginal.

SUZY: Every once in a while we have a real sit-down dinner and we use my grandmother's silverware. I think it's nice to do, and I think we need to do it. I do try to cook something on Sunday nights.

SCOTT: There were times over the years when I made valiant efforts to contribute to household chores, but I have no taste for it and I have no discipline. We rub against each other because neither of us wants to do them and so we've looked for alternate means of being able to do it. Fortunately, because we're both working at jobs that pay reasonably well, we've been able to hire other people to do them.

SUZY: There have been many times when I've wanted more

from Scott, mainly having to do with the logistics of the children. It's easy now because they're older, but I used to wish he'd be more involved in making arrangements for who would visit whom and how they'd get picked up and where they would be after school, that kind of thing. It was easier for me because I was closer to the kids physically because my office was near their school.

Sometimes I'm a martyr. Sometimes I end up running around, like last week Alicia had to have a miniskirt. I was under a lot of pressure at work with a new job, but she was going to a roller disco party. I ran home, picked her up, and ran around town to find a miniskirt. I was exhausted. Sometimes I feel the pressure and I get headaches.

But, I can't think of any other people I'd rather spend time with than our kids. As far as being working parents is concerned, it is much easier to have twins. They are on the same schedule. I have friends with one child in first grade and one child in nursery school, and they're in two different schools with two different schedules, and that I think is much more difficult. My children are never really left alone—they always have each other; so when we walk out the door with a babysitter here it is easier for them because they're together. But then, they'll both be grown up at the same time, too. That is the biggest drawback. I realized that when they were less than twenty-four hours old. They'll both be going to college at the same time. I think about it a lot. We only have seven more years with them.

Part III

Strategies for Coping—Today and Tomorrow

Women often feel that they're alone, struggling to provide for their families financially, emotionally, and physically, with little understanding or help from their families, their communities, or their work places. The sense of loneliness and isolation, of frustration and exhaustion, that comes from working long, hard hours with little or no support emerges in conversations with all kinds of women, in all kinds of situations. But there are also many women who have learned to work within the status quo to create more fulfilling and less stressful lives.

Through our research and interviews, we discovered that women who have learned to work within the possible and who have developed concrete strategies that produce results are making a difference *now*. They've done it by developing a new perspective conducive to change, by utilizing their skills, and by taking action.

Ideally, women in our society should have equality of opportunity. There should be equal pay for equal work. But the subtle discriminatory practices which preclude promotions for women—hiring practices which keep women at entry or middle management levels without allowing them to move up and into decision-making positions of power—have contributed to ways in which women, especially those with family responsibilities, form the bottom of a two-tier work force. In the ideal, women should be considered as essential providers for their families, just as men are. Women should not be regarded as supplementary, temporary wage earners who are gathering discretionary income.

But the ideal is not the real. Statistics underscore that. So do firsthand accounts. In the meantime, it's possible for working mothers to shape their lives in ways that reflect their circumstances and fill their needs.

Taking the Initiative

Central to the success of women who are making a difference now is the fact that *they're taking the initiative.* They're not shouting that society ought to respond to their needs because it's the right thing to do or because society has been unfair to working mothers in the past. Such angry rhetoric is unproductive. American history has certainly shown that merely having a just cause has never been the determining factor in enlisting the support of the established society so that things could be changed. To achieve greater democracy in this country, we've always had to fight for it, even if justice or right was on our side! Lunch counters weren't integrated or women given the vote because it was the democratic thing to do. These rights were won because people took the initiative, and the risks, and fought for them.

While women have become more politicized since the early 1960s, many are reluctant to fight for their rights. Most middle-class women were taught that it's not nice to fight. They were raised to be passive and to look for approval, not justice. But in order to forge a more egalitarian society, one has to stand up for one's rights. In so doing, you may be considered a troublemaker. Women tend to judge themselves, or are judged, more harshly than men when they advocate and fight for a just cause. Men are often called courageous and determined, whereas women can be labeled bitchy and demanding when they stand up to the established order. This isn't to say that women have to be militant and strident in order to change procedures and traditions. We've seen how women have restructured their jobs and their families in ways that reflect mutual respect for individual rights, and commitment to their responsibilities.

Those who have power in a given situation are not eager to relinquish their hold; the established order, whether it's in an office or a home, will perpetuate itself unless an impetus for change comes from those who need or want it the most. In order to change the status quo, one has to develop a realistic strategy or plan of action and then learn to negotiate calmly, clearly, and consistently for well-defined objectives.

Mothers who work *well* have learned the importance of: (1) developing a new perspective; (2) utilizing skills; and (3) taking action.

Developing a New Perspective

Women need to think of themselves as adults whose needs are as legitimate as those of their husbands, partners, children, colleagues, and others in their lives. If a woman feels ambivalent about whether she's entitled to work in the first place, she won't advocate after-school programs very vigorously. If a mother is defensive about not cooking for her family, she won't support alternative meal preparation that may be available to her. Blacks who questioned whether or not they really had a right to vote didn't make very committed demonstrators during the civil rights movement of the 1960s. It's essential to believe in oneself and the legitimacy of what one is advocating before anyone else will believe in you.

Suzy Newman, for instance, didn't question her right to return to law school, nor did she question her expectation that her husband would share in the parenting. Her right was a given, and they worked out the logistics of raising the children based on that premise.

Likewise, Randee Pierson did not expend her energy debating whether she should put her baby's needs first and stay at home for the first two years; she looked for day care that fit into her schedule.

One woman told us that "you need not apologize for having a baby. It is your right." That statement reflects the fundamental acceptance of one's legitimacy and entitlement that allows a working mother to negotiate from a position of psychological strength, not defensiveness.

Utilizing Skills

Most working mothers have acquired skills that can change their lives once they develop a perspective that's conducive to such thinking.

A Georgia professional took the initiative to create a part-time job for herself, for example, in two separate corporations that had never offered such management positions before. She negotiated to work on a part-time basis as a well-paid professional. Rather than bemoan the fact that these companies were not responsive to the needs of working mothers, she initiated an option which fit her needs and benefited her employer.

Several executives told us how they had acquired executive and administrative skills which could be utilized in all kinds of situations. They've learned how to handle unrealistic demands upon their time and energy in a manner which is both firm and professional. When faced with impossible assignments, for instance, they told us that they assess their resources and determine how and why the task is not feasible as outlined. They then clarify an alternate, more realistic way in which the job *can* be done. The bottom line, said one executive, is to have a plan and then learn to negotiate, not request, changes. If a job schedule is unworkable, tell your superior that it's not possible to get it done efficiently within the prescribed period, and then present a realistic alternative describing how you will get the job done effectively and on time. One executive said, "Your boss wants the job delivered on time. If it can't be done according to his or her requirements, then propose what can be done and how." Impossible demands should be dealt with clearly, and alternative plans proposed. However, it must be noted that no employer is interested in carrying someone who cannot or will not fulfill his or her responsibilities.

Skills that are developed in the work place can be transferred to family life too, although many women indicated how difficult it is to apply business skills to the more emotional environment of the home. It's easier to be objective and a clear thinker when there is not such high emotional investment. But women are doing it, and their families are changing to reflect a more flexible structure.

Taking Action

In order to change one's life, it's necessary to take action. Someone else will not take care of us, and to be taken care of suggests the passivity and dependence that many contemporary women find unacceptable. Women as activists are not a new phenomenon, but many women do not know where to begin.

First, it's essential to define one's needs, to create programs, and to work together with other interested parties for common goals. Working mothers have several possible groups with which to work: the PTA; the League of Women Voters; National Organization for Women; American Association of University Women; religious institutions; community centers; professional organizations and assocations; senior citizen groups; local government; political groups; and informal grassroots organizations. Families can be allies, too. Husbands, partners, children, friends, and extended families are often more receptive to combined efforts than one at first perceives. It may not be easy for them to understand what it is one wants, and they don't always cooperate to the extent that one would like, but the fact is that they, too, can be seen as individuals with whom one can negotiate in order to achieve mutually acceptable goals.

Thinking creatively is a hallmark of change. Marjorie Kennedy, for example, suggested to us that volunteer organizations begin to reassess their attitudes about working mothers. She contends that her school's Mothers' Club calls upon women to bake cookies or participate in telephone chains when they should begin to think of ways they can call upon the business-related skills of working mothers. She would be happy to print brochures, for instance, but does not have the time to go to monthly board meetings or to make coffee. She also suggested that such boards need to have more long-range vision, especially when it comes to fund-raising. Because of the greater experience that many women now have in the business world, they find bake sales and car washes to be inadequate ways to raise the large sums needed for schools. Private schools especially need the financial expertise as well as the traditional involvement of mothers who can provide them with long-range planning. One suggestion that Marjorie gave was the possibility of working with a neighborhood bank to invest in the private school in their neighborhood. Since the bank has a vested interest in the neighborhood, she believes they would invest in the school the same way they do in politics. Discussing such possibilities as financial grants for private schools or private investments on the part of banks is a practical way in which a volunteer group can utilize the talent and experience of potentially involved parents who have little or no time for traditional volunteer activities such as bake sales in order to raise funds.

It's up to working parents to suggest such uses of their time and expertise if they feel that the schools are unresponsive to their situation, or that groups are rigid in their demands upon their time. Instead of feeling guilty about not being able to make costumes for the school play, working mothers can suggest that they'll print the tickets or provide some other business-related service. Too many communities are locked into thinking of mothers as cookie specialists and become frustrated by the seeming unresponsiveness of working mothers to the traditional needs of volunteer organizations. An innovative approach on the part of organizations and initiative on the part of working mothers could bring about change in that regard.

Much can be done within the present structure of our society. And it can be done simply. A government worker from Maryland complained to us that she would "like a complete restructuring of schools so that my child's schedule is more in line with mine and my husband's. Elimination of half-days, parent-teacher conferences between nine and two, teachers' professional days, and six-hour school days instead of eight-hour days" were some of the items she listed. No doubt these changes will take years, if they're *ever* made. In the meantime, however, there are ways to handle some of these frustrations.

Barbara Matthies told us how she dealt with the midday parent-teacher conferences that she's had scheduled for her over the years. When she gets a note from a teacher informing her of a two-thirty appointment, she sends a note back saying that "my child is important to me. However, in order for me to make a two-thirty appointment with you, I have to take a half-day off from work. I would like to reschedule our appointment for either the first thing in the morning or the last thing in the afternoon. Thank you." She says it's rare that a teacher doesn't reschedule the conference. Certainly, schools should be more responsive, but until they are changed, it is up to working parents to take every opportunity to make their needs known, in a calm, civilized manner, so that some pressures are eliminated or reduced. It's also up to parents to let the realities of contemporary family life be known to local school boards, principals, and teachers. More would be changed if working parents themselves were on more school boards, but short of that, a clear presentation, plus a workable alternative—a plan—can help.

Specific ways in which working parents can implement the philosophical framework we've presented briefly here are discussed in the next chapter. There are concrete ways that people have changed their family and job structures, and they're making a difference now.

Making a Difference Now

Women are changing their lives—redefining their family roles, expanding their professional opportunities, and even altering the social structure—right now, even though their families, their employers, and the whole society are not necessarily responsive to or supportive of their efforts. In their personal lives, in the public sector, and in the business world, working mothers (and fathers) are developing new ways to reinforce family life without denying women the right to work outside the home.

Our survey revealed that all kinds of women, whether they are married, divorced, widowed, single, young, old, financially comfortable or struggling, working full- or part-time, have developed constructive, efficient ways of getting things done. Most have given up the myth of Supermom, and most admit that their homes are a little less clean, their social contacts a little less frequent, their entertaining a little less elaborate, their intellectual development a little less satisfying, than if they were not working. But still, homes were livable, friends were seen, parties given, and reading done. The women shared with us suggestions for getting chores done faster, with less duplication of effort, and for finding time for other aspects of their lives that they found rewarding.

A key to eliminating stress is to find, or to make, a supportive work environment. In terms of personal life, of the women who said that they never felt torn between families and jobs, 75% said that their relationship with their husband or partner was positive. Moreover, of those who never felt conflict between families and careers, 89% felt that their children's general development was positive. Presumably, good feelings about partners and children have a positive carryover into one's professional life as well. Having, or creating, a supportive home life is essential to eliminating the stress and the conflicts that working mothers feel.

One of the key elements to making a difference now, especially in women's personal lives, is the development of a *psychology of sharing*. Women who have begun to see that families must work together to create a viable family life have been able to free themselves from some of the onerous responsibilities of being Supermom.

At Home

Women who advocate a psychology of sharing have begun to see the home as *ours,* not *mine.* It's not for the woman to put dinner on the table every night, it's the family's responsibility to see that there's a meal. Therefore, whoever can best do the job does it. A woman's success as a wife and mother is not dependent solely upon how many tasks she can take care of for her family. She shares the household responsibilities with her partner, her children, outside help, members of her extended family, or even friends. It's not always easy to retrain our minds, but it's possible!

Most of the women surveyed expressed the need for more help from members of their families; the women who received the most help seemed to experience the least amount of stress. The kinds of help varied from doing household chores to taking care of the children or making meals and shopping. Some help took the form of doing the laundry or taking care of financial matters. A communications designer from Nebraska devised a schedule with her husband whereby each has designated chores. Each does housecleaning for approximately four hours on a weekend. They take turns cooking, each for one week at a time, and the one who is cooking has primary responsibility for the care of their twelve-year-old son. "By Saturday evening the person who has cooked is pretty much on vacation until a week from Monday. It's a great psychological lift and leaves no guilt—you've really done your part."

Another woman, a suburban New Yorker, recently hired a housekeeper who lives in. "It has changed our lives dramatically for the better," she said. "It has given us back some of the flexibility we lost when we had to arrange for a babysitter in advance. And having the housework, laundry, and cleaning done makes everything workable." A director of an undergraduate program in the Washington, D.C., area has some assistance from a "dependable mother substitute who is on salary with benefits. If it weren't for her, I would be up a creek."

An added bonus of sharing child-rearing is that fathers have an opportunity to parent, and children get to know their fathers as well as their mothers. Some parents are able to do this to a fairly large degree because of flexible work schedules. A government worker from Iowa was grateful that her husband is a university professor. "He can work flexible hours, do errands, come home if a child is ill. He is also only five minutes from home. This is why he now manages more household business." A young woman with a new baby was able to return to her job as a self-employed lawyer by taking the baby to work with her, or trading off with her husband. "For the first three months, my husband and I traded taking him to work with us, although I had him most of the time because I was nursing. Later we had a babysitter care for him beginning with a half-day a week and increasing to three days a week. My husband and I each work four-day weeks, and we can each stay home one day a week with our child."

In the most successful families, the children are expected to do their share as well. It is only in the last few generations that children have been encouraged to be carefree—to be able to play, to dream, to be taken care of without having to contribute to the family in return. In earlier times, children worked alongside their parents in the home, on farms or in shops. We are not suggesting that child labor ought to be encouraged, but certainly there are jobs that children can and should do around the home. In one family, a toddler has been taught to help unload the dishwasher every day. His mother makes a game out of it, and he thinks it's fun. In another family, the woman, a project director from Michigan told us, "I stress to my children that to maintain order we all have to pitch in. We rotate chores to alleviate boredom. My ten-year-old son loves to cook and also takes his turn doing dishes, just as my eleven-year-old daughter is expected to take out the trash when it's her turn. She has also helped to scrape the house for painting."

An entry-level government worker with five children felt strongly that her primary goal as a parent was to have her children become self-sufficient, responsible, self-confident members of the community. "All of us cook one dinner a week, and we all have two rooms to clean (or an equal chore) on Saturday. I ask the children to participate in painting, yardwork, and so forth. I told them at the beginning that if one person had to be the servant, that person would shrivel up, and if some people did not do survival chores, they too would be incomplete human beings." A New York professional "assigns specific jobs to children on a monthly rotation system; for example, setting the table, taking out the garbage, clearing the table." A woman who lives on an island in Maine "has the children help with the meals, which makes them feel important and gives me a little extra time to read a bedtime story or listen to a report for school."

A secretary who lives in the center of a large city explained: "We are very programmed. All members of the household have at least one duty to perform during the course of the day, and are responsible for seeing that it gets done. If problems arise, my husband and I discuss that particular problem and decide on the solution. Things generally work themselves out."

An insurance agent from Wisconsin believes that it's good that "we have no male or female jobs and all seven children do everything on an alternating basis, more according to size and age than sex."

Our survey results indicated that about 25% of the children help with meal preparation, housecleaning, and laundry, while only about 18% help with the marketing. Although many of the women did not feel that their children *should* be required to help, in those families where they did, the women told us that the relationship between responsibility for sharing family chores and the results of that sharing included the development of a sense of fairness, independence, equality, and the satisfaction of having contributed something essential to the family.

A woman from Colorado with two children hires her children to perform essential chores. She told us, "I find that my children (sixteen and fourteen) perform better if I hire them on a businesslike basis to do weekly cleaning, yardwork, laundry, and other chores, and then leave home and let them do their jobs with payment upon completion. They work harder and better without my presence. Also we agreed that I cook all weekend meals and they each cook two nights a week. . . .

This arrangement leaves me time to paint for pleasure and gives me evenings to do free-lance design work to earn extra income."

In a family with two young boys, a schedule was developed and a contract drawn up listing each boy's chores, when they must be completed, and the payment that would be due upon completion.

A mother in Philadelphia told us that she belongs to a cooperative group that "helps with babysitting, yardwork, and other services through bartering." The woman continued, "We have a somewhat unusual lifestyle in this culture. We are vegetarians, nonsmokers, and nondrinkers. We seldom go to movies or watch TV. We enjoy working together and keep busy seven days a week. We also go to church several times a week and pray together at home so that minor frustrations and irritations remain minor." Not only does her husband share in daily tasks, but community members help each other as well, reinforcing the idea that the more sharing there is, the less stress on the individual.

A woman with four children who is a manager of a communications department called herself a "superorganizer." She has two huge calendars, one for the office and one for home. The family of six has two planning sessions each week where children outline their weekly schedules and the household chores are assigned. Menus are posted on the bulletin board, and members sign out when they leave the house so that everyone will know where the other is. There is also scheduled free time before dinner when the mother is available for whatever the children need.

Divorced and single women do not have another adult with whom to share either the burdens or the joys of caring for children. Although the survey indicated that they did not experience significantly more stress in the areas of home and child care, they did experience somewhat more stress connected with housecleaning, marketing, doing the laundry, and providing for car-pooling for their children. Many commented that life got easier for them when their children learned to drive and could help with family errands.

Essential to the smooth functioning of the family, it became clear, is organization. A secretary from Colorado declared, "The longer I am a single working mother, the more organized I get. My son and I come first, and being organized helps me find time for all the together and alone activities we want to do. A calendar and a generous number of tote bags, one for each activity, are essential to our way of life. When we moved, my top priority was making everything convenient for us; with a lot of effort I found a good school, nice house, babysitter, piano teacher, and a job in one neighborhood. From this stable base, we're able to weather everything from changing schedules to broken legs."

A suburban New Yorker expects her thirteen-year-old son to assist with household chores. She commented, "Since he is alone for quite a few hours per day, I have established a point system (alloting specific numbers of points for each job) which at the end of the week must total up to and go beyond the week's goal in order for him to receive a specially decided upon gift or treat. This gives him something to do after school while waiting for me to get home, as well as encourages him to take part in keeping up the house. It also relieves my guilt feelings about his being home alone for so many hours a day."

A computer programmer from Ohio solved her needs since her divorce by living in an extended family setting in order to provide for help in child care, cooking, housework, and shopping. "We are living with my lonely seventy-year-old grandmother who is more than delighted to do half the housework. I am thus free to work overtime, as well as to be an active member of several organizations. My personal conflicts as a working mother have been drastically reduced in the last two years, thanks to a helpful grandmother." Another idea was presented by a divorced administrator from Oklahoma who brings home friends to serve as surrogate aunts and uncles for her children.

An assistant to the superintendent of a nuclear generating station feels enormous pressure as a single mother. She has given her older son the responsibility for caring for her younger son, who is mentally and physically handicapped. This "has matured him and given him an extra sense of responsibility that many men in their fifties do not have." She went on to caution, "Never lie to your children, and don't try to be Supermom. It's amazing how unselfish and understanding children can be if they know they are loved and that they are not being lied to."

Husbands, partners, children, relatives, and friends are working together to make life easier and more manageable. The bonus of this kind of cooperative effort is the closeness of the family unit and the common investment in shared goals and objectives that all family members have.

There are several ways in which other women have manifested a psychology of sharing in order to get chores done, divide up work, and make time for other, more rewarding activities.

Managing the House

Many women suggested lists as the best way to organize one's life. Lists for appointments, lists for chores (which can be rotated daily or weekly), lists announcing the menu for the week, ongoing shopping lists so that each family member adds needed items, lists indicating schedules of family members, and even lists itemizing short-term and long-range goals! The idea is that no effort is duplicated and no time is wasted.

A Florida woman told us that she lives by lists. "I keep lists handy and jot down things I need so that when I get in the car to go someplace such as the cleaners, I will not forget to go to the hardware store or the drugstore while I'm out. I keep a note pad on my vanity for morning thoughts while getting dressed, one pad by my bed for thoughts and needs at night, and a pad in the kitchen to keep track of things I need before I run out."

In many families, children were given contracts for work done, listing price details and time specifications. Other suggestions for effective management included shopping by mail, using catalogs, using the telephone whenever possible to locate required goods and services, making hair appointments for the evening, and scheduling repairmen in the evening when possible. Another suggestion was always to trade at the same store, even if it's more expensive, because there's a time advantage in knowing where every item is located.

Many women gave us such widely known recommendations for food preparations as getting a good slow-cooker for roasts and putting them in the night before; cooking in quantity and freezing meal-sized portions; using a microwave; preparing menus and shopping for a week or two at a time; baking desserts and bread on weekends; and having each family member prepare his or her own Sunday night dinner. One mother offered a means to treat the children and still reduce the stress on her—she designates Monday night as Friends' Night. Each child is allowed to invite one or more friends for spaghetti or stew. The meal is quite simple and can be stretched if need be, and the children are given an opportunity to entertain even though their mother works. Several women suggested that the best way to deal with the house is to get up early each day and get a head start on the family. Other women, on the other hand, told us they just don't do the things in the house that require such commitment to housework—the closets aren't as clean, the furniture isn't dusted as often, and the dishes aren't always put away right after dinner.

One of thc greatest difficulties cited by working mothers in our survey was the lack of responsible, dependable domestic help. It's not easy to find reliable, responsible caretakers for children and professional housekeepers for a home. Even those for whom the expense is not a problem expressed concern about finding help.

The issue is complex and reaches far beyond the need for help for working mothers. Domestic work is a low-status and low-paying occupation in our society and consequently attracts unskilled and uneducated people whose ideas of proper child care often conflict with those of the middle class. However, it does seem possible to approach the need for domestic help as well as the lack of jobs for the unskilled, especially women, by developing ways in which domestic services could be professionalized. Possibly, high schools or vocational schools could offer training programs in domestic services in an attempt to upgrade and professionalize the industry. Learning such basic skills as punctuality, respect for the property of employers, caring for the young or the elderly, pride in one's work, and other rudimentary domestic knowledge would certainly help in fostering mutual respect between workers and employers. Employers need to begin to view workers as trained professionals, entitled to reasonable working conditions, pay, and benefits. No doubt costs would be increased, probably substantially, causing difficulties for some people. But the benefits to both workers and employers would be great.

One way to attract responsible people to the field is to have a reasonable work situation. Provisions for eight-hour days, lunch hours, sick days, vacation days, Social Security, liability insurance, and, possibly, other benefits would help establish the rights of domestic workers. Both employees and employers need to be educated about such benefits and the responsibilities on both sides that are a part of upgrading the field. More training of the workers and more realistic demands from the employers should lead, eventually, to a more equitable arrangement within the industry. Apparently the government, through CETA (Comprehensive Employment Training Act) programs, has attempted such training, but the initiative has not been taken by the private sector to any appreciable degree. Cost is a factor, too, and a high degree of profitability may not exist in the development of such programs. Therefore, training offered through the public school system seems to be the most viable possibility.

Another option available to working mothers, especially in terms of home care, is the use of housecleaning services that are organized to provide domestic help to families. Usually they provide only for housecleaning, but they could be developed to provide all kinds of services, similar to caretaking services provided in home nursing. An individual could arrange with a company for specified days or times, and the company would then provide trained workers. All benefits would be provided by the company, and the company could supply necessary machines and materials, eliminating the duplication of such equipment at home. Workers could be bonded so that the risk to both employer and employee is minimized. The disadvantages include the fact that there is no ongoing relationship between worker and the employing family; in addition, the costs of such services would no doubt be higher. Such ventures require innovative workers and adaptable families, but they can be embarked upon, and they have also offered enterprising young women ways to build businesses! Clearly, there is a need for reliable help, and with more mothers working outside the home, the possibilities in the industry could be very good.

Meeting Family Needs

One important way that many women deal with the complexities of careers and families is by simplifying their lives as much as possible. The most successful know that it's impossible to spend hours in the house polishing silver, dusting collectibles, and washing walls. Likewise, many advised that it is important to live in a home that's convenient to everything—schools, buses, stores—all of the services which family members need. It is also helpful to live in an area where older children can walk where they need to go, to libraries, community centers, doctors, museums, music teachers, and sports facilities. This kind of planning cuts down on car-pooling, at least during the day when parents are working. One apartment dweller told us that she uses the doorman to handle daytime deliveries and service calls for appliances or home maintenance. Another woman suggested giving up such activities as sending Christmas cards, especially if this kind of thing is more burdensome than pleasurable! Over and over again we were told that the most important aid to working outside the home is living as near to the work place as possible, enabling the parent to get to the child if there's an emergency. Women feel less anxious and guilty if they are able to get home quickly.

The needs of children are of great concern to working mothers, and all of the women surveyed attested to the importance of their children. Most expressed some guilt over providing for their needs. Those who were self-employed felt that they had the flexibility necessary to deal with children's illnesses, school vacations, emergencies, and activities. Others said that they take their children with them to work when necessary and that the work place is supportive to them. This alleviates sitter problems and also shows the children what the mother does when she goes to work. One mother met the needs of her children by providing after-school care for two days a week and a teenage babysitter for the other three. Another had her baby fed by the sitter before she picked her up in the evening so that the child could eat earlier and more calmly. One of the best pieces of advice given applies to all working parents—when at work, concentrate on work issues, and when at home, concentrate on family needs. Don't bring the office home and don't take family concerns to the office.

More than 50% of the women we surveyed felt that they didn't have enough time for their husbands or partners. However, some women solved the problem creatively by using the limited time available in innovative ways. Some said they had daily or weekly meetings to set goals, go over financial matters, set up schedules, plan menus, clear the air, or just be together. One woman spoke about a Friday night "debriefing" session she and her husband had to discuss job concerns and conflicts so that they could then spend a calm weekend together. She added that they often talked frankly about overextending themselves and the need to say no without feeling guilty. One couple used business trips as minivacations. Another set a 10:00 P.M. curfew when they retired to the bedroom, and the children knew that it was off-limits unless they were sick or something very important happened. One working mother explained that she must make time for her partner because he needs to know that he's still the most important focus in her life, even though their time together is limited.

Another concern of working mothers is finding time for the

family. Many of the women we surveyed recommended family outings, trips to museums, art galleries, or sporting events, many of which are free, as ways that the family can enjoy each other. One mother suggested that a family outing be planned once every few weeks so that the family can be together *enjoying* something, not discussing, planning, scheduling, or arguing about something. One family goes through the newspaper once a week to plan a weekend activity. Many parents schedule vacations to coincide with the children's vacations so that they can all be together. Another family does outside chores as a family where they can talk and work at the same time.

In still another family, when the father travels, the entire family joins him whenever a business trip is on the weekend. Other women told us of taking long walks together or spending evenings talking to one another. The most important issue is that the family needs to establish time together as a priority so that plans are made and schedules are devised to provide for it. One woman put it succinctly—after working hours "my children and my husband come first."

Throughout the survey responses, women underscored again and again their lack of time for self. Too many women had no time or energy to regenerate themselves after meeting all of the other demands and needs in their harried lives. Some women, however, were able to find personal time for reading, exercising, and socializing. Again, the key to shaping a satisfying life was organization. One woman solved her energy needs by taking a nap on the train on the way home. She told us, "Then I have the strength to face being a mother again."

One woman spent her lunch hour taking piano lessons, shopping for clothes, pursuing hobbies, exercising, or reading. Several women suggested the use of personal shoppers to help them organize and select their wardrobes, in an effort to save time and needless expenditures. These shoppers often work for large department stores and see people by appointment only, helping them to choose entire wardrobes, including shoes and other accessories. In some cities, there are stores especially designed for the needs of the working woman.

A commuter used time on the train to balance her checkbook, read, sleep, knit, and study. Optimum use of time is essential to working mothers, and setting priorities, making lists, and then using the lists can be both time and cost effective. Other suggestions from working mothers included:

finding support networks such as professional organizations, magazines, books, and other working mothers to share common needs and concerns; managing activities realistically—not spreading oneself too thin; keeping perspective on what's important in the long run and having a sense of humor!

Again and again, women stated, "Be selfish about your spare time outside the family," "Learn to say NO," "Set priorities," "Take time for yourself." One woman just started her fifth career at age forty-five, this time as a small business owner. She told us, "It has been important for me to tune out the trivia. I choose my friends from active, stimulating, creative women. They are worth my time." Responses from women clearly indicated that they desire more time for themselves, their intellectual, physical, social, and spiritual needs, as well as for their children, their partners, and their homes. A woman from Florida who is a director of public affairs affirmed the need for "time to rebuild one's emotional and spiritual reserves." She continued that she was filling out the questionnaire while "I am house-sitting for friends in a neighboring town—five glorious days of solitude and silence. This is the second time in two years and it works marvels for me, better than a costly spa. I go home renewed, refreshed, feeling whole again, and ready to meet the demands of home and office."

Our research emphasized the fact that the most successful families, in terms of lessened stress and heightened satisfaction, were those in which each member of the family unit is cooperating and sharing in the goals and values of the family. Certainly, mothers cannot do it alone, not only because there isn't enough time, but also because it works against the idea of the family unit itself. The strength of the family comes from the fact that members learn interdependency, mutual respect, love, and working together for common goals. This can't happen optimally if mother is the only one providing for everyone's needs, or if the children don't contribute to the family's well-being, or if the father's only focus is on his work.

In many ways, it's simpler for women to reshape their family roles and the way that the family structure is defined than it is for them to form a more responsive work place. Their tentativeness, lack of negotiating skill, and tenuous power base in the working world all contribute to the helplessness they feel, and the ineffectiveness that often results. However, large numbers of women have learned that they needn't merely adapt to current inflexible conditions within their work places, and some work places have begun to explore ways in which the work world can be restructured. In the public sector, as well as in the private sector, things are changing.

In the Work Place

In the public sector and in the business world, there has been a reluctance to meet the needs of working parents. Too often corporations and businesses operate as if their employees were *only* men with wives who are at home caring for children. Since the United States Department of Labor, Bureau of Labor Statistics, has indicated that in 1980 56.6% of all women with children under eighteen were in the labor force, corporations and businesses need to recognize that many of their employees are *women* and those women often have children at home who require care and attention. Also according to the Bureau of Labor Statistics, the number of married women who are working is increasing, with 24.4 million wives either working or looking for work in 1980. The statistics shatter the myth of traditional American families' having nonworking mothers at home caring for children. Corporations and businesses are increasingly facing the reality that the statistics reveal: American mothers are working, and the private sector will be changing to meet the needs of that ever-increasing group.

Some companies have begun to deal realistically with family needs as they now exist, and are developing programs, such as flex-time and job-sharing, and benefits that address and support American family life.

In the public sector, the government—federal, state, and local—is both an employer and a resource. Its status as employer is evident. Its position as resource is often less clear. For example, certain governmental agencies have developed progressive policies, such as flex-time, that can be implemented by the business world. Because of its role in affirmative action, the government has initiated creative uses of funds and personnel, especially in some poverty programs, that the middle class can adapt to its own needs. For example, Foster Grandparent programs have existed for poverty-level senior citizens and day care groups whereby the two share facilities, allowing for close interaction between children in need of supervision and senior citizens in need of programming. The mutual benefits are far-reaching; children have the attention and talents of surrogate grandparents, and senior citizens can have the joy and satisfaction of being involved with youngsters who need their care. Certainly, the use of community centers or churches or other private institutions for combined senior citizen and child care programs ought to be more thoroughly explored than it now seems to be. No doubt there are isolated instances in the country where after-school programs are taught by retired people, or where healthy, active senior citizens are helping to care for children, but these programs are not far-reaching and are not widely publicized. Such artificial extended families could serve many purposes and could save money as well! Researching the established Foster Grandparents programs in one's community could provide an excellent foundation for the creation of middle-class programs that gather children and older citizens in a mutually satisfying, beneficial, growing, and caring environment.

The legislative branch of the government can also be a resource for working parents in that it *can* respond to grass-roots petitions for tax revisions, corporate incentives, and other benefits that lend support to middle-class working families. Recent polls indicate that women are becoming more active in the political process and are more inclined to be reformers than men; as more women become legislators, and as more women vote, it's conceivable that more supportive family programs can be developed and implemented—programs that address themselves to the realities of family structures and family situations, not to some idealized vision of father supporting the family, mother at home baking, and two children being carpooled and pampered according to the romanticized dream of the 1950s.

Flexible Working Arrangements

Some concrete advancements have been made in our society to make the work place more responsive. To date there have been some tax incentives included in legislation that encourage corporations to provide flexible benefits, including child care, to middle-class working parents.

One of the most salient ways in which the government has been resourceful is in initiating a number of flex-time programs for the benefit of several federal agencies.

The Women's Bureau of the Department of Labor, for example, as one of the many federal agencies involved in flex-time programs, offers several possibilities for work schedules. Fundamental to these programs, however, are the following: all work must get done by the deadlines given, and all departments must be adequately staffed. Employees are accountable for making certain that the coverage is adequate, and if such coverage doesn't exist, supervisors can preempt flex-time. Given those limits, employees of various federal agencies have had some of the following flex-time arrangements available to them (policies change, however, and not all programs remain intact).

In certain agencies, federal employees negotiate with department heads to work flexible hours on a given day, with certain restrictions. There are many ways this can be done. One possibility is that within a department, each person selects his or her work hours (9:00–5:30; 8:30–5:00; 10:00–6:30) and then works those hours every day. Another possibility is the four-day ten-hour-a-day week. Still another option involves core hours of, for example, 10:00 A.M. to 3:00 P.M., when all employees of the department must work, and then negotiated fringe hours that individuals schedule so that the department is covered. In this arrangement, the employee must work eighty hours every two-week period, but an individual's day can be structured so that more hours can be worked late in the day, for example, or early in the morning.

Yet another variation on flex-time in the government is called maxi-flex whereby core days exist—Tuesday, Wednesday and Thursday, for instance—when everyone must be present. The remaining hours worked can be scheduled flexibly. Another possibility is called 5-4-9 whereby people work nine hours a day the first week and then nine hours a day for four days the second week, thereby allowing them to take either Friday or Monday off every other week. Some people prefer to schedule their flex-time so that they take a longer lunch hour every day. Other employees prefer a waiver of flex-time because they want regular hours and don't want to sign in and out.

The Economic Recovery Tax Act of 1981 provided tax benefits for corporations if they chose to give their employees flexible benefits. Child care, for example, became a cost of doing business and was therefore deductible by the employer and not taxable to the employee, because it was considered a benefit. In addition, the maximum tax write-offs for child care for middle-class parents have been increased, but many women in our survey expressed a need for a more realistic tax deduction or credit than the ones already existing. Clearly, there is some movement toward more innovative and responsive policies for middle-class working parents, but unfortunately, such practices are not widespread. Here again the necessity for taking the initiative is clear. There are provisions for flexible benefits; it becomes incumbent upon working parents to negotiate with their employers for such options.

One of the most innovative programs has been developed by the American Can Company of Greenwich, Connecticut. They have created a flexible benefit program which can serve as a model for other programs. It's open to all employees who are salaried; that is, not members of a union. Before the flexible program existed, benefits included medical, dental, and various insurance benefits, depending upon eligibility. In 1977, they instituted a pilot program with a more flexible selection of benefits, including options for those that had existed formerly, now called the preflex program. In the flexible benefit program a value has been placed on each benefit, and employees can select benefits based on a credit line that has been extended to them. For example, a married employee with 1500 credits could select more benefits than a single employee with 800 credits. Each credit has a value of $1.00, and the employee benefits include various medical plans, life insurance options, income disability, vacation and capital accumulation options. The preflex plan can be used as a core program, with other benefits added, or an entirely individualized program (within the options available) can be created. For example, a woman whose husband has the core benefits from his employer may opt entirely for capital accumulation or vacation benefits from American Can. Beginning in January 1983, American Can will begin to offer a day-care benefit which allows an employee to elect to use some or all of the credits toward day care. Since the credits are considered unearned income, the individual does not have to pay tax on those benefits. A woman theoretically, then, could have 1500 credits, or $1500, for day care if she worked at American Can. Of course, that does not cover the entire cost of day care, but it is a beginning, and it demonstrates the feasibility of such flexible, innovative programs.

Child Care

Several of our surveyed mothers voiced concern about the unresponsiveness of schools to the needs of middle-class working parents. Sick-child care provisions are especially problematic, and many of the women expressed a need for such care when a child becomes ill at school and the parents (or neighbors) are unavailable. These are issues that could be addressed by parents through their PTA groups, school boards, and other community organizations. Resistance to implementing such provisions will no doubt be strong, and local codes may even be restrictive in some areas, but it may be that intransigent people or lack of initiative are more stifling. Once it has been acknowledged formally that large numbers of local mothers are working during the day and are not able to do what mothers twenty years ago could do, schools will not automatically assume that Mother is out for a while and can be reached later, or that a neighbor can be reached in case of emergency. The school will not provide such options just to be magnanimous; it is up to working parents to make their needs known and to create possible programs within the limits of local regulations to provide adequate care for children who become ill during school.

Schools, often with the impetus provided by hard-working parents, have begun to respond to middle-class needs. One such example is Ardsley, New York, a suburban community that generated a parent-sponsored day-care program that linked day care to the public schools by utilizing school facilities. Underutilized or closed school buildings can be used for such programs as day care or after-school activities, since taxpayers are already paying for the buildings. According to some professionals in the field, it's important to make sure that such programs are school-*based,* not school-*sponsored,* because the administration of the programs should be independent of the schools.

After-school programs for children of school age have grown out of mutual efforts of the PTA and other organizations. Such activities as puppetry, hiking, guitar, dance, cooking, and other programs can be offered in school buildings after school, but organized and run by the PTA, parents' groups, privately hired teachers, or others, approved by some responsible body. Programs can be supervised by adult volunteers, or they can be run by high school or junior high school students who could be involved in worthwhile activities after school themselves while they work with the younger children.

Enlisting the aid of such organizations as the League of Women Voters and the Junior League may provide support resources for programming, too. Opposition to innovative programs has to be expected, and it is prudent to have realistic, well-thought-out plans that benefit the community and are not merely self-serving for working parents. One group in Westchester County in New York found out how difficult the opposition to a seemingly benign program can be. Their local school board defeated a proposal to bring day care into the public schools. Another group found that a private nursery school owner charged that a parents' group that wanted to use the school was in competition with private enterprise. Such issues may require legal counsel before programs are proposed—an ideal way to call upon the community service of an interested mother/lawyer who's never been available for traditional volunteer service!

On-site day care on the grounds of a corporation has become one way in which the business world has responded to needs of working parents. Day care is an issue that has been handled more creatively and successfully in Europe than in this country. Middle-class families and American companies seem to share a resistance to such programs. However, there are companies that are formulating day care policies and are instituting day care programs.

An urban company has difficulty in establishing on-site day care because, as one woman noted, commuting on buses or subways with large numbers of children would certainly make rush hour even more of a nightmare than it already is! It's also difficult to provide adequate play space for children in some of the older inner-city structures that house many companies. But some companies in outlying areas have created on-site day care.

The Stride Rite Children's Center in Boston, Massachusetts, has become a model for on-site programs. It accommodates fifty children, as of this writing, from the ages of two years and nine months to six years, and it's open from 7:00 A.M. to 5:00 P.M., Monday through Friday. It serves the employees of The Stride Rite Corporation, although it reserves about half of its places for children in the community. There is a waiting list for the employees' children, but Stride Rite believes that it has a responsibility to the community at large to provide some facilities for them. (Eligibility for government funds may also be a factor.)

The cost of the program is 10% of an employee's salary, while the Massachusetts Department of Public Welfare provides for the children from the community. A federal program paid for 75% of the installation of the kitchen at the center, and the Massachusetts School Lunch and Nutrition Bureau provides cash reimbursements for about seventy percent of the cost of the food program, which includes breakfast, lunch, and a light snack. Lunch at the center coincides with the factory lunch hour; so parents can come and have lunch with their children, if they wish.

The center is staffed by ten full-time people as well as volunteers. There is also a director and a part-time cook. Employees of the center receive benefits and vacation time. Many attend college to improve their training, and that is paid for in part by the federal government through a new careers program.

Stride Rite believes that this children's center has become a valuable investment; not only does it enable the company to attract and keep more desirable personnel, but it also provides a valuable asset to the community in which it operates.

In New York City, the Ford Foundation maintains a Child Care Assistance Program for employees. This program is available only to workers whose family income does not exceed $25,000. The foundation pays up to 50% of the cost of day care, depending on the types of care and the age of the child, with forty-five to fifty dollars per week being the maximum paid. Depending on the kind of care, benefits are paid from full-time preschool programs to part-time after-school programs. In the summer, the foundation pays more for school-age children than in the winter because they spend more time in a day care or camp situation.

Another benefit that the Ford Foundation provides is child care leave. It is available for the mother or the father, and it provides them with eight weeks of leave with pay, and up to eighteen weeks without pay. Although their jobs cannot be guaranteed for the eighteen-week period, they will be reinstated to an equivalent position in terms of grade and salary, if at all possible. Because the Ford Foundation is a nonprofit institution, employees are allowed tax deferred annuities, which is a helpful benefit in terms of saving money for retirement and reducing taxes. A spokesperson for the foundation noted that this procedure is most likely to be followed by an employee with another family member who is working. Child care, or maternity, leave is not uncommon in American companies now.

Intermedics, Inc., a corporation based in Freeport, Texas,

has a day care program which it operates three miles from the headquarters, which are located fifty miles south of Houston. The program accommodates 260 children at the present time. They range in age from six weeks to six years, including kindergarten children. It's available to all families of employees with both parents working, but only one parent needs to be working at Intermedics.

The center is open from 7:00 A.M. to 6:00 P.M., with some flexibility allowed in the times of attendance for the children. The cost to the family is 25% of the going rate of day care in the area, which is around fifty dollars a week. There are approximately 170 children on the waiting list, but Intermedics plans to build a center for approximately 500 children when it moves to a new location about twenty miles from the present site. There is a registered nurse at the facility.

In the winter months, the program is basically educational; whereas in the summer the focus is on recreational activities. Parents are not entitled to bring their children to the center when they themselves are on vacation, but they can bring them in if they are traveling for business or if they are going to medical appointments.

The Polaroid Corporation in Waltham, Massachusetts, provides its employees with a voucher system for day care. Employees can either find their own day care facility near their homes, and the company will supply a voucher, or the company will make a contract with an existing licensed day-care center to provide placement for the child. The company pays from ten to eighty percent of the day care, with the lower salaried employees receiving the higher percentage of the cost. The benefit applies to all employees earning $25,000 or less; however, those with higher incomes can avail themselves of the referral service run by the company. Although Polaroid operates three shifts during the day, only the employees on the day shift can take advantage of the benefit because day care is only available during daylight hours. Only one percent of Polaroid employees take advantage of the voucher system.

The concept of day care, however, has not been one that has been historically embraced by American families. The extended family has been seen as the resource used by working parents, especially those in the lower classes or the immigrant groups that needed to work. Mothers have worked throughout the history of this country, and children have either taken care of one another, or been cared for by other family members, or have worked alongside their parents in family stores and businesses. Now that these arrangements are often impossible, we seem to have large numbers of latchkey children who come home to empty houses after school, or who have no supervised arrangement. School-based programs, on-site day care, voucher day-care systems, and flexible benefits that would allow for funds to be channeled into acceptable, structured, and professionally administered programs should help provide for the millions of children whose mothers and fathers are working.

Thus far, corporations have not been too responsive to human needs and contemporary family life, and with the unemployment rate high, they are even more unlikely to provide extra services and benefits in order to attract employees. As one vice-president of a corporation put it, the individual can negotiate situations to help her in working out a schedule that is advantageous for her career and family obligations, but it is unlikely that the corporation will make such policy decisions at the top. New programs will develop, but they will probably be the result of management people working from the grass roots to spark change, not the result of beneficent corporate officers providing for family needs. Again, it is clear that working parents, especially mothers, must define what they need and create workable, realistic plans which will benefit both them and the company so that they can effectively meet the needs of their families and the responsibilities of their jobs.

In Society

Many women have come to understand that in order to have a more responsive society, they have to make their needs known. As women reach policy-making and decision-making levels in business and government, they are in a position to change society for the benefit of themselves and others. Even the ordinary woman, however, has power; she can *vote,* and can make her needs known, in spite of the fact that she may have no interest in obtaining power for herself.

Women are becoming more expert in asking political candidates where they stand on issues relating to women. No longer do women discount the importance of "women's issues" as automatically secondary or unimportant in the scheme of things; such issues have subtly discriminated against women and the equal opportunities they want. Lack of day care, policies advantageous to men or one-worker families, and nonverbal or informal company traditions which assume someone in the home who cares for family needs have all contributed, directly or indirectly, outwardly or covertly, to discrimination against working mothers. Many women are beginning to understand that they *can* change things through political action. Such issues as safe mass transportation, for instance, deeply affect the logistics of a working mother's life. If her children could get around more easily to after-school programs or to lessons or friends' homes, then their lives would be less complicated.

Women can also instigate change through their collective economic power. If working mothers can establish themselves as an identifiable group of consumers, businesses will arise in response to their needs. Widespread availability of home-cooked meals, for instance, provided by a small business owner to working mothers in his or her area, is one way in which needs could be served and businesses developed.

As long as women feel guilt and ambivalence about their *need* to work and the concurrent need to have someone else provide family services, then they will not be unified or decisive enough to initiate the change needed to offer these services. Disenfranchised people in America, whether they have been poor or black or female, have historically not been given their rights—even in a democracy, which rhetorically promises equality, and the right to pursue life, liberty, and happiness. Women have a great deal of economic power in this country, and they now have a political majority as well.

Change occurs because certain groups find ways in which the present system can be acceptably reshaped to accommodate their demands *without* arbitrarily and unilaterally withdrawing all rights of the established groups. Businesses will not automatically institute flex-time because it is good for families or because it is fair to working parents. To wait passively for the system to understand and act upon what is just is naive and, in the long run, not productive. Women have tended to wait for someone to take care of things. If they want changes, they will have to do what other powerless groups have done in the past, take risks and pay a price in order to get an equitable share. But many women are doing just that and have forged for themselves and their families a meaningful and well-balanced life within the limitations of the present system.

Not only do women need to become more vocal about the

legitimate needs of working mothers, but they must become more active about running for political office themselves if they really want the society to reflect more realistically their priorities. Just as in business, women at the top who understand the specific needs and problems of working parents can be more responsive and helpful than people who lack fundamental understanding of the problems involved. The more leaders elected who are knowledgeable about and responsive to the real needs of working parents, the more chance there will be that special needs will be addressed. At the very least, however, women need to understand the power of the vote, and that they have within their grasp an important tool for effecting social change. Every time they make their needs known, and demand (nicely!) accountability from their candidates, they move closer to achieving their goals.

Times are changing. The fact that some corporations have initiated flexible benefits and the government has provided for flex-time in some of its departments is indicative of the enormous steps taken over the past few years. The struggle has been long and hard, and the inroads have not been substantial. Compared to what needs to be done, little has been accomplished. But the fact is, attitudes are different now in some places, and policies aren't as rigid everywhere as they were ten years ago. Families and companies are proving that something can be done to accommodate the needs of individual family members and still get a job done. There are opportunities for hard-working, courageous, dedicated, and creative people to make the personal, public, and business sectors more responsive. But it takes determination, and firm resolution to make a difference—now, or in the future.

Surviving in the Future

Unquestionably, our world is changing. Roles are less gender-defined, opportunities are expanding, social structures are less rigid, and family life-styles are more individualized than they were a generation ago. The premise in our society has traditionally been that each generation learns from the previous one, both cognitively and affectively, in ways that better the quality of our lives. This attitude has occasionally led us blindly to accept scientific breakthroughs without questioning the larger implications of such technology. But the fact remains, we are a society that rapidly adopts what we perceive as technological advancement. One such advancement that has been enthusiastically accepted is the computer, and its use has implications for working mothers.

The Computer Age

The computer, especially the growing use of home computers, is an ever-increasing reality in contemporary American society. Our children are learning BASIC, the computer language, with the same frequency that previous generations learned French or Spanish. They are computer literate; the computer is becoming an integral part of their everyday lives. Professional use of computers has been with us for decades, but bringing the computer into the home may change the next generation's lives in ways that we are only beginning to understand.

The homes of the future may be equipped with computers that can provide families with several different options. They can provide security for the home, help us to conserve energy, facilitate shopping and banking, and regulate use of home appliances. Home computers will be a source of home entertainment, offering a wide variety of games and educational functions. However, the most important way in which home computers will affect family life is the increased ability of people to work at home efficiently and effectively. Computers will enable office workers to do whatever they would do in the office in their own homes. Computers will allow them to store, disseminate, retrieve, and have access to all the information they will need, both interoffice and intraoffice. Communications services such as teletext and videotext (which communicate both written and pictorial messages onto screens in homes or other places) will add to the effectiveness of these systems.

One suburban New York couple exemplify the interlinking of professional and family life in the computer age. They developed new ways to structure their jobs with New York Telephone when their daughter was born. They both now work in their suburban home some days of the week and in their New York City office on other days. They arrange their schedules so that one of them is working at home with their child on any given day.

This couple is in the communications industry; so the operating system which they have in their home stores and retrieves information that can be communicated to others. Whatever information they have that needs to be dispatched to other individuals or other offices can be routed through their telephone wires to other similar systems. In short, they can be in communication with their own office in the city or the suburbs, or with other offices they need to reach. The computer age allows them to work as effectively at home as they can work in the office.

The advantage to working at home is that each of them is able to have time for their child when, and if, the child requires it. This couple, as well as others we talked to, have found advantages to integrating the work place with the home. The child grows up with a clearer view of the kind of work the parent does, and feels a part of the professional life of the parents. Men can be more available to their families than the traditional commuting father, and mothers do not feel the intensified pressure of commuting in addition to balancing career and family.

One three-year-old child, whose parents are partners in business and work from their home, announced, "Do you want to hear something ridiculous? My friend's mommy and daddy don't even work together!" This child's view of reality is that parents work together, and they work from home.

Parents who work at home can structure their lives so that they are more a part of the community where they live. A by-product of professionals' working at home can be the enrichment of so-called bedroom communities because more middle-class parents would be working within, rather than outside, of the community. Their investment, then, may be greater than if they perceive home as merely a place where the children are. Another factor in increased instances of people working at home could be the reduction in the number of homes empty during the day, thereby reducing crime and the large numbers of latchkey children who come home to empty houses after school.

Of course, there are disadvantages to such working conditions. Those who work at home suggest that their day never ends—they work after dinner, on weekends, and whenever they have a few minutes. Clients or business associates often feel free to call at any time because the distinctions between business hours and private hours are more diffused. Moreover, there is a sense of isolation that people who work at home refer to; there is little interaction with colleagues, and the lack of contact with peers can mean the loss of the tacit support system they provide; there is little contact with superiors, producing an "out of sight, out of mind" syndrome; in addition, there can be a diminished sense of professionalism. Interruptions from the family or from those who are servicing the home (repair people, for instance) can be disruptive also. Couples who work together at home can experience tension from spending too much time together; there is increased need to redefine family and professional roles and to establish private space. As with all other aspects of combining careers and families, there is a trade-off in working at home.

But there is no question that computers provide a wide range of professional possibilities at home, and the options will be increasing. One woman, an investment analyst, decided to install a computer in her home rather than work in an office when she had her baby. Another woman left her job as a computer programmer when she had children to start a software business at home, part-time. The business quickly went from part-time to a multimillion-dollar corporation. No longer working from home, this woman is now a corporation president who runs her complex company by working long hours and traveling extensively. Her husband, who has a nine-to-five job, has become the primary caretaker and it is the mother who indulges the children with presents after a business trip.

The computer age allows for decentralization of tasks, thereby eliminating the need for management personnel and clerical workers to be in the same place at the same time. It offers opportunities for growth in both traditional and innovative fields. Computer skills have introduced new ways for creative thinkers to become entrepreneurs, and since computers can't see whether the programmer is male or female, there's been no sexual discrimination in the possibilities for dramatic success in this field. The computer age may well intensify the social changes that we've begun to experience in the last few years.

Changing the Way We Live

In assessing the complexities of managing careers and families, a fundamental question arises: Is it possible to change the way we live? If we could simplify our life-styles and could align our actual lives with our expressed priorities more closely, we should be able to reduce the pressure that we feel. However, Americans have been socialized to measure status and success in terms of private ownership—owning a house, car, appliances, and other material things. Private ownership can be a psychological stumbling block which interferes with a more reasoned, logical approach to combining careers and families appropriate to our current life-styles.

With more women working, individual homes, with all their attendant care and maintenance, become burdensome. Energy and resources are needed for home management of single-family dwellings that could be more profitably spent on families and careers. And the costs keep going up. Although it certainly doesn't seem to be the American Way, it would make more sense if we could learn to share some of our more expensive possessions, such as lawn mowers and snow blowers, or if we would be willing to limit the size and luxury of our homes so that they are more consistent with our needs in the way that European middle-class homes have tended to be simple and utilitarian. It would seem more prudent if we would limit our consumption, too, and buy fewer but higher quality items rather than trendier things. Some have said that we've become a disposable society, with disposable pens, lighters, bottles—even mates. Of course, our private enterprise system is based upon mass consumption, but the heretofore accepted script, that man produces and woman's role in society is to consume, which Betty Friedan so aptly presented in *The Feminine Mystique,* no longer is commonly acted out in American families, and the need to simplify our lives is increasingly becoming evident. Smaller, maintenance-free, efficiently built houses with little yard space serve changing family needs.

Cluster housing is another option which would presumably serve family needs more effectively. These communities could provide for a day care center, shared appliances, a maintenance corps, communal resources for cooking and other shared services. Possibly one person, or group of people, could be responsible for the preparation of meals, thereby eliminating the need for repeated single-family meal preparation by working parents. Perhaps people could eat communally, or in a small family-style dining room. These ideas tend to sound radical to mainstream American families, and they don't reflect American life-styles of the past, but the trade-off is duplication of effort in single-family home after single-family home in suburban, urban, and rural areas, with increased pressures on all family members.

A possible model for such innovative homes is Roosevelt Island in New York City. This six-year-old community is three and a half minutes by tramway from the center of Manhattan. It was designed in part to meet the needs of working parents, to provide a life-style within a large urban area which is safe for families and easily accessible. The complex provides housing for 5500 residents, representing all socioeconomic groups. There is an elementary school and a junior high school, a day-care center, and an after-school program—all surrounded by grass and trees on the East River. Shops and services are within walking distance or are accessible by free minibus service, which eliminates the need for a car.

Other possible ways that people are simplifying their lives include living in condominiums and cooperative apartments. Even though they often do not share facilities or household items, they do share many services and resources. Household problems are taken care of by a staff of hired electricians, plumbers, and maintenance personnel who are often managed by a superintendent. The outside areas are cared for by professionals, thereby freeing individual owners from the responsibilities of home maintenance, inside and out. These housing situations often provide recreational facilities such as tennis courts, swimming pools, and game rooms. The trade-off is that people do not have a high level of privacy, and often don't have their own yards.

Even within single-family dwellings, however, there are ways that life can be simplified. Many women in our survey expressed a desire for more carefree materials—paneling instead of painting; platform beds with drawers in the bottom instead of dressers; cedar shingles or other siding instead of wood that needs repair; deck areas instead of lawns for outside entertaining; fewer collectibles and bric-a-brac that need dusting; window blinds or other window treatments instead of draperies—in other words, less of everything that requires time and care that only a full-time housekeeper can give. Other requests that women made were for decorating, food preparation, and cleaning services which were easily available and affordable; for car pool drivers to take children to after-school activities, and for senior citizen services which would provide care and talent for families with no extended family nearby. Moreover, women wanted accessible credit and financial planning services.

The lives of working parents are undergoing changes on many levels—they entertain simply and no longer prepare elaborate dinner parties. Groups sometimes cook together, and the process of preparing dinner becomes the evening's focal point, with men and women making pasta or Chinese food or other meals together, making the kitchen an entertaining area. Working parents often include children in the evening's activities. One woman told us that friends tend to be other working parents; they get together on Saturday nights, with all the children, and hire a sitter in common to take care of the children.

As the changing needs of working parents are identified, the opportunities to provide services to meet those needs are increased, and enterprising individuals will create successful businesses in meeting those needs. Perhaps a good cook in a suburban neighborhood could start her own business by preparing quantities of home-cooked meals to sell to working mothers in her area. Stopping by a neighbor's house to pick up freshly made lasagna or stew or other main courses could benefit both families. Weekly menus could be posted and orders could be called in early in the week, thereby organizing the working mother's life and helping to build the business of someone else who wants to work at home.

There is growing awareness on the part of working couples that changes need to be made in the way they live so that more time can be spent with families or involved in leisure activities that are more individually satisfying than home maintenance. The economic factor may make some of the changes necessary, in that many young couples will no longer be able to buy single-family dwellings, even if they're both working, forcing them to opt for cluster housing or smaller homes. As women in the work force increase their numbers and gain more status, the home may become less of a reflection of a woman's identity and more a place where one goes as a refuge, a sanctuary of sorts. Perhaps home products and the industries that have such a huge stake in consumerism will become more responsive to the changing needs of families and will begin to provide the kinds of products and materials which will make home maintenance easier and less time-consuming. Making those needs known is one way in which working parents can begin to initiate product development and widespread marketing of such goods and services.

Part IV

Becoming Families that Work

Being a working mother is not so much a fact as it is a process. As a process, it's constantly changing and redefining itself. It requires enormous energy, ingenuity, adaptability, and perseverance. Being a working mother is not simply a matter of getting a job and then existing. Or of having children at the optimal time in one's life, given a commitment to a career. It's not, of course, a matter of getting married and just living happily ever after, either. It requires sustained effort and continual reassessment of priorities, needs, and goals. It's a way of life that demands the clarification of shared values and objectives, as well as individual needs and feelings. More than that, it is a continuous commitment to the well-being of loved ones—all the loved ones in the family—including oneself!

Whatever their situation—whether they're professionals living in urban areas, or small business owners living in rural communities; whether they're in first marriages of long standing, are divorced heads of households, or are women in alternate, less traditional family structures—working mothers are demonstrating to themselves and to others that they're capable, independent, resilient, determined, assertive, creative, and resourceful. They're strong. And ever more confident. What's more, they are increasingly rejecting the roles of the victim, the martyr, and the vision of passive, dependent femaleness that many of them grew up with. Our research, although based on a limited group of women in the upper socioeconomic strata, seems representative of the attitudes of contemporary middle-class working mothers.

They feel good about themselves. They see work as a given, and themselves as providers as well as nurturers. They feel good about their children too, and their husbands or partners, if they have them. They see themselves as successful people, and others see them that way too. They do, however, experience stress. Sometimes they feel overwhelmed by the enormity of the two jobs they're carrying—home and career. Occasionally, some working mothers have moments of panic. Of those who indicated such incidents, they suggested that those moments are more likely to occur in relation to their private role, and its human, emotional demands, not to their professional role and its intellectual or occupational demands. They see themselves as primarily responsible for their homes and their families, in addition to their responsibility as providers. Their position is not the same as that of traditional working fathers; they are in no way relieved of personal responsibilities when they work. Right now, they tend to be sustaining traditional female, as well as male, responsibilities.

They often feel as if they're doing everything alone, and their response to us and their behavior as a group indicate that they do feel isolated. Clearly, the more help and support they get, be it emotional or physical, from family or from the work place, the less stress they feel. Whether women are married, single, in first or in later marriages, whether they live in the city or the suburbs, have a family income of over or under $40,000, and whether they're thirty-five years old or over, our research showed that they all experience similar conflict. They did not, however, exhibit symptoms of health-related problems in our survey.

Contrary to our expectations, high-powered career women responded differently to the daily family pressures than successful men have traditionally responded. That is, they still consider themselves to be the primary caretaker and nurturer, no matter what their professional position. What's more, women who work full-time and women who work part-time feel equal levels of stress with respect to conflicts between family and career. It makes no difference if women work from home, either.

Moreover, women who feel a sense of personal satisfaction professionally experience less stress and are presumably happier. Surprisingly, working mothers do not evidence ambivalence about the impact of working on their families—they emphatically stated that they feel good about themselves, their partners, and their children. What's more, they wouldn't want to be full-time wives and mothers. In short, we found that working mothers feel positive about themselves personally and professionally.

Working mothers are becoming increasingly aware that they can't be Supermom, and that their working or not working is not the sole determinant in the well-being of their children. Other things have impact, too. Working mothers know that they can't do everything well all the time. There are trade-offs, there are prices to be paid. They're learning to gauge what they can and cannot do. They're learning to say no, when that's appropriate, and to use their talent and their energy in focused efforts that coincide with their long-term goals. They're becoming more realistic about what they can and cannot do despite their family's continued pressure on them to be the all-giving, selfless, mother of the past. They're comprehending that they can be maternal without being domestic. They're learning to assess what only they can do for their families, and what their families can learn to do for themselves. In an effort to free themselves from the bondage of voluntary enslavement to real or imagined needs of families, they are helping their children and their partners to become more independent and resourceful. Mother is no longer the only one who can cook, sew, car-pool, clean, and do other family chores—so can fathers, and so can other people. Women are also discovering what society will and will not do in terms of expanding its services and broadening its attitude.

To the extent that individual women have resolved the issues of legitimacy, entitlement, independence, and autonomy, they experience less conflict and are better able to integrate their personal and professional selves. Essential to the ability to reconcile these roles is the psychology of sharing, which allows them to view family life as a cooperative venture, and their professional life as legitimate, but not all-consuming.

The thread unifying the women who feel the most fulfilled and the least pressured in terms of time, relationships, commitments, and expectations is a positive attitude toward oneself, one's role in the family, one's career, and one's place in society. These women feel a sense of control over their own destiny, and the direction of their lives; what's more, they do not see themselves as dependent extensions of their families on the one hand, or driven careerists on the other. They are able to synthesize the cognitive and affective areas of their personalities in ways that are satisfying for them and productive for their families. They feel that they are independent and can take care of themselves; yet they choose to share their lives with families. They are not subordinate females or slaves, they are autonomous, loving adults.

It's not easy to affirm one's autonomy, especially at a time when most males, and indeed most of society, perceive a loving woman as one who caters to the needs of others, while denying the existence of her own needs. Many men, whether consciously or subconsciously, intellectually or emotionally, overtly or covertly, still believe that the woman's role is to make their lives comfortable and happy, even if the woman happens to be working as many hours outside the home as the man is. Often women, on a subconscious level, acquiesce to that view, and find themselves embroiled in a Superwoman role in spite of protestations to the contrary. Many men and women are working hard to overcome that attitude, and they've developed shared family responsibilities that supplant the inequity of such impossible, relentless expectations. It requires diligence and openness and a great deal of respect for the rights of each family member, on the part of each family member, to create an environment that reflects such true sharing of home responsibilities.

Women would like to see a spirit of cooperation and support permeate American society as a whole, too. They'd like to have the burdens of their many roles eased by an increase in the availability of services such as day care, flex-time, mass transportation, and other systems which alleviate the unremitting and unrealistic demands upon working mothers. It's not possible for women to attend to all family needs and all professional responsibilities at the same moment, yet that's what society seems to assume. Although individual women have shaped their lives in ways that ease the pressures, women consistently indicated to us that they'd like to see society reflect the realities of contemporary American family life by becoming more supportive of their multifaceted roles, both attitudinally and actually.

There aren't widespread support services available to working mothers right now, but there are opportunities for the public and the private sector to address those needs. Day care, after-school programs, meal preparation, financial planning services for women, home maintenance services, professionalized domestic services, and others need to be expanded and redesigned to coincide with the real, not the idealized, family structures that exist today. Women are becoming increasingly aware of the imperative to initiate change themselves, and to take action themselves, especially through politics, if they want society to respond to their legitimate needs. Educated, articulate, assertive mothers are beginning to recognize that special interest groups represent the needs of all kinds of people in society, and if the common good is being ignored, or if social services are neglected, then it's up to concerned, interested people to organize and make their needs known. Working together for common goals is the democratic way! Women are also learning that to be powerful is not necessarily to be Machiavellian, and that power means making decisions and formulating policy. Increasingly, women are learning that it's far more effective and productive to work from within to get to leadership positions than it is to scream hysterically for someone else to give you what's fair and right. To be taken seriously, one must learn the skills needed to negotiate, and one must form power bases. Women are learning that. And they're learning what men, and what adults, ultimately come to know—there are no easy answers. Only tough questions.

Working mothers are discovering that the traditionally feminine, nurturing, supportive qualities and the newfound providing, independent, assertive characteristics work synergistically, giving a woman both personal and professional fulfillment. As working mothers venture forth in greater numbers, and achieve more significant positions of leadership, they'll become even stronger, and surer, individually and together, than they are now. They believe that they're raising new generations of children who see women as people, not just as mothers, and they're forging new relationships with partners that are built on mutual respect and strength and trust. They don't see themselves as passive or helpless or victims. They see themselves as adults. As mothers who work. And with their courage, their strength, and their dedication, they're moving beyond being mothers who work—they're creating families that work, too.

Appendix

This is the self-administered questionnaire that was sent to women all over the country.

Summer 1981

Dear Working Mother:

We are writing a book for Ballantine Books, tentatively entitled *Choices for Working Mothers*, and we'd like to gather some information from you about your complicated life as a working mother.

Our purpose is information, and we're taking a survey of women all over the country to gather data about the common conflicts and solutions that working mothers have.

We, too, are combining careers and families. Between us, we have five children ranging in age from 2–17. We are teachers and business women in addition to being writers.

We know how busy you are and how precious your time is, but we'd appreciate your taking some time to fill out this questionnaire and return it to us in the enclosed envelope as soon as you possibly can. We'll share the results of the questionnaire with you when we have tabulated and analyzed them. We also want to assure you that your name will remain confidential.

Thanks for your help and cooperation.

Sincerely,

Jeanne Bodin and Bonnie Mitelman
Choices for Working Mothers

This survey is divided into three sections: your working/professional life, your personal/family life, and you and your background. Most questions can be answered by placing an "X" in the appropriate box(es). Should you like to add something, there is room for comments at the end of each section. All answers will, of course, be kept strictly confidential.

I. Your Professional Life

1. Please put an "X" next to the category that best describes your occupation.

   Professional (e.g., attorney, editor, stock broker, teacher, psychologist, doctor, engineer, etc.) . . . . ☐
   Managerial or administrative . . . . ☐
   Sales (e.g., real estate, retail, etc.) . . . . ☐
   Secretarial or clerical (e.g., bank teller, bookkeeper, cashier, etc.). . . . . ☐
   Artistic work (e.g., artist, designer, writer, performer, etc.) . . . . ☐
   Service work (e.g., hair stylist, chef, dental assistant, etc.) . . . . ☐
   Small business owner . . . . ☐
   Government or military worker. . . . . ☐
   Other (PLEASE SPECIFY YOUR JOB TITLE AND DESCRIBE BRIEFLY WHAT YOU DO:)

2. Do you work . . . ?

   a) Part-time (less than 30 hours/week) . . . . ☐
   Or Full-time . . . . ☐
   b) Do you work from home at all?
   Yes ☐ Approximate # hrs/week___________
   No ☐

3. About how much time do you spend commuting to and from work?

   ____
   \# hours a week

4. Do you consider yourself to have . . . ?

A job to supplement income . . . . ☐
Or A career to which you are committed . . . . ☐

5. Do you supervise men?

Yes ☐ Does this role make you feel awkward?
Usually. . . . . ☐
Sometimes . . . . ☐
Rarely . . . . ☐
No ☐

6. Do you travel with men in your professional capacity?

Yes ☐ Does this role make you feel awkward?
Usually. . . . . ☐
Sometimes . . . . ☐
Rarely . . . . ☐
No ☐

6a. Do you entertain men in your professional capacity?

Yes ☐ Does this role make you feel awkward?
Usually. . . . . ☐
Sometimes . . . . ☐
Rarely . . . . ☐
No ☐

7. Do you find the time demands of your work excessive?

Usually . . . . ☐
Sometimes . . . . ☐
Rarely . . . . ☐

8. At this point in your career, have you achieved . . . ?

More than you thought you would have . . . . ☐
Just about what you thought you would have. . . . . . ☐
Or Less than you thought you would have . . . . ☐

9. How successful are you in your working life?

	I Consider Myself	Others See Me As
Very successful	☐	☐
Somewhat successful	☐	☐
Not very successful	☐	☐

Please feel free to comment below about your working life—conflicts, satisfactions, anything at all.

____

____

____

II. Your Personal/Family Life

1. Please indicate whether or not you feel you have enough time for each of the areas listed below. For each area you say you *do not* have enough time, please indicate how much this lack of time bothers you.

	Have Enough Time	Do Not Have Enough Time	Bothers Me: A Lot	A Little	Not At All
Community involvement	☐	☐	☐	☐	☐
Your home	☐	☐	☐	☐	☐
Your wardrobe	☐	☐	☐	☐	☐
Physical fitness	☐	☐	☐	☐	☐
Your husband/partner	☐	☐	☐	☐	☐
Your children	☐	☐	☐	☐	☐
Hobbies	☐	☐	☐	☐	☐
Friends	☐	☐	☐	☐	☐
Extended family	☐	☐	☐	☐	☐
Travel	☐	☐	☐	☐	☐
Personal care (hair, nails, etc.)	☐	☐	☐	☐	☐
Intellectual development	☐	☐	☐	☐	☐
Reading	☐	☐	☐	☐	☐
Entertaining	☐	☐	☐	☐	☐
Social/cultural activities	☐	☐	☐	☐	☐

	Have Enough Time	Do Not Have Enough Time	Bothers Me: A Lot	A Little	Not At All
Personal health care	☐	☐	☐	☐	☐
Children's activities (watching sports, school visits, etc.)	☐	☐	☐	☐	☐
Other (SPECIFY)__________	☐	☐	☐	☐	☐
______________________	☐	☐	☐	☐	☐

2. For each of the areas listed below, please indicate who takes care of the function currently and who you would like to take care of the function ideally.

	Currently Taken Care Of By (X One or More Boxes)				Ideally Should Be Taken Care Of By (X One or More Boxes)			
	Self	Male Partner	Kids	Help Outside Immediate Family	Self	Male Partner	Kids	Help Outside Immediate Family
General household management	☐	☐	☐	☐	☐	☐	☐	☐
Meal preparation	☐	☐	☐	☐	☐	☐	☐	☐
Home cleaning	☐	☐	☐	☐	☐	☐	☐	☐
Financial management .	☐	☐	☐	☐	☐	☐	☐	☐
Marketing/shopping	☐	☐	☐	☐	☐	☐	☐	☐
Laundry	☐	☐	☐	☐	☐	☐	☐	☐
Child care	☐	☐	☐	☐	☐	☐	☐	☐
Sick-child care	☐	☐	☐	☐	☐	☐	☐	☐
Arrangements for lessons and special activities	☐	☐	☐	☐	☐	☐	☐	☐
Resolving family problems	☐	☐	☐	☐	☐	☐	☐	☐
Car pooling	☐	☐	☐	☐	☐	☐	☐	☐

3. The functions you just answered Q.2 about are repeated below. Regardless of who takes care of the function currently or ideally, please indicate whether or not each of these functions is an area of conflict for you (stress, pressure, guilt, conflict with partner, etc.)

	Area of Conflict Yes	No
General household management	☐	☐
Meal preparation	☐	☐
Home cleaning	☐	☐
Financial management	☐	☐
Marketing/shopping	☐	☐
Laundry	☐	☐
Child care	☐	☐
Sick-child care	☐	☐
Arrangements for lessons and special activities	☐	☐
Resolving family problems	☐	☐
Car pooling	☐	☐

4. For each of the following areas, please indicate the impact you feel your working has on that area.

	Very Positive	Somewhat Positive	Somewhat Negative	Very Negative	No Impact At All
Your general relationship with your husband/partner	☐	☐	☐	☐	☐
Your children's general development	☐	☐	☐	☐	☐
Your children emotionally	☐	☐	☐	☐	☐
You emotionally	☐	☐	☐	☐	☐
Your sense of control over your life	☐	☐	☐	☐	☐
The kind of wife/partner you are	☐	☐	☐	☐	☐
The kind of mother you are	☐	☐	☐	☐	☐
The way your husband/partner sees you	☐	☐	☐	☐	☐
The way your children see you	☐	☐	☐	☐	☐

	Very Positive	Somewhat Positive	Somewhat Negative	Very Negative	No Impact At All
Your satisfaction with your sexual activity ..	☐	☐	☐	☐	☐
Your husband/partner's satisfaction with your sexual activity	☐	☐	☐	☐	☐

5. Listed below are pairs of phrases that describe attitudes toward work. There is a phrase on each side of the page with six boxes in between, and we'd like you to indicate which phrase best describes your attitude. For example, the first pair says "I like my work" on one side and "There is other work I'd rather be doing" on the other side. The more you like your work, the closer the box your "X" will be to the left side of the page, the more you'd rather be doing something else, the closer your "X" would be to the right side of the page. Please do this for each pair of phrases.

I like my work	☐☐☐☐☐☐	There is other work I'd rather be doing
I am adequately paid for what I do	☐☐☐☐☐☐	I feel I am underpaid
My primary reason for working is personal satisfaction	☐☐☐☐☐☐	My primary reason for working is economic
My work environment is generally supportive	☐☐☐☐☐☐	My work environment causes conflict for me
I am well trained for my work	☐☐☐☐☐☐	I need to learn a lot more to do my job well
My family responsibilities have not affected me professionally	☐☐☐☐☐☐	My family responsibilities have kept me from realizing my professional goals
I am confident in my relationship with professional peers	☐☐☐☐☐☐	I would like to feel more self-confident with peers

I am assertive with supervisors	☐☐☐☐☐☐	I feel very subordinate with supervisors
I never feel torn in my allegiances to my family and my job/career	☐☐☐☐☐☐	I often feel conflict about family needs versus job/career needs

6. Please put an "X" next to each of the supports/services listed below that you would like to have *more* accessible. For each one you "X", please indicate how important it would be to you.

	Would Like to Have More Available	Very Important	Somewhat Important	Not Very Important
Day care	☐	☐	☐	☐
Sitter services	☐	☐	☐	☐
Home cleaning services	☐	☐	☐	☐
Meal preparation	☐	☐	☐	☐
After school programs	☐	☐	☐	☐
Safe mass transportation	☐	☐	☐	☐
Home repair services	☐	☐	☐	☐
Adequate arrangements for a sick child at school	☐	☐	☐	☐
Flexible work schedule	☐	☐	☐	☐
Personal time off	☐	☐	☐	☐
Communal kitchens	☐	☐	☐	☐
Community centers with supervised activities	☐	☐	☐	☐
Maintenance free home furnishings	☐	☐	☐	☐

	Would Like to Have More Available	Very Important	Somewhat Important	Not Very Important
Credit and financial counseling	☐	☐	☐	☐
Recreational facilities	☐	☐	☐	☐
Dependable help (housekeeper, service people)	☐	☐	☐	☐
Shopping/marketing and home delivery	☐	☐	☐	☐
Others (SPECIFY)				
________________	☐	☐	☐	☐
________________	☐	☐	☐	☐
________________	☐	☐	☐	☐

7. Please look at all of the supports/services you said you would like to have more accesible to you and write in those you would rank 1st, 2nd and 3rd most desirable.

1st________________________
2nd________________________
3rd________________________

8. Please note below any constructive ways you have of dealing with the demands of your multiple roles that other people could use. Be sure to indicate the areas that your solution(s) apply to.

____
____
____
____
____
____
____
____

9. Please feel free to add any other comments you'd like.

____
____
____
____
____
____

III. You And Your Background

The following questions are included only in order to help us interpret and classify responses.

1. Counting yourself, how many people live in your household?

One .... ☐
Two .... ☐
Three .... ☐
Four .... ☐
Five .... ☐
Six or more .... ☐

2. And, how many are children under 18?

One .... ☐
Two .... ☐
Three .... ☐
Four .... ☐
Five .... ☐
Six or more .... ☐

3. What is your marital status?

First marriage .... ☐
Second or later marriage .... ☐
Living together, not married .... ☐
Divorced .... ☐
Widowed .... ☐
Separated .... ☐
Single, never married .... ☐

4. What is your age?

18–24 . . . . ☐
25–29 . . . . ☐
30–34 . . . . ☐
35–44 . . . . ☐
45–54 . . . . ☐
55–64 . . . . ☐
65 and over . . . . ☐

5. What was the last grade of school you completed?

Some high school or less . . . . ☐
Completed high school . . . . ☐
Some college . . . . ☐
Completed college . . . . ☐
Some graduate school . . . . ☐
Completed graduate school . . . . ☐
Other education beyond high school,
(business, nursing, etc.) . . . . ☐

6. What is your family's total yearly income?

Under $10,000 . . . . ☐
$10,000 to $19,999 . . . . ☐
$20,000 to $29,999 . . . . ☐
$30,000 to $39,999 . . . . ☐
Over $40,000 . . . . ☐

7. What ethnic group do you consider yourself to be a member of?

Caucasian or white . . . . ☐
Black . . . . ☐
Hispanic or Spanish origin . . . . ☐
Other (SPECIFY)____________________ ☐

8. Do you live in . . .?

A single- or two-family house . . . . ☐
Or An apartment . . . . ☐
Do you . . .?
Own . . . . ☐
Or Rent . . . . ☐

9. Is your home in . . .?

   A central city area . . . . ☐
   A suburban area. . . . . ☐
   Or A rural area . . . . ☐

10. Do you have family nearby?

    Yes ☐ No ☐

11. What state do you live in?

    ____

12. How would you describe your weight situation?

    Currently close to my perfect weight. . . . . ☐
    Underweight by more than I'd like to be . . . . . . ☐
    Overweight by more than I'd like to be . . . . ☐

13. How would you describe your smoking status?

Currently	Would Like It To Be
Non-smoker . . . . ☐	Non-smoker . . . . ☐
Light smoker . . . . ☐	Light smoker . . . . ☐
Moderate smoker . . . . . ☐	Moderate smoker . . . . . ☐
Heavy smoker . . . . ☐	Heavy smoker . . . . ☐

14. How would you describe your consumption of alcoholic beverages?

    Two or more drinks daily . . . . ☐
    One drink a day . . . . ☐
    Two or three drinks a week . . . . ☐
    Once in a while at parties or on special occasions . . . . ☐
    Rarely or never . . . . ☐

15. Do you suffer from allergies?

    Yes ☐ Have you always . . .? Yes ☐ No ☐
    No ☐

16. How frequently do you take antacids?

Daily or almost daily.......................... ☐
Once or twice a week .... ☐
Only occasionally .... ☐
Rarely or never .... ☐

17. How often do you have headaches?

Daily or almost daily.......................... ☐
Once or twice a week .... ☐
Only occasionally .... ☐
Rarely or never .... ☐

18. How often do you get the amount of sleep you'd like to?

Daily or almost daily.......................... ☐
Once or twice a week .... ☐
Only occasionally .... ☐
Rarely or never .... ☐

19a. In retrospect, would you have preferred to be a full-time wife and mother, that is, not be employed outside the home?

Yes ☐ No ☐

19b. If it were possible, would your husband/partner prefer you to be a full-time wife and mother?

Yes ☐ No ☐

Are there any comments you'd like to add?

____
____
____
____

Once again, thank you for your time and interest. We would like to be able to talk further with some of you and of course would like to send you the results of this study. Therefore, at your option, please fill in your name, address and phone number below. Please be assured that your name will remain confidential.

Name:____
Address:____
____
____
Phone #: (_______)______________________________
Area Code

Selected Bibliography

The following is a selective bibliography that would serve as background information for further understanding of the role of women in American history and culture. This is a limited list, and in no way reflects the vast amount of material on the subject. In addition to the books cited, there are scores of articles published with increasing frequency, many of them in professional journals.

Agonito, Rosemary. *History of Ideas on Woman: A Source Book.* New York: Capricorn Books, G. P. Putnam's Sons, 1977.

Bardwick, Judith, ed. *Readings on the Psychology of Women.* New York: Harper & Row, Publishers, 1972.

Baxandall, Rosalyn; Gordon, Linda; and Reverby, Susan, eds. *America's Working Women: A Documentary History—1600 to the Present.* New York: Vintage Books, 1976.

Bell, Susan Groag, ed. *Women: From the Greeks to the French Revolution.* Belmont: Wadsworth Publishing Company, Inc., 1973.

Berkin, Carol Ruth and Norton, Mary Beth. *Women of America: A History.* Boston: Houghton Mifflin Company, 1979.

Boserup, Ester. *Women's Role in Economic Development.* New York: St. Martin's Press, Inc., 1970.

Brownmiller, Susan. *Against Our Will: Men, Women and Rape.* New York: Simon and Schuster, Inc., 1975.

Brugger, Robert J., ed. *Our Selves/Our Past: Psychological Approaches to American History.* Baltimore: The Johns Hopkins University Press, 1981.

Cott, Nancy F. and Pleck, Elizabeth H. *A Heritage of Her Own: Toward a New Social History of American Women.* New York: A Touchstone Book, Published by Simon and Schuster, Inc., 1979.

de Beauvoir, Simone. *The Second Sex.* New York: Alfred A. Knopf, Inc., 1953.

Flexner, Eleanor. *Century of Struggle: The Woman's Rights Movement in the United States*. Cambridge: The Belknap Press, Harvard University Press, 1979.

Friedan, Betty. *The Feminine Mystique*. New York: Dell Publishing Co., Inc., 1963.

———. *The Second Stage*. New York: Summit Books, 1981.

Gilligan, Carol. *In A Different Voice: Psychological Theory and Women's Development*. Cambridge: Harvard University Press, 1982.

Goodfriend, Joyce D. and Christie, Claudia M. *Lives of American Women: A History with Documents*. Boston: Little, Brown and Company, 1981.

Harris, Barbara J. *Beyond Her Sphere: Women and the Professions in American History*. Westport: Greenwood Press, 1978.

Hayden, Dolores. *The Grand Domestic Revolution: A History of Feminist Designs for American Homes, Neighborhoods, and Cities*. Cambridge: The MIT Press, 1982.

Janeway, Elizabeth. *Man's World, Woman's Place: A Study in Social Mythology*. New York: A Delta Book, Published by Dell Publishing Co., Inc., 1971.

———. *Powers of the Weak*. New York: Morrow Quill Paperbacks, 1981.

Kanowitz, Leo. *Women and the Law: The Unfinished Revolution*. Albuquerque: University of New Mexico Press, 1969.

Kessler-Harris, Alice. *A History of Wage-Earning Women in the United States*. New York: Oxford University Press, 1982.

Matthaei, Julie A. *Women's Work, the Sexual Division of Labor, and the Development of Capitalism*. New York: Schocken Books, 1982.

Millstein, Beth and Bodin, Jeanne. *We, the American Women: A Documentary History*. New York: Jerome S. Ozer, Publisher, 1977.

Morgan, Robin ed. *Sisterhood is Powerful: An Anthology of Writings from the Women's Liberation Movement.* New York: Vintage Books, 1970.

Norton, Mary Beth. *Liberty's Daughters: The Revolutionary Experience of American Women 1750–1800.* Boston: Little, Brown and Company, 1980.

O'Neill, William L. *Everyone Was Brave: A History of Feminism in America.* New York: Quadrangle/The New York Times Book Co., 1969.

Quint, Howard H. and Cantor, Milton. *Men, Women, and Issues in American History, Volumes I and II.* Homewood: The Dorsey Press, 1980.

Rosaldo, Michelle Zimbalist and Lamphere, Louise. *Women, Culture, and Society.* Stanford: Stanford University Press, 1974.

Schneir, Miriam, ed. *Feminism: The Essential Historical Writings.* New York: Vintage Books, 1972.

Stein, Leon, ed. *Out of the Sweatshop: The Struggle for Industrial Democracy.* New York: Quadrangle/The New York Times Book Co., 1977.

Strasser, Susan. *A History of American Housework.* New York: Pantheon, 1982.

Wertheimer, Barbara Mayer. *We Were There: The Story of Working Women in America.* New York: Pantheon Books, 1977.

Index

About the Authors

Jeanne Bodin and Bonnie Mitelman have been involved in the field of Women's Studies for years. Jeanne Bodin teaches history at Harrison High School and is the coauthor of a textbook entitled *We, The American Women*. She resides in Hartsdale, New York.

Bonnie Mitelman is an adjunct lecturer at Mercy College, where she teaches History of Women among other courses. Her articles appear in various publications, including *The New York Times*. She is also a partner in an advertising and public relations firm. She makes her home in Briarcliff Manor, New York.

Both authors have been working for approximately twenty years and during that time have combined careers and families, both as married women and as single parents.